Give My Secrets Back

An Alison Kaine Mystery

by Kate Allen

Give My Secrets Back

An Alison Kaine Mystery
by Kate Allen

New Victoria Publishers Inc.

Published by New Victoria Publishers Inc., a feminist, literary, and cultural organization, PO Box 27, Norwich, VT 05055-0027.

Cover Photo by Judy M. Sanchez

Printed and Bound in the USA
1 2 3 4 5 6 1999 1998 1997 1996 1995

Authors Note

I have used the names of many actual institutions and places in Denver, both current and past. A women's bookstore, Big Mama Rag—the women's news-paper, and Virago—the women's production company actually existed. However, such references are only for fun—all characters are completely fictional and any resemblance to actual people is coincidental

Library of Congress Cataloging-in-Publication Data

Allen, Kate, 1957-
  Give my secrets back : an Alison Kaine mystery / by Kate Allen.
      p.   cm.
    ISBN 0-934678-6-42
    I Title.
  PS3551. L3956G58   1995   94-38403
  813'.54- -dc20   CIP

1

"**A**nd here she is in the new dress that her mother made her for Easter." Officer Robert Ellis, when not behind the wheel of the squad car he shared with his partner, Officer Alison Kaine, did two things. He lit up a cigarette—his wife was under the impression he had stopped almost three years before in response to her fears about being a young widow—and he pulled out photos of his two year old daughter, Timica, who was the apple of his eye. This was the seventh photo of Timica in her lacy Easter dress Alison had been forced to admire that day. Robert didn't seem to quite get the idea that though, yes, Sears would give you five poses and one hundred and forty pictures for under fifteen dollars, you didn't have to actually *look* at every picture, for godsake.

"Oh," said Alison, as she scanned the street—everybody on *Hill Street Blues* reruns always busted their big cases while on the way to coffee, so why not them? —"She looks *so* cute." What she wanted to say was, "Stop doing the lace thing, Rob, you'll turn her into a dyke in self defense, that's what did it to me," but she bit her tongue. Yes, Robert was her friend and, next to her father, the most avid supporter of what he insisted on calling 'her lifestyle' on the force. But that didn't mean he would take hearing his daughter's chances were one in ten—just like everybody else—graciously. What she said instead was, "She has such a beautifully shaped head. She's going to look great when she starts wearing dreadlocks and a nose ring."

Robert, who was in some ways more conservative than Ward Cleaver, blanched visibly. "Don't say that," he said, pushing the fan of photos back into a stack like a deck of cards.

"Or a shaved head," said Alison. "All the guys like a girl with a shaved head."

Robert began to wail aloud—this was his standard response whenever anyone brought up the possibility that one day the apple of his eye, the little girl whom he insisted had walked and talked before anyone else in her preschool, and was even now learning to read, might want to have anything to do with boys. Officer Ellis, before settling into such a suburban life that he owned two gas grills and a battalion of lawn equipment bigger than the infantry sections of some third world countries, had been a wild young man who had lead many a young girl astray. He was convinced God was going to punish him for that period, just as his mother always said He would. God would do it by sending young men who wore pants with the crotch at the knee and admired Ice Cube to court his daughter.

Alison knew from experience that Robert could keep up his dreadful keening for half an hour, but she had planned well, and he was just taking a second breath by the time she turned the car into the parking lot of the Gay, Lesbian and Bisexual Services Center of Colorado.

"You didn't tell me this was going to be a goddamn *party*," said Robert, looking out the passenger window and then hastily lighting up a cigarette. Although Robert was a vocal advocate of Gay Rights, and got along wonderfully with all of Alison's lesbian friends, he tended to act kind of like a jerk around gay men, convinced they were always cruising him. Nothing Alison had been able to say, including all the standard responses like, 'Aren't you flattering yourself?' and 'For christsake, we don't think about sex all the time any more than you do', had been able to change his mind. This was because, most of the time, gay men *were* cruising him. Robert was a nice looking guy in a Black Republican kind of way, and he looked almost as good in his uniform as Alison did in hers.

"Gay culture. Enjoy it." Alison made an expansive gesture towards what, except for all the same sex couples, looked pretty much like your standard church bazaar. The community center, which until the year before had been located in an office building on Colfax, had benefited unexpectedly in March, when one of their founding members had finally lost his five year struggle with AIDS. Much to the surprise of not only the staff, but the man's partner, who had not realized his discreet little affairs had not been quite discreet enough, the former president had left the center his spacious Victorian home. After they had gotten over the shock, and the first stages of mourning, everyone had been delighted, except for the boyfriend, who, when last heard of, was bagging groceries at the gay King Soopers, rather than living the life of ease he had projected to those various indiscretions who no longer called. The house was much more spacious than the windowless offices had been, and it also offered a lawn upon which a yard sale was in process. All kinds of queers, most in unflattering shorts, were picking through each other's cast offs. The stone lion by the front walk was wearing a former Miss Gay Colorado's tiara and lucky rhinestone necklace. Over by the side of the lawn, a big leather girl in full gear, despite the heat, was grilling hot dogs and Polish sausages and selling them for two dollars. Robert cast a critical eye at the grill and turned up his nose just a bit.

In the tiny parking lot, the gay youth group, OUTEEN was running a car wash. Or, at least, that's what their sign said. What was really happening was a huge water fight, and Alison kept a wary eye on the girl holding the hose as she got out of the car. This was just her lunch hour—she didn't want to spend the rest of the afternoon in a wet polyester uniform. The girl was a sight to behold even without the hose: thin as a rail, dressed all in black right down to her lipstick. She was wearing a baseball cap backwards over her long blonde hair, and there was a tiny padlock locked through the side of her nose.

Robert walked around to the driver's side in a nervous-macho kind of way, pretending not to look over his shoulder at two queenie men selling balloons and very obviously talking about his ass.

"Don't flatter yourself," Alison lied as she handed him the keys. "Meet you in forty-five. You can stay in the car if you're afraid to get out."

Because it *was* her lunch break, Alison stopped to buy a hot dog and chat up the leather girl, who was a friend of her girlfriend, Stacy. Stacy had been big on the dungeon scene this year, and Alison, who had been dragged to a few herself, was still not quite up on next day etiquette. What did you say to someone, for example, whom you had last seen in restraints and on fire? Alison settled for a few remarks about the weather, and admired the flannel pajamas, hardly worn, the woman had purchased for $1.50 from the yard sale.

Up on the big Victorian porch, a thin man at a draped table was telling fortunes with a tarot deck. He was dressed in full, if stereotypical, gypsy drag, up to and including a fringed shawl, head scarf and hoop earrings. There were also two face painters, who were doing such beautiful things with the pink triangle and rainbow motifs that for a moment Alison thought of indulging. That'd freak out anybody they pulled over for a tail light violation.

She resisted both this temptation, and the even stronger one to get a quick piercing at the next booth. Stacy had hinted a pierced nipple would be most pleasing, and Alison could go back to work with it hidden under her shirt and Robert none the wiser. There were, however, all kinds of people wandering around taking photos for the local gay rags, so she thought better of it. She'd never make detective with that kind of publicity photo. Face it, she was never going to make detective at all. Too maverick, too queer.

In the main room downstairs, a local vintage photographer was donating her efforts to the cause. For fifteen dollars, you and your friends could dress up as pioneers or outlaws or dance hall girls and have your picture taken in front of a saloon door back drop. As Alison walked by, two portly men, one in a lace wedding gown with a parasol and one in a tail coat and top hat, were saying cheese. A whole slew of dykes dressed like Butch Cassidy were waiting to be next.

"Alison! In here!" Michelle Martin, Alison's oldest friend and upstairs neighbor, had separatist leanings. She really did think it was best lesbians save their energy for other lesbians and the straights and gay men be allowed to go to hell in a hand basket. Therefore, she had been put in quite a quandary the previous spring when, out of all the candidates applying, she had been chosen by the GLBSCC (the name had been changed as a gesture to the bisexual community earlier in the year, and everybody was still trying to get their mouths around the string of initials) as the dyke they wanted the very most to put together the Denver Lesbian History and Archive project. Working at the center meant working, at least peripherally, with men.

Even more dismaying, Alison suspected, was the fact that Michelle found herself actually liking several of the boys at the center. It was hard to be a purist in the real world.

At any rate, this explained how Michelle happened to be involved in the big summer GAY-la, and why, by extension, Alison was dropping by on her lunch hour with her little envelope of papers under her arm. Michelle, who was beckoning to her from the top of the showpiece staircase, was wearing a nametag identifying her as a staff member, and carrying a cardboard box. The staircase, which was so wide as to immediately give rise to debutante fantasies, had lavender crepe paper wound in and out among the banisters and helium balloons were tied to the newel posts. A number of the balloons had been liberated and were now tied to the wrists of small children who were either tailing a parent or running madly.

"Up *here*," said Michelle again, and then disappeared, with a last cross look at two children who were running amuck. Obediently, Alison crossed the hall. Off the main room, in what had probably once been the dining room, men and women from the mixed chorus, dressed elegantly in their performance outfits, black pants, tux shirt, cummerbund and bow tie, were serving coffee and tea to those who'd had a little too much festival. Through another door, Alison spotted Michelle's lover, Janka Weaversong, off in one of the side rooms running a cardboard weaving workshop.

On the big landing of the staircase, Alison passed what was obviously a book signing table, though there was no author beside the stacks of paperbacks. Michelle pulled an apple and a bottle of spring water out of her box and set them on the table.

A small child tobogganed past them in a cardboard box. On the balcony, Alison could see the boys from the gay salon on Colfax giving new punk haircuts to two of the OUTEEN kids. Alison reached a hand out to pick up one of the books, but before she could Michelle, in a dour voice, said, "Ol' Heather there better find her two mommies really quick, or she's going to lose her head." Casting daggers at the tobogganing child, who was pulling her box upstairs for another run, she started briskly up the stairs again, Alison trailing her. "They're doing the wills in here." She gestured toward the closed door of what had once been a bedroom.

Although every little festive piece of the GAY-la brought in a little money, the event which brought in the really big bucks was the will-a-thon. Local gay and lesbian lawyers spent the day behind card tables fixing up simple wills for ex-lovers and GLBSCC staff and potential dates—in short, anybody who had sixty dollars and an estate that wasn't too complicated. That description fit Alison perfectly, and was the reason she was settling for a hot dog here instead of making Robert, who did carbohydrates like he did cigarettes—constantly and behind his wife's back—go to Healthy Habits.

The will room was a bit less noisy than the rest of the center, but a little festivity had crept in. Two of the lawyers were wearing crowns made out of gold, sparkly pipe cleaners, and someone had let a whole bouquet of balloons loose near the door, so you had to dodge through their long ribbons to reach the desks. There were clients with all three lawyers, which made Alison's heart sink a little. She had hoped to be in and out so fast Michelle would have no time at all to question her about the details she had filled into her pre-will paperwork.

"So lemme see what you put," said Michelle, shooting that hope all to shit. Ah, it had been a fantasy anyway—Michelle was bound to find out sooner or later. Silently, Alison handed the envelope over. Then, since Michelle seemed to have forgotten she was in the middle of a job, Alison picked up the box and passed out fruit and water to the lawyers. One, Stacy's friend Liz, caught her eye and winked.

Michelle was still looking at the papers, working up to blow, so Alison cracked the door and looked into the hall. The hall made an L about twenty feet down, and around the corner someone was having a crisis. She could not see it, of course, but she could hear the muted weeping and, in the window of the sun porch, she could see two wavery reflections, too distorted even to tell the sex, though there seemed to be a lot of long blonde hair in the picture.

"It meant nothing," said a voice that, especially considering this crew, could have belonged to either a man or a woman. "It didn't mean anything! It was just a good time!"

This conversation was a bit too close to several Alison had been on the receiving end of in the past few years, so she decided to shut the door and check on Michelle, who she figured was probably close to boiling.

"You didn't put me down as the executor!" Michelle's little baby butch face was crinkled with astonishment and indignation. "You put your dad down!"

Alison looked longingly over at Liz, who was nodding seriously as the woman in front of her listed who would take her cats upon her death. "Well, yes..." she began.

"I put you down on mine!" said Michelle, in a voice containing such hurt the topic could have been monogamy.

"Well, yes..." repeated Alison. She peeped into the hall again, just to steel herself for the scene that was sure to follow. The weeping was still going on, but, so far as the reflection in the window could be trusted, it appeared that one of the original two players had left, probably the person to whom the encounter had meant nothing, and someone new was comforting the blonde weeper.

"Michelle." Alison shut the door again and took a deep breath. "Michelle. I did the living will. But it doesn't make any difference if you don't have someone who is going to make them pull the plug."

"Oh!" Michelle put her hand up to her heart as if she had been shot. "Oh! And you can't trust *me* with that, but you can trust your *father*?"

"My dad's done it before. Remember?" Alison pleaded. Pleading was preferable to hurting Michelle's feelings, which was coming next. "Remember—he had to get them to unplug my granddad—had to get a court order to back it up?"

"And so you don't trust me because I haven't done it before? Does that also mean you wouldn't elect a woman president because she hasn't done it yet? How can we expect the Straights to respect our relationships if we don't even honor them ourselves? How can..." She was working herself up for a good twenty minute tirade. Obviously Alison was not going to get away with being vague, so she leapt right in with the word she had been hoping to avoid.

"Michelle," she said, holding up a finger to indicate this issue should not be pushed any further for both their sakes, "Rover."

Rover had been Michelle's old dog who should have been put down three years before Alison and Janka had sneaked him off to the vet's themselves. It was still a touchy topic.

"Oh!" said Michelle, holding her heart again. "Well!" She swept out of the room, carrying her box with her. Through the open door, Alison could see that the hall was suddenly full to bursting with dripping wet teenagers, all of whom appeared to be speaking at once.

"No, if you do that they'll just..."

"We're supposed to be safe here, how can we trust..."

"Marnie, no, Marnie, no, don't..."

Over the top of the din, Alison could hear a woman saying over and over, in a voice of forced calm, "I need some help here. If you're a Youth Facilitator, I want you to take the people around you and go downstairs. We'll talk about it later. I need some help here..." For a moment Alison wondered if she should step into the hall and try to give a hand, but then she saw that the two men giving haircuts had put down their clippers and come out into the confusion, talking in the same calm voice as the unseen woman.

"Youth Facilitators, please take the hands of the two people next to you and go down to the coffee room. We'll be down in a minute." A boy who looked so young Alison thought his parents might be horrified to find out not only that he was gay, but that he had taken the Colfax bus alone, pushed past Alison. He was holding the hands of another boy and a girl, both of whom were weeping. His face was torn with indecision—he wanted to stay with the crisis, but was determined to be responsible as a facilitator. The exit of the trio turned the tide. Hesitantly, the other youth, many of whom were also crying, began to follow them.

"Get everybody food," said one of the haircutters, slapping a twenty into the hand of one of the older girls, who was ushering a small group in front of her.

"Next!" sang Liz from her cramped little desk, and reluctantly Alison shut the door. This was the kind of drama in which Michelle absolutely reveled, but she had disappeared.

"So here she is, the Big A," said Liz, bobbing her head so that the spires of her crown dipped graciously. Liz was small, and had been freckled with a generous hand. She had just lately let her young girl-friend, Carla, who she was sending to beauty school, cut her hair in a new experimental style that had turned out badly. The crown, frankly, was a mistake, because it drew attention to her head. "So what'd you do, leave all your dough to the Sisterhood of Steel instead of Michelle?" Liz and Michelle were open antagonists.

"No. Michelle thinks it is my right to do anything I want with my worldly possessions." Alison said this firmly, although she kind of thought, in Michelle's book, that probably meant to any of the approved people and causes, not to the leathergirls' bike club. "Michelle is objecting to the fact that I did not make her executor of my living will."

"Oh," said Liz, sorting through the forms Alison had handed her. "Rover." Alison had already told Stacy the story of Michelle's old dog and what Stacy knew, Liz knew. "Wise move, there, Alison. I'd hate to have to smuggle you to the vet."

The whole will-making process did not take more than fifteen minutes. Alison had carefully listed who was to get her car and her stocks and her savings—Michelle; and who was to take her cat—Michelle again; and who was to make sure her personal things were distributed to her family and friends—Michelle, of course. She had not left anything at all to Stacy, the woman she had been dating for a year, which was a little embarrassing, considering Liz was Stacy's best friend. She had thought about it. But the truth was, she had been striving very hard to avoid the dreaded lesbian relationship merge, and it seemed rather silly to leave her Holly Near albums and cat fabric to someone to whom she wouldn't even give a spare key yet, and with whom she might break up at any time over cleaning habits or personal quirks. It happened. Whereas she and Michelle had been friends since grade school; they were practically joined at the hip. Michelle could be trusted to use anything she was given wisely and spread it around the community like a cranky little fairy godmother. If she was still speaking to Alison.

The hoopla in the hall had vanished by the time Alison exited, though there were still puddles of water on the hardwood floor where the OUTEENS had stood. Alison hoped that someone would find a mop before the poor ex-president turned over in his grave. From the top of the stairs, Alison could see that the youth group had all but taken over the tea room. They were earnestly processing while putting away tea cakes.

Michelle was standing on the landing, talking to a stocky woman with dark hair.

"Well," she said, upon seeing Alison. Alison steeled herself for another chapter of the lecture, but all Michelle said was, "You remember Tamsin, don't you?" One never knew with Michelle whether or what she was going to blow off or keep close in her heart as a death grudge. Michelle liked to keep people on their toes. Grateful that, at least for the moment, she seemed to have chosen the former, Alison stuck out her hand. Tamsin, Tamsin. The woman did indeed seem familiar, but she could not place her.

"I'm sorry," she said, looking to Michelle for help. "I just don't..." She stopped, whipping her head back around. "Tamsin? From *Big Mama Rag?*"

Michelle laughed with delight. "I told you she'd remember," she said, as if Alison had done something very clever. Which she almost had. Let's see, *Big Mama Rag,* the Denver lesbian paper, had closed the door of its basement room in the late seventies, and she hadn't seen Tamsin since the last time she had picked up Michelle at a staff meeting. Thirteen years? That was pretty damn good identification, especially considering the metamorphosis Tamsin had undergone. Back in the seventies, Tamsin had been, like Michelle and Alison and all of their friends, a political flannel-shirt dyke. They had all worn, day after day, outfits that were similar enough to be a uniform. They had gone to the same barber for three dollar hair cuts, or not bothered at all, and just pulled their hair back in a one length ponytail. From that mold, Tamsin, who had been one of the ponytail set, had butterflied into a very butch gal, her dark, grey-flecked hair gelled into almost a ducktail. She was wearing a tank-top with a March on Washington logo, and though she had gained weight (and who hadn't?) her shoulders and arms were firm, as if she had been lifting weights.

"So you're still in town?" Alison asked politely, thinking she had to get out more. Thirteen years was a long time not to run into another local dyke. She had made a vow to go to more concerts and women's events this year, but the last show in town had featured Ferron and Buffy St. Marie together, and that had seemed just a little too eclectic— kind of like putting Joan Baez and Phranc on the same bill.

"Kind of back in town," Tamsin interrupted that little flight of fancy in a firm voice, as if she had not only detected Alison's wandering mind, but wished to reprimand her for it as well. You could tell right away that Tamsin was the kind of gal who wanted to top everything. Oh, shit. Alison's smile wavered just a little. She hated these top and only top gals, and it didn't matter whether they really were leather girls or just GUPPYS with control issues. However—she did a quick scan that took in Tamsin's fly, bottom button left undone, and landed on the subtle black bandanna sticking out of the back left pocket of her 501's—she'd bet twenty dollars that Tamsin *had* gotten into the leather scene since last they met, and another twenty said Michelle didn't realize it. Alison chuckled to herself. Far be it from her to spoil Michelle's little reunion.

Tamsin's grip tightened on her hand, bringing her back to attention. "I lived in Tacoma for quite a little while, then I finally decided to come back home." She gazed directly into Alison's eyes, and Alison gazed directly, unwaveringly back. She had been around this kind of woman before, and she was familiar with the lead dog technique.

"But guess what?" Michelle was dancing up and down with excitement and pleasure at meeting an old friend. The bottles in her box clinked together. She stepped back and made an expansive motion towards the table. "Tam is Katie Copper!"

"Really?" The firm handshake, the top dog stare, the black bandanna had not impressed Alison, but this news did. Katie Copper was one of their favorite lesbian authors—they owned all of her books and followed the adventures of her protagonist, Blaze Badgirl, eagerly. Blaze was a punk baby butch with plenty of time for adventure and mystery, because instead of holding a job she received a monthly disability check for living just a little too far on the wrong side of reality. "We love your books!"

"That's what I've been telling her!" Michelle broke in eagerly. "Of course, I knew that Katie Copper was going to be here," she gave Alison a look that said, and so would you if you'd read the leaflet I gave you, "but I had no idea it was Tam!"

There was a commotion downstairs, caused by the OUTEEN group all exiting the tea room at one time.

"What was that all about?" Alison asked, inclining her head. A couple of the kids were still mopping tears. "There was all this screaming and yelling upstairs…"

"Oh, god, it was awful," said Michelle. "I thought we were going to have a riot. One of the kids was threatening suicide or something, and the facilitators wanted to call the police and have her taken to the hospital, and the other kids got wind of it and freaked. They don't realize that the center has liability, we *have* to report runaways, we *have* to turn in suicides…."

Alison gave her a look. This was the same Michelle who had personally busted women from the loony bin and raved about psychiatric abuse to the point that Alison went to therapy for six months before telling her? Michelle had the good grace to blush. "Anyway," she went on, with a marked loss of momentum, "some little baby dyke had lost her first love or something…"

"Excuse me," Tamsin interrupted, "but do you have an ice pack in that box for me?"

"Oh, yeah!" Michelle, obviously seeing this as a chance to get off the hot seat, abandoned the story and began rooting in the box.

"Drinks for the lawyers, Girl Scout cookies for the fortune teller, here they are!" She handed over two blue ice packs. Tamsin held one in each hand, curling her fingers around them. Alison struggled for a comment. Katie Copper she would have inquired solicitously after—Tamsin McArthur she suspected of putting on a little show—the important author deals bravely with her writer's cramp.

"Pardon me." A tall woman dressed in one of those shapeless, low waisted jumpers made popular by LL Bean, interrupted. "I hope you don't mind," she said to Alison, who by the third word realized that this was the person who went with the calm voice in the upper hall. "My name is Marnie, and I'm with the OUTEEN group...."

Please, God, thought Alison, Let that kid be already out of here. Don't let her ask me to take her away. Please just this one thing, and I'll never ask for anything again.

It was not easy being a lesbian cop. On the one side were the straight and narrow boys in uniform who thought, despite the fact Amendment two had been declared unconstitutional and Denver's gay rights law was back on the books, no goddamn queer should be disgracing the uniform. On the other side were the dykes and fags who, every time she showed up anywhere in uniform, took it upon themselves to confront her about every atrocity ever committed by the boys in blue, from Rodney King to Stonewall. If she had to strong-arm a weeping teenage lesbian into the squad car and take her to Denver General, she would never live down the stigma.

"...we're having career day soon," Marnie went on, blithely unaware of the panic she was causing, "and I wondered if you'd come speak to the kids..."

So relieved was Alison it was only this and not *that*, that she agreed immediately, and even passed over one of the business cards that her father, Captain Kaine of Denver District Four, had proudly printed for her every Christmas. She had a backlog of about five hundred.

"Why'd you do...?" asked Michelle loudly, on the verge of revealing Alison's fear of public speaking.

Hastily, Alison broke in. "Michelle's a stained glass artist," she said, presenting her with a flourish, as if she were the first lesbian supreme court judge. "Would you like her to come, too?"

"They don't want artists." This was from Janka, who had come quietly up the stairs behind Marnie. Her event was over; she was carrying a pile of samples. "They have a special day when crafts women come in and talk about living on rice for a month and try to encourage the kids to become doctors and lawyers."

"But Tamsin is a successful lesbian author," said Michelle, getting into the spirit of throwing your friends to the wolves.

There was a sudden and complete pause Alison did not understand. Tamsin looked steadily at Marnie, and Marnie looked steadily at Tamsin. Marnie was the first to look away, but she did it with disdain, rather than submission.

"I think not," she said.

There was another small pause.

"Robert is here," said Janka to Alison. "That's what I came to tell you. The gay teens are forcing him to get the squad car washed."

"I'd better go save him." Alison looked around a last time. "I thought I was going to see Stacy here, but it looks like we're going to miss each other."

The OUTEENS had not only bullied Robert into a wash, they were busily vacuuming the seats and floor, commenting loudly on the doughnut ends and fast food wrappers with which Officer Ellis marked his territory. Officer Ellis himself was standing off to one side, trying to look cool rather than panicked as two of the seventeen year old boys tried to hit on him. Time for a rescue. Alison waved at Michelle, who was trying to keep a pack of small, unsupervised children from making away with her free juice. Although she had not particularly liked Tamsin McArthur upon re-acquaintance, she wished she had been able to talk writing with Katie Copper, who she suspected was as much a separate entity as Stacy's top personality, Anastasia. Oh, well, Tam was a local now, and local authors were always being pressed into charity book signings and readings. Alison would run into her again soon.

She just didn't realize that she'd be dead.

2

"I can't believe I was roped in to this," Alison groused four weeks later. She adjusted her shirt collar, as if wearing it up or down was going to make her look like anything but a middle-aged mommy to these kids. "It's bad enough that I have to wear this thing five days a week, I shouldn't have to wear it on my day off, too." She had been whining and moaning for over an hour—everybody had been over it long ago.

"Take your gun," advised Michelle. "You might have to shoot some of the kids. They were on the verge of rioting the whole time I was there." She was draped over one end of Alison's couch, reading from a short stack of laser-printed computer paper. As she finished each page, she placed it on the coffee table and Stacy, who was draped over the other end of the couch, picked it up.

"Yeah, take your gun," agreed Janka, who was sitting on the floor and having a little love fest with Alison's tattered old grey cat, KP. "The week *I* was there two of the baby dykes were at each other's throats. One of them had slept with the other's girlfriend. They had to lock them in separate rooms. And," she added, rubbing KP under the chin in that special way only she understood, "while the facilitator was dealing with *that,* one of the other kids pulled out a potato and an ice cube and offered to do piercings. In places my mother doesn't even wash."

"And these are the same kids who wept because Marnie called the cops on a runaway?" Alison marveled. "We are talking about that same sensitive group?"

"They are sensitive," said Michelle, without looking up. "They are also walking hormone machines. Just watch your back."

Stacy, who read a little faster than Michelle, and so had a little lag time at the end of each page, looked up. "Okay, now, how did you two get roped into being speakers?" she asked. "And what did you talk about?"

"The same way as everybody else," said Janka. "We were at the GAY-la, we were adults, we didn't seem to be drunk and we didn't have any spikes sticking out of our cheeks or tongues."

"I don't know if that last is a necessary qualification," interjected Stacy. "Marnie caught me at the piercing booth."

Janka shrugged. "Anyway, I got to talk about the anti-violence project. They took four smoke breaks in an hour and a half. I haven't seen that many people in one place smoking in ten years."

"Oh, man, I don't want to do this," Alison whined. She eyed the manuscript Stacy and Michelle were sharing enviously. "I want..."

"Stop whining," said Stacy, "or I'll have to beat you later." This was not something she would have normally said in front of Michelle, but Michelle was tuned out to the world, engrossed in the new adventures of Blaze Badgirl.

"Well, there's a confusing thought," said Janka. "You mean the punishment is the same as the reward?"

"It does get a little difficult," Stacy admitted. "We certainly would have fucked with Pavlov's head. So what did Michelle talk about?"

"The Archives. She got to give her slide show. At least as much as there is so far. I understand the kids made shadow puppets on the screen through the whole thing. I further understand that the puppets performed a number of unsafe acts with one another."

"Have fun, honey," said Stacy, returning to the manuscript.

Alison pouted. She didn't want to spend the afternoon with a bunch of horny teenagers who might make fun of her. She, too, wanted to spend it with Blaze Badgirl and her femme sidekick, Diamond. "How did Michelle get this manuscript, anyway?" she asked Janka.

KP opened one eye. Even he was sick of the whining.

"Oh, they've hung out a couple of times since the GAY-la. Tamsin doesn't really know anybody else in town yet. I guess it's been hard to connect with her old crowd. It's not the whole manuscript, anyway, it's just the first chapter."

Alison lowered her voice. "Does Michelle realize Tam is in the leather scene, yet?"

Janka's lips twitched and she tucked her head without answering. Michelle had gone through great agony when Alison had gotten involved with Stacy. She was totally opposed to S/M and thought that the leather girls were the poorest of representatives for the lesbian community. Twenty years of friendship, however, was hard to discard. She had finally come to grips with Alison's new proclivities through a combination of ignoring the whole thing and being mean to Stacy when the mood struck her. It was unkind, Alison knew, to keep her in the dark about Tamsin, but if even Janka wasn't saying anything, she certainly was not going to be the one to spill the beans.

"So," Janka inclined her head towards the manuscript, "I guess if you go to the baths with Katie Copper, you get to preview the new book." She glanced over at Michelle and asked, sotto voce, "Do you know that for sure about Tam, or are you still guessing?"

"For sure," Alison whispered. She inclined her head towards Stacy. "Stacy saw her at Powersurge. She was chickenhawking." Powersurge was the big lesbian leather conference Stacy had attended that spring in Seattle. Without Alison. They were still working that one through. The agreement she and Stacy had after a year was they were not 'partners' or 'lovers' or 'life companions.' They were girl-friends. Period. They were dating. Period. They were not yet ready to buy a house or land or a business together, they didn't want both names on their checks or cute Christmas photos to include in jointly signed cards. They did not want to co-habitat. And, since it was Alison who was pushing hardest for all this space and non-commitment, she had not felt she had any right at all to complain when Stacy announced she was going to Powersurge and made it clear Alison was not invited along. But, just because Alison was resigned about the trip, did not mean she wanted to hear the details about the workshops and the dungeons and the old friends Stacy had seen. The snippet of information about Tamsin McArthur, which Stacy had volunteered the evening of the GAY-la, when she had shown up for dinner carrying an autographed Blaze Badgirl mystery, was the only detail Alison had heard.

"How do you like her?" Alison asked Janka.

Janka shrugged. KP was on his back now, offering his beautiful white belly up for admiration and homage. "I like the Katie Copper part. I mean—if you can get her talking about books and writing, she's great. She's funny, she's witty—you can see a lot of Blaze in her. But other than that..." she gave another shrug. "Power issues."

"Full time top," Alison agreed. "Did she try that eye thing with you?"

"Yes, and I apparently did not pass, because she treated me like a servant the whole time she was here. Needless to say, I did not say, 'Come back soon.'"

"Did she try it with Michelle?"

"Probably. But can you imagine anyone topping Michelle?" They both laughed. Stacy, during one of her exchanges with Michelle, had politely asked her, "Now, were you medicated as a child?" and it was true she was the most hyperactive adult Alison had ever met. Even now, as she read, she was tapping one foot and bobbing her head. Luckily for all involved, Michelle channeled her energy into a number of productive skills. She was a wonderful Jill-of-all-trades who could wire your cabin or sand your floor or re-shingle your roof, and she was likely to start any of these projects if you spent too much time in the bathroom while you were supposed to be entertaining her. Michelle wouldn't hold still long enough for anyone to give her the domination stare, and she would be oblivious to anything more subtle, like the bandanna or the button on Tamsin's jeans.

"Are you sure you don't want to come with me, just for support?" Alison turned wheedlingly to Stacy.

"No way." Stacy didn't even look up. "Liz and I have to go next week and speak on Leather and Drag. We're the leather part, in case you couldn't figure it out. Don't ask me how they came up with that combination."

"Two aspects of the community that everybody else hates and denies and puts down?" offered Michelle. It was not clear whether she was merely offering, or endorsing this explanation but still, Alison thought it best to leave.

****

Janka had been right about one thing. Practically every single one of the kids in the group smoked. It was like a bad seventies flashback.

But she had been wrong about another. Alison had not taken her gun, and she was very glad she had not taken it. The group was gregarious and bright and not at all shy. From the way they pushed in to stroke her uniform and fondle her props during the smoke break, had she been armed she would have been fearful that one of them might have lifted it and used it to shoot up either the skinheads on Colfax, or an unrequited love. There were plenty of both.

"Oooh, let me play with your handcuffs," said one of the boys, who was dressed in leather drag and had piercings in his lips, nose, ears and tongue. One of the other boys, a preppie type from the suburbs, had lifted her nightstick and was making highly lewd and recognizable gestures with it.

"Give me that," she said, swatting at them like mosquitoes. "Go away. Go talk to the doctors and plumbers." She jerked her head towards the other adults Marnie had bullied into making a career appearance.

"Ooo, love a girl in uniform," said one of the girls, as if it were something original, rather than something Alison heard so often she wouldn't even play with Stacy in her uniform. Which was a shame, because Stacy really *did* love a girl in uniform. The girl was all leathered up herself, wearing chaps and a jacket that Alison, who had a decent job, certainly couldn't afford. And little else. Her black and red zebra striped panties were little more than a g-string. She stood close to Alison, playing with the little chain that went from her nose to her ear in a seductive way that made Alison nervous.

"I have to talk to Marnie," Alison blurted and pushed her way out of the group.

"I see they almost ate you alive," said Marnie, offering her a cigarette. It had been five years since Alison had smoked, but she took one anyway.

"No shit!" They watched the girl in leather run a finger up the arm of one of the gay boys, who merely looked startled. Her long hair was shaved on both sides of her head, and the middle strip either hung down her back or stood up in purple and green spikes.

"Thanks for coming," said Marnie. "These kids *really* need good role models. Half of them can't get anything but phone work." She nodded towards a knot of young men who were critiquing each other's hair cuts. "One of our kids is even some kind of AT&T phone supervisor—he recruits every week. I mean, it's not that it's *bad* to do phone work, but they can't *imagine* ever doing anything else. We've got a lot of dropouts, you know—that holds them back." She sighed and was silent a moment. "You were lucky to escape that crowd with your life," she said finally, blowing a long stream of smoke out her nose, and looking back over her shoulder at the girl in leather. "We just call this place 'Hormone Central'. The group breaks up around January every year, over the boyfriend, girlfriend thing. They sleep with each other. They trick with their friends' main squeezes. Then they get mad and divide into camps and don't come to group for a couple of months. Except for the really nerdie kids. I love the nerdie kids."

"I saw that scene at the GAY-la," Alison said. "They all seemed really freaked."

Marnie sighed heavily. "I hate it," she said, "when I have to turn someone over to authorities. I hate it, and it's especially bad if there are any other kids around. They don't understand—what am I going to do with someone who is suicidal? I'm not trained to handle a major freak out scene. I'm just not, and I can't turn a kid loose on the street like that. And if a kid's a runaway we're bound by law to report her. By law! Most of the time, if I think a kid is on the streets, I try real hard not to ask her. I try to steer her towards one of the other kids, somebody who has their own place, and might put her up. Or I try to have the Safe House information out. I figure, if they ran, there must be something badly wrong at home—how is it my business to put them back? But sometimes they're really out of control, and you have to do *something*." She sighed again.

"Oh, was the kid involved a runaway?" asked Alison vaguely. She was watching with the intensity of an anthropologist how the gay kids laughed and joked with each other. What must it be like to have that kind of support at sixteen and seventeen?

"Actually not," said Marnie. "I was wrong about that one. Thank God. It's bad enough to call the parents, but if you have to call the police, the kids never trust you again."

"Marnie," one of the youth facilitators pulled on her arm, "I think maybe someone set the trash on fire in the bathroom."

Marnie appeared neither to be alarmed or surprised. "Back in a minute," she said to Alison.

The lesbian doctor, who was pretty much the primary caregiver for all the dykes in Capital Hill, was heading Alison's way with a look of grim determination on her face. Uh, oh, she was going to ask if Alison had made an appointment with a rheumatologist, as she had been promising and failing to do for six months. Hastily Alison flaunted her cigarette. As she'd thought, this stopped the doctor like an invisible wall. "I'm going to get you yet!" she called from ten feet away.

Alison smiled mysteriously and let a huge mouthful of smoke trickle over her lips and nose. She waited in vain for Marnie to reappear. There was some secret signal, and everyone, except Alison, threw down their cigarette and trooped back inside. It was the first time she had smoked in five years, she wasn't about to throw it down halfway. The young leathergirl, who was talking to one of the boys whom she referred to as 'Boss', gave her a slow wink as she slouched in the door.

"Don't hit on the speakers, Obsidian," scolded one of the younger boys, pulling her by the hand.

Alison stood propped against the building, inhaling deeply. She didn't care what Marnie said about runaways, that kid was or had been a sex worker. Alison could feel it. She was just about to enter a smokers' Zen state when a familiar voice sounded shrilly right in her ear.

"Hey! Are you done yet? Can you leave? What are you doing?!"

Michelle was better at blindsiding people than anyone Alison knew. The first two questions were startling simply because Alison had not seen Michelle approaching on her hybrid mountain bike. The third, shrieked as if Alison had been caught trying to give Tammy Faye, Michelle's dignified long-haired cat, a punk cut, made Alison jump and fan her hand down in the direction of her holster.

"What am *I* doing? What are *you* doing? I thought you were at home reading about Blaze Badgirl!"

"You're smoking! Is this what you do every time you go out? Have you been smoking the whole time?" Michelle was understandably peeved. She and Alison had gone on the weed together, and they had gotten off together. Alison could see Michelle's little mind ticking like a clock—if Alison had smoked just one cigarette every time she had gone out without her, then, well, damnit, she was thousands ahead of her! You could practically see her looking around for a Seven-Eleven.

"Get a grip," said Alison crossly, tossing the butt, which still had at least three good drags left on it, to the ground. "This was the first one. This will be the last one. What are you doing here?"

"I need a ride. I've got to go over to Tamsin's right away—it's an emergency—you know our car is in the shop."

"Why didn't you ask Stacy to give you a ride?" Alison asked nastily, still pissed about the surprise attack.

A lesser woman might have decided to play that one mellow, considering she *was* asking for a favor, but Michelle was not such a woman.

"I didn't ask her because I didn't want anybody to think that I begged her to tie me up and beat me," answered Michelle, just as nastily.

"Oh, you ride with her all the time."

"Okay, I didn't ask because she had already gone home by the time I got the call. Is that good enough? Will you give me the ride? Or trade with me?"

"I'll take you. And, incidentally, I don't have to beg."

Michelle ignored this, contenting herself with putting a huge scratch on the top of Alison's car as she hoisted her bike up.

22

"So, what's wrong with Tamsin?" Alison asked as they cruised down Lincoln towards the north side of town. Knowing Michelle, it could be anything. Tam could have chipped her tooth. She could need help deciding if her shirt matched her socks. Michelle liked to inject a little drama into every situation, like a cook overly fond of seasoning with garlic.

"Nothing's wrong with Tamsin. In fact, I think she went out of town for the weekend." Michelle paused for dramatic effect. After a moment, Alison clicked on the radio. This was a little game they played. About half the time she let Michelle win, saying eagerly, "Then tell me! What, What!?" but she wasn't in the mood today.

"It was her neighbor who called," said Michelle sullenly, after they had heard Mary-Chapin Carpenter demand passionate kisses. "Apparently Tamsin left her tub running or something. The downstairs neighbors' ceiling is leaking and she's afraid it's going to come through at any minute if it isn't stopped. Tam left her my name in case of emergency—she gave me her extra keys."

"Hmm." That didn't sound too exciting. Even Michelle was going to have to work awfully hard to milk this one. Alison wondered if it would be possible to start smoking again. Moderately. Just one cigarette a day, as a little treat. Right.

Michelle must have agreed with her analysis of Tam's situation, for she changed the subject. "You haven't forgotten about tomorrow, have you?" she asked anxiously. As if there was any chance. As if the date had not been ringed on Alison's calendar for months, as if Alison didn't know that, even if her father keeled right over dead, she'd better choose Michelle and Janka's conception ceremony over the funeral. For a minute, Alison considered saying yes, as a matter of fact, she had forgotten and planned something else. It might give Michelle something new to chew on, something to make up for the fact Tamsin's emergency was nothing more than a clogged drain. But, though Michelle could dissolve into and recover from a full blown, screaming and shouting tirade in less than five minutes, it tended to take anyone else within earshot just a little longer, and Alison wasn't up to it, even as a favor. She hummed along with Clint Black.

≈ 3 ≈

The woman downstairs, whom Alison instantly identified as Family, answered the door immediately. She was obviously trying to make the best of things. Through her open door Alison could see a mop bucket, surrounded by towels, but just as obviously she did not want to make small talk. She wanted the damn tub turned off and it was right up the stairs. The landlady lived just around the corner, but she wasn't home *either*, the neighbor said in a voice that told them it had been a bad day.

Actually, Tam's apartment was right up either of two sets of stairs, an inside set that the neighbor showed them, leading them around a pile of power tools and lumber in the lobby, and a metal stair case outside, little better than a fire escape, but still, a private entrance. Like the house in which Michelle, Janka, and Alison lived, this had once been a single family dwelling. There were two closed doors on the upper landing. Michelle turned towards the one marked Number Three.

"So Tam's out of town?" Alison asked, popping the can of Diet Pepsi she had insisted on stopping for over Michelle's protests. It was not just concern for Alison's body that had fueled the objection on the way over. Michelle knew damn good and well the caffeine-in-a-can habit was something Alison had picked up from Stacy, and therefore to be viewed with suspicion.

"I guess. She's been talking about it. I didn't know she'd decided." Michelle was having trouble with the lock, but Alison didn't sweat it. Nothing mechanical ever beat Michelle. If she couldn't do the lock she'd figure out a way to take the door off its hinges or something. Nope, it wasn't going to take that. With a small click of triumph the key was turned and the door was open.

Alison crowded up close behind Michelle, eager to see what the apartment was like. She loved looking at other women's living spaces, particularly if they were not home. The first thing she always looked for in women her own age were old dyke posters from the seventies, which she collected. Bingo, immediate score. Not only did Tamsin have 'The common woman', which Alison still had hung in her own bathroom, but also the fairly rare 'Butterfly woman', which had sold at the Denver women's bookstore for only a few months. Alison wondered if she would sell it.

"Mep! Mep!" Kitten sounds, but Alison could not locate the kittens themselves. Shy kittens. Shy kittens who were unhappy and had something to say about it. She walked through the living room—pleasant, not too-cluttered, a futon couch and sea shells on the mantle—and into the kitchen. There were the kittens, two little black heads peering out from beneath the refrigerator. There, too, was the source of the complaint, an empty food dish and a bone dry water bowl. Alison's mouth tightened in disapproval. She opened the cupboard beneath the sink—that was where *she* kept the Iams—and sure enough, there was the familiar purple bag. Twenty pound size, and stamped with the name of the dyke pet store over on sixth. She scooped a double handful into the bowl, and the kittens immediately forgot she was Satan in their hurry to chow down. KP regularly went directly from his bowl and straight out to tell strangers how bad things were at home, but this was not just a case of kitty lying. These guys seemed really hungry. She filled the water dish to the top, but neither seemed interested. The smaller kitten put her back foot, the only white appendage out of the eight, into the water dish in her haste to get the best kibbies.

Michelle was still in the other room.

"What are you doing?" Alison called.

"Just looking." Michelle was even nosier than Alison was—she was probably going through Tamsin's diaries and back bills. "Come and see her office."

Many of the divided houses in the north end had a little room that had been created by closing in a second story balcony. Most of these, the carpentry done by a landlord with more enthusiasm than actual experience, were actually livable only for a short period in the fall and spring. The little room in which Tamsin had her computer was the exception. Someone had actually taken the time to put up walls along two sides, instead of the usual bank of windows. The one long window that looked out over the yard was double paned so the room could actually be used as a workspace rather than converting to a walk-in refrigerator by November.

It was, beyond that, a delightful space, and Alison could see why Michelle had called her in. From the ceiling hung two mobiles, one featuring cranes, the other tropical fish, and a flying tiger made of balsa wood. The room was circled with waist high book shelves, and among the eclectic collection of books including *Hers Was the Sky*, *Macho Sluts* and a whole collection of Bebo Brinker, were crammed little pieces of folk art and personal trinkets. A stuffed cat in a harlequin costume with a porcelain head. A fat cat with a hollow body and an oil wick coming out of his head. A line of smooth black river rocks. A tiny Navajo doll working at her loom. Of course Michelle loved it. It was much like the pleasant apartment that she shared with Janka.

A bulletin board covered the entire upper wall, except for one place right by the computer, where there was a black board. The bulletin board looked like a giant collage created by a child who had not yet heard of theme. There were newspaper and magazine clippings—*Dolly Parton is Space Alien!* screamed one. There were photographs of women and cats. There were comics—Mo got lost at the March on Washington and Maybonne explained what life after death would be like. But, mostly, there were notes. Cryptic little notes, like the one written on the edge of the torn off menu that said, "Linda is selectively dyslexic" or the piece of notebook paper that read, "There's the doings report, and the death report and the depression report."

"Look at this one," Michelle said, laughing with delight. "'Pavlov's tacos.'"

"What does that mean?"

Michelle shrugged. "I don't know. Pavlov's tacos—they make you drool?"

Drooling reminded Alison. "Aren't you supposed to be here to turn off the water? That woman downstairs is probably freaking."

"Eh." Michelle shrugged again. "If the ceiling hasn't come down yet, three minutes isn't going to make a difference. Actually," she looked over her shoulder, "I've only been here one other time. I'm not sure where the bathroom is." They both did a three-sixty.

"Off the bedroom?" guessed Michelle, heading that way.

"Off the kitchen?" guessed Alison, going back. In these converted houses, one guess was just as good as another, for rooms had been crammed in wherever they might fit, witness the office as an example.

The kittens, now that their tiny little bellies were full, suddenly realized that Alison was an evil interloper and bolted for the refrigerator. She was quick enough to catch the one with the white foot. Kitten-like, she immediately changed her mind and settled, purring, into Alison's arms.

She had guessed right. The bathroom was off the kitchen, or, at least, off a little pantry that had probably once been a closet. It was a narrow little corridor, lined with shelves, and the doorway itself was also narrow. There was no door—they probably would have had to get one custom made, and that was expensive. Instead, a brightly patterned sheet had been tacked up for privacy. The bottom of the sheet dragged the ground. It was wet. An extension cord, plugged into an outlet on the shelves between Tamsin's clean linen and her canned goods, snaked out under the sheet.

"Found it," Alison called back to Michelle. The kitten had begun to knead and suck her hair enthusiastically, and she put her on the floor. She pushed the sheet aside and then stopped in horror.

The woman in the bathtub was not only obviously dead, but had been dead some time. Alison had seen a number of dead bodies in her career, and each time, after the initial shock, she was struck anew by their gracelessness. Tamsin's head was underwater. It was a big tub, but it had been necessary for her to fold up in an ugly, ungainly way in order to fit in that manner. One arm stuck straight up in the air. The hand dangled limply.

"Oh, Jesus." Alison held up a futile hand as if to prevent Michelle from coming into the room. "Oh, god." Michelle made a motion towards the woman, but Alison grabbed her shirt and pulled her back. Already she was clicking into that protective cop mode that masked her feelings and helped her get through things like this. "No, honey," she said, the 'honey' merely a concession because it was Michelle. "She's dead for sure—we can't do anything. We're going to have to call the police."

"We can't just...what if..." in a moment, unchanneled, Michelle would be hyperventilating.

"Go call the police," Alison said, automatically scanning the pantry for a paper bag just in case the channeling didn't work. It was a measure of Michelle's distress that she did exactly what she was told without arguing. Alison edged slightly into the room. There was a smoking smell in the room, and she saw, on the lip of the tub, one candle still burning, and another that had melted to a puddle, the red wax running down into and fanning out over the water. By the side of the tub was a plastic bucket, half full of water, and beside it an ice tray. She knew that, professionally, she should probably stay at the door. But what had happened here? Obviously Tam had drowned. But why? She could have dozed in the tub and sunk down, but why hadn't she just pushed her head up out of the water when it woke her? Surely no one was that sound a sleeper. Had she suffered a stroke or heart attack? She looked young for it, but age was not always a good indicator. The water was still running. Most of the overflow was going out the safety drain, but there was a towel that had fallen over the side of the tub, one end in the water, and it was acting as an aqueduct. Alison assumed the puddle at its other end was this causing the leak in the downstairs apartment. The woman downstairs was lucky, Alison thought, that nothing had floated against the drain. If the overflow had gone on unchecked for the entire weekend, then she might have arrived home to find a collapsed ceiling and a dead body in her kitchen. It was a sobering thought. But still, all of that aside, why had Tam drowned to begin with? Alison took one more tiny step into the room, and almost tripped over the mostly black kitten. Before she could put out a hand, the kitten leapt onto the side of the tub and drank daintily from the water. Alison recoiled. Not many things made her sick any more, but for some reason this did. She had to put her hand to her mouth to keep from losing the cookies and chips they had fed her at the OUTEEN meeting. Only after her stomach settled did she look back, and only then did she see the long black extension cord going into the water.

⤬ 4 ⤬

There was no place in the world more comforting than the apartment of Michelle and her lover, Janka Weaversong. The walls were always covered with their art work. Old projects disappeared as they were sold, and new took their place. Throughout the apartment were scattered signs of the many other skills with which Michelle bartered for her needs. Currently there was a bicycle upside down on a tarp in the living room and, a few feet away, a stringless guitar in the process of being refinished. In and among the plants (which were almost all vegetables) and the books (which were almost all by women) was a pleasant clutter of things the two had picked up on their travels or traded for at women's festivals. There were tiny vertebrae from mice and voles and owl feathers and river-worn stones and dancing goddesses made of fimo. There were chimes made of obsidian and porcelain and old forks hanging up in front of the windows, and during the summer they would catch the breeze from the open windows and tinkle softly all day. It was a most pleasant space to spend an afternoon.

"You've got to be kidding," Janka said, as she placed a bowl of carrot soup in front of Alison. She and Michelle had recently become committed vegetarians and Alison, who believed in the philosophy, but found old habits hard to shake, was trying rather unsuccessfully to follow suit.

"No," replied Alison with one eye on the bathroom door. She had waited until Michelle left the room to tell Janka the actual cause of death just in case her initial reaction was to giggle. Michelle, who had gone into a fairly major, and understandable freak-out at the scene of the crime, would be in no mood to make allowances for anyone else's nervous reactions. "No, I'm not, and let me hasten to add that Michelle is currently very sensitive on the subject." Alison hesitantly tasted the soup with the air of someone doing a noble but unpleasant duty.

"I guess *so*." Janka set a plate of bran muffins on the table. The smell that engulfed the apartment was like an olfactory sound track to *Leave it to Beaver*. Everything good and comforting was promised in it, and for a moment Alison was able to forget how awful it had been to sit in the downstairs neighbor's apartment, waiting for the boys from the Homicide Bureau to talk to them one last time. Not knowing what to say, pretending not to see when the ambulance crew hauled the body bag across the wooden porch a foot from the front window.

In Alison's opinion, it hadn't been necessary to detain them so long. The questions they were asked three hours after the Homicide Squad arrived were no different than the ones they were asked half an hour after they arrived. It was true that a death could not be categorized—accident, suicide, murder—until the coroner's report was issued, but come on, she and Michelle obviously had not been suspects in anything. Keeping them waiting had just been more gay bashing. Detectives Jones and Jorgenson, old nemeses of Alison's, just weren't about to miss a chance to make her uncomfortable while they had her in the unique role of citizen rather than fellow officer. They weren't impressed by her explanation about why she was in uniform either. It had sickened her to know that their homophobia reached into even a situation like this, but it had not surprised her. The year before, when she had discovered the identity of the person killing women at the local lesbian bars, they had not only never given her any kind of credit, but had actually tried to railroad her as being a nuisance and a hindrance on the case. That had gone nowhere, and Alison suspected it had been squelched internally by her father. He denied it, of course—he knew how strongly she felt about getting by on her own accomplishments.

But her father hadn't been there to metaphorically slap heads in Tam's apartment. If Jones and Jorgenson had said anything at all outright, Alison would have filed a complaint—Liz had a lawyer friend who was dying to take on *that* discrimination case. But it had just been the looks, the undertone, the hours of waiting.

"Her vibrator had fallen into the tub with her," Alison repeated to Janka, keeping a wary eye on the bathroom door. The problem was it *was* kind of funny, in a sick way, and laughing actually would have been a great way to relieve tension—one of those hysterical laughter scenes that ends up with everybody's head down on the table sobbing—if the men at the scene hadn't already been such pigs about it and pissed Michelle off so badly.

"Why in the world would anyone be using a vibrator in the bathtub?" Janka asked. She set a large glass jug of unfiltered apple juice on the table. Alison eyed it with some trepidation. She didn't like chunks of anything in her drinks. It seemed to her a mixing of categories not meant by nature. She got up and filled her mug, which was hand thrown and painted with a design of unclothed, buxom women, from the tap.

"I have no idea," she said, "and it bothers me. I mean, it's not something that I've ever done. I should tell you it *was* inside a zip-lock, which I guess was supposed to prevent this kind of problem from occurring." Again that shameful twitching of lips and that almost uncontrollable desire to laugh.

"I mean," Janka pursued, sitting across from her and digging into the carrot soup as if it were, Alison thought with nostalgia, an order of kung pao chicken, "if you want to get yourself off, you're in the tub anyway. Why not just do a water scene?" Since Alison had decided she was a leather girl the previous fall, Janka had picked up her habit of referring to everything as a 'scene'. It irritated Michelle to no end.

"Wrong kind of tub. You need a claw foot to get the right angle." Alison decided the time to attack the soup was while overwhelmed by the smell of the muffins. She took a large mouthful and rolled it around on her tongue as if it were fine wine. It wasn't bad. Her problem with vegetarianism was the same as her problem with monogamy.

Yeah, it would work for right now, but could she live with it for the rest of her life?

"Alison. You don't need a claw foot to get yourself off in the tub."

"Okay. This is true. I've done it in my parents' tub, and the faucets are set right into the wall. But. This woman was as old as we are. I was eighteen when I did that. I don't know about you, but I am no longer that limber."

"You know, you guys are such assholes." Oops, in the struggle with the soup, Alison had forgotten to watch the bathroom. She exchanged a quick cringing look with Janka. Michelle went for drama in the best of circumstances, and something this upsetting was bound to bring out her most aggressive and obnoxious side. "Ass-fucking-holes," she repeated slowly, like they were probably also too damn stupid to have gotten it the first time. "You're just like those goddamn pigs—'Heh, heh, guess she flew to heaven on the Big O, huh?' Did it ever occur to you that you can use a vibrator on anything but your clit?"

"Well, I never have," said Alison.

"I'm not surprised," said Michelle in a disparaging tone, and for a minute Alison thought she was also going to seize the moment to slip in a little anti-S/M rhetoric.

"I've never heard of anybody using a vibrator for anything but sex," chimed in Janka. "I know they're called massagers, but I figured that was just a face-saving device."

"Look," said Michelle in her dealing-with-idiots voice, "when my granddad had emphysema, my grandma used a vibrator just like that one on his chest and back twice a day. It broke the shit in his lungs up."

"I don't get it," said Alison. "Tamsin had emphysema?"

"No, but she could have had a cold! She could have had bronchitis! She could have had any of this shit that's going around and clogs you up so bad—it would have been great to sit in the steam and use a vibrator on your chest or your face."

Alison looked at Janka and Janka looked at Alison.

"Michelle," said Alison, "it's summer time. It's not cold season. There's not anything 'going around'."

"Michelle," said Janka, "that woman was over here two days ago. She didn't even have a sign of the sniffles."

"Well," said Michelle, and they bowed to the word, which said that it was *her* friend who had died, who she had seen floating beneath the water like a ghastly specimen in a bottle. What did it matter what Alison thought?

"Where are those kittens?" she said to change the subject, and as if on cue, there was a terrible yowl from the front room. Alison stood up, fearing that either her cat, KP, or Michelle's cat, Tammy Faye, had disemboweled one of the black kittens. What she saw instead was Tammy Faye, bristled up to twice her already formidable size, screaming with outrage because one of the kittens had *tried to sniff her tail!* KP, she saw, was up on the high bookcase. KP and Tammy Faye regularly played a game of chase and stalk, but they could ally themselves in an emergency, and it was obvious that the two kittens definitely fell into that category.

"Kittens downstairs?" Alison asked, picking up one in each hand.

"Yeah. And don't forget about tomorrow."

"Like I could." She turned to KP. "Do you want to come and help me pick out a festive outfit?" KP turned his head in the other direction as if she had said something crass.

"See you tomorrow," said Janka.

****

"Janka." Alison, glancing around her neighbors' kitchen, resisting the urge to go 'Ssstt!'—the grade school alert that something was up. "Is Michelle here?"

"No, she's down in her shop." Janka, who was well known for being the epitome of patience, looked a little cross. Maybe a hasty retreat was in order. No, a couple of things must be settled.

"Look," Alison said, stepping through the door, "is this okay?" Since she had started dating Stacy, Alison had really embraced the butch thing. It had been hard then, to decide how to respond to the request that everyone attending the conception ritual dress festively. She had gotten rid of anything remotely robe-like from her wardrobe, except for her black and red flannel bathrobe, and she didn't think that Michelle would see the humor in that.

"Fine," said Janka, taking a cursory glance at the flowing black pants she had put together with a loose rainbow top. It was a kind of soft-butch-goes-to-the-music-festival look. "Just try to stay out of Michelle's way before the ceremony, okay? She's itching to fly off the handle. Chop these for me, please." She handed Alison a paring knife and a bowl of apples. Obediently Alison set to work. She and Janka often cooked together, and had long since worked out all the details like where to stand in the tiny kitchen and how to share the sink and counters. When they were really going, they looked like a modern dance routine.

"Now, I need to know something else," Alison said after a moment, knowing the question was probably going to piss Janka off. She set down her knife and pulled Michelle's blue denim butch apron over her head. The damn outfit had been hard to put together—if she stained it she was going to have to come to the ceremony naked. "Am I going to have to watch... I mean is...."

"Oh, for Christsake!" Janka slammed down her bread knife with a thump that sent crumbs flying. "I am so tired of this bullshit between the two of you! 'I can't watch Michelle do anything sexual, it really grosses me out.' 'I hate the way Alison's new girlfriend is always kissing on her, I can't stand it when she's sexual around me.' Yes, Alison, we are going to use a turkey baster, and yes, we are going to put it in right there with you in the room being grossed out. So figure out a way to deal with it that does *not* involve talking to Michelle, because she and I have already had this scene, and she came this close," she motioned recklessly with the bread knife, "to calling the whole fucking thing off so she wouldn't have to deal with you being in the room. She's already freaked out about the thing with Tamsin—wanted to call the whole thing off. You know we're trying to be on a schedule—if one of us doesn't get pregnant soon, we're going to be hitting nine months right in the middle of next summer, no thanks!"

"Maybe I could help in the kitchen during that part," Alison suggested.

"Maybe you could just get a grip. I'm going to inseminate her. I'm not going to fuck her. It's not an orgy."

"Thank god for small favors" muttered Alison. "Why did you decide to do this at a party instead of the privacy of your own bedroom?" Janka gave a huge sigh and said nothing. Which was actually fine, because Alison really knew the answer to the question. It had to do with Michelle and her whole attitude towards lesbianism.

In 1978 Michelle and Alison had attended their first Michigan Women's Music Festival, back when the C in the WWTMC had meant collective, rather than company. They had hitchhiked out with their forty dollar festival tickets and twenty dollars between them, staying at the house of any dyke they met without a second thought, and then gone back to annoy everyone in Denver with their fierce little baby-dyke-we-are-all-sisters energy. That was the year the bookstore and the newspaper were both run by fervently feminist nineteen-year-olds. Alison could still remember that fierce glow of sisterhood, but she had become somewhat—she hated to use the word cynical—acclimated with time. She no longer believed that she was safe with any group of lesbians, that no lesbian would hurt her or lie to her or rip her off. She was sad sometimes about this loss of innocence, particularly as she realized it was somehow paired with her upward mobility. Looking back now at seventy-eight she could say *of course* they had felt totally safe from rip-off—they'd had fucking nothing anyone would want. She didn't want to invite strangers off the street in to stay with her anymore, as she and Michelle had done for years when they lived in a collective household. Now she had a VCR and leathers to worry about getting ripped off. She had changed the lesbian-supporting things she did. Now, rather than taking women in off the street, she gave money to the groups who had worked on overturning Two, she looked up dentists and photographers in the *Gay Yellow Pages* and went out of her way to buy all her birthday cards at the Book Garden, even though her choices sometimes puzzled her father and her brother. She loved lesbians, but she no longer had that feeling of sisterhood she had once had. She remembered when running into a dyke anywhere at all had necessitated some type of contact, a nod at least, and more often at least a snatch of conversation. Now she and three friends could go out to dinner and be seated next to a table of dykes and not even make eye contact. This, too, was part of that same loss.

But Michelle had managed to save and nurture a part of that 'we-are-family' feeling. At times like this, when Alison didn't want to have to attend the fucking ritual, it irritated the hell out of her. Michelle had been fucked over by other dykes just as often as any one of them. Yet, at the same time, she respected Michelle's cultivating of dyke family. If she could have put it into words, Alison would have described Michelle as the equivalent of a monk in the middle ages, preserving the written word and the knowledge until the populace at general was ready to receive it again. She could not bear to believe that she would never again feel that heady lesbian loving she had experienced that first year at Michigan when she was twenty. It comforted her to think of Michelle and women like her keeping the culture and faith until she could believe again. Which was why she was going to attend the damn ritual and be gracious about it if it killed her, and was also why Michelle, who was just as uneasy about Alison's presence as she was, was insisting upon it. Because Alison was Michelle's best friend, and that was the way lesbians did best friends, often making them, in fact, more important and primary than lovers.

Alison gave an imitation of Janka's sigh.

"Close your eyes and think of England," Janka advised.

Alison tried to keep this advice in mind later that evening, as the fifteen or so women arranged themselves into a candlelit circle under Janka's direction. It was actually quite easy to distract herself—she spent several moments just going around the circle and deciding by what virtue each guest was present. Michelle had an interesting little mixture of friends. She had her moments of rigidness, but she was gregarious and outgoing and was genuinely interested in other dykes. And she held on to her friends. There was a smattering of new friends—women she had met within the last couple of years—but for the most part she, and by extension, Alison, had known the women sitting cross-legged on the floor for a good long time. There was Vicki, her very first, just-out-of-high-school lover. Michelle was one of those dykes who did not believe in discarding lovers, no matter what the breakup was like. If you had truly loved her, then how could you just push her out of your life like an old pair of culottes that had gone out of style, just because you weren't sleeping together anymore? This was another tenet of the basic dyke philosophy from which Alison had grown away. Once she broke up, she wanted to put as much distance between herself and her exs as possible. She had been known to change her laundromat, her grocery store, and her whole work schedule to avoid chance encounters. She and Michelle had argued about it. Michelle saw maintaining old lovers as holding the threads of a web that bound and defined their lesbian lives. Alison saw it as needlessly keeping open a painful wound. Yet, though she thought she was right, she felt a twinge of jealousy as she looked around the circle and saw so many of Michelle's ex-lovers.

Michelle's exs were like a time line into her own life. In some ways, she was always surprised to see them with current lives, clothes and haircuts. They were like the Beatles, whom she always pictured as they had first appeared on Ed Sullivan. She looked at photos of a middle-aged George and Ringo with no interest or belief what-so-ever— as if they were only a marker in her youth, a marker which had frozen in time that night her parents had let her stay up late.

Similarly, Nadine, sitting next to Vicki, was always seen first in the context of *Big Mama Rag*, the local women's newspaper which had folded ten years before. Nadine as an exhibit in the lesbian wing of the Smithsonian would have been shown wearing overalls and a plaid jacket someone had put in the alley for scavengers, a cigarette in her hand. The set would have been the basement apartment that one of the Radical Information Project lefties had rented to the *BMR* at an excellent guilt-controlled price—after all, he did need to make up for being a white, middle class male—and all decorated with crudely printed political posters, while sporting an actual printing press which would have to be explained to all the baby dykes who had grown up in the era of desktop publishing. Nadine had some kind of desk job now to which she wore a power suit and beeper. She could make hours of conversation that had nothing at all to do with separatism, but Alison could still not help that first little wince of anticipated confrontation whenever she saw her. Nadine and Vicki, both eating dip out of a bowl shaped like a cunt, were icons of an age of confrontation. Alison had only to look at them to flashback onto hundreds of hours spent in the basement of the bookstore trying to figure out collectively what recipe they would use for lemonade and whether they were going to make an exception to general policy and let the members of L.U.N.A., the lesbian alcoholics group who met weekly in the basement, smoke at meetings so they wouldn't have to deal simultaneously with two addictions. It was an age when it was permitted and fair for one PC lesbian (and the straight press was picking up that term as if it were brand new!) to say any hurtful thing at all to another as long as it were presented in the name of openness and honest confrontation. A collective member's wardrobe, diet, private life or job all were up for grabs. Alison winced when she thought of the women they had totally rejected because they wore high heels or were secretaries, and she winced more when she thought of the totally unmendable purges and confrontation wars that had split every group regularly. It was as if, she had argued to Michelle not long ago, they had not felt they'd had enough energy to attack and conquer an outside oppressor, so they had practiced on one another, not realizing they were playing with real bullets that actually diminished their ranks. She hated the fact that, while so many of the truly good parts of the 70s lesbian movement had been lost, the inalienable right to criticize and judge other dykes seemed to be as strong as ever.

Some soft drumming had started, and Alison was amused to see that several other women were wearing the face of apprehension she was trying so hard to suppress, that oh-shit-I hope-we-don't-have-to chant look. Probably they wouldn't. Later the background would no doubt change to one of the ninety minute Holly Near tapes Michelle had put together from the vast collection of albums she and her friends had collected over the last fifteen years. Michelle herself had major trouble with cosmic-goddess dykes and all trappings she associated with them. She saw anyone with a crystal as a generic type—

Sparrow's friend Milkweed, as drawn by Alison Bechdel. They changed their names to something she could not say with a straight face and wouldn't work because they didn't want to support the war machine with their taxes, or couldn't stand florescent lighting, or patriarchy made them physically ill, and then confronted the women they expected to subsidize them for what was in their refrigerators and where it was bought. Michelle had the ability to run further with a dyke stereotype than any Ku-Kluxer and at the same time push all her prejudices to one side without a moment's hesitation if she found herself drawn to a woman. She saw nothing oxymoronic about sneering over a woman who called herself Moon or Hawk and being married (at a ceremony where they had evoked the goddess and jumped the broom!) to a woman who not only called herself Janka Weaversong but had lived on women's land for years. Still, the drumming was probably Janka's contribution to the ceremony.

Alison found herself inexplicably cheered by the thought of Michelle's prejudices. So often she felt like she was not a good dyke— it was cheering to know that even Michelle had a few problems with sisters-loving-sisters-loving-sisters.

It was getting uncomfortably close to actual insemination time, so to distract herself, Alison looked across the circle to where Stacy was sitting cross-legged with her skirts spread out around her, a look of spiritual rapture on her face. Stacy's very presence was an example of Michelle's wrestling of standards. There was nothing about Stacy of which Michelle could approve. Though Stacy was an artist, she supported her quiltmaking by working as a kind of prostitute, and the fact that it was with women and did not involve genital sex did not make supporting that traditionally oppressive and detrimental occupation any better in Michelle's eyes. Stacy not only practiced and promoted sadomasochist activity, she had, like all those college roommates, older women and camp counselors upon whom generations of upset parents blamed lesbian daughters, led Michelle's best friend down that same primrose path. On that hand alone she was clearly a candidate for that lesbian-feminist-pacifist version of the death penalty— ostracism. ("Though why," Stacy had said to Alison after a particularly ugly incident in the Michigan S/M wars, "PC dykes think that shunning is a punishment is beyond me—I'd pay some of them money not to talk to me.")

On the other hand, though, Stacy was Alison's lover, and if you couldn't respect that, well, what was left? Michelle was a big believer in the theory most lesbian relationships failed because the community did not afford them the same respect and support the heterosexual community did their married counterparts. Michelle would have cut off her right hand before having an affair with a dyke while in a relationship, and though her commitment to letting Alison make her own mistakes about the kind of low life she wanted to hang out with was not nearly as intense, conscience had made her include Stacy in Alison's invitation. Besides which Janka, much to Michelle's dismay, liked Stacy and could spend hours talking textile shop with her.

Alison's attention shifted back to Vicki, who had put down the chips but was still holding the cunt-shaped bowl with both hands in front of her. Alison would have thought this was part of the ceremony, had she not happened to know Michelle's feelings about this particular bowl, which had not only been made by one of Alison's exs whom Michelle could not stand, but in addition was unattractive enough to make even the most experienced lesbian wonder for a moment if she were not in the wrong line. Alison hoped Michelle would not glance up and see it at the wrong moment or she would probably spontaneously abort. Vicki, besides being Michelle's first passionate heartbreak, was also from the *Big Mama Rag* era. She had been one of the 'older' (she must have been twenty-four!) women Alison and Michelle had passionately pursued after that eye opening trip to Michigan. At the time of which Alison was thinking, Vicki had lived in a tiny one room apartment, the size of which she was constantly reducing by bringing home stacks of books from the used bookstore down the street from the Volmers' bakery. Like Nadine, Vicki had done her fair share of confrontations, but because Alison had known her better, she also had shared a number of—usually drug related— pleasant experiences with her. Vicki had worked at the women's bookstore as well as the newspaper, and she and Alison had staffed a number of book tables at concerts, fairs and political rallies in a companionably mind-altered state. That was when, Alison thought with a touch of nostalgia, you could still buy a bag for fifteen dollars. The breakup of Vicki and Michelle was the first major dyke drama Alison had seen up close, and though she could now laugh stiffly at some of their theatrics, she could also remember holding Michelle as she wept hysterically and the choking hatred she had felt then towards Vicki for hurting her friend. Michelle had forgiven Vicki much sooner than Alison had, a pattern that followed them both up to this day. Alison still snubbed women whom Michelle couldn't even remember dating. Now Vicki was drug-free, installed phone systems for AT&T, danced with the mixed gay and lesbian square dance group (she who had been such a separatist that she had been known to verbally castrate innocent men on the street who were just trying to get directions to the 7-11) and for the past year had lived two doors down from Alison and the Martin-Weaversongs. They had established a nice borrowing flour and dropping in for dinner relationship. Vicki, Alison thought with a sudden flash that was unrelated to anything except trying to ignore the insemination, had undoubtedly known Tamsin.

The woman to the right of Alison, a weaving buddy of Janka's named Seven Yellow Moons, who usually lived on women's land in New Mexico, gave her a gentle nudge. With a start Alison realized, the actual act apparently completed, the women were taking turns coming forward to place their hands on Michelle's stomach—her uterus, she corrected herself quickly. This correction did not arise from her radical lesbian-feminist background, but because she herself was of a generation of children who had imagined younger siblings growing in a mess of half-digested pot roast and chicken pot pies in Mom's stomach. As an aunt she was determined *she* was not going to perpetuate such a disturbing myth.

"A sense of humor," said Nadine, who had at one time boycotted *Monty Python and the Holy Grail* because of the scene with the fey prince, as she laid her hands, and Alison belatedly realized they were doing a dyke version of that famous Grimm-cum-Disney scene where the fairy godmothers clustered around to bless poor baby Sleeping

Beauty, destined to be trapped in stereotyped print and film forever. Damn it, why hadn't Janka warned her? She had nothing touching in mind. Now it was Stacy's turn and the eyes of Michelle, who had been maintaining an amazingly—considering her propensity towards hyperactivity—tranquil stance flew open and fixed on Stacy with a mind-controlling intensity, as if this way she could she keep Stacy from bestowing a spindle-pricking gift like loving spike heels. Stacy, much to her credit, totally ignored this implied insult towards both her appropriateness as a role model and her ability to behave at a ritual, and said, "Love to read."

"Work with your hands," said Seven Yellow Moons, laying her own, which were large, scarred and capable, upon Michelle.

Then it was Alison's turn, and she had no wish at all to bestow upon this child they hoped had been conceived. Tongue-tied, she touched Michelle only because she could think of no way to gracefully avoid it. Then she looked into the still-open eyes of her friend, and without conscious thought said, "Have a friend like I have."

A smile from Michelle told her this was the right thing to have said, and, with a stifled sigh of relief, Alison pushed herself back out of the way. For the first time she imagined Michelle actually holding a baby in her arms, and the thought was both exciting and frightening.

5

S tacy was in the mood. She had signaled this to Alison at the party, while everyone was mingling, carrying their plates of bran muffins and carrot cake around Michelle as she lay on the floor with her knees up.

"Rrrr," Stacy had growled into Alison's ear, as she was talking to Seven Yellow Moons. Growling was a form of communication they had picked up from Worf, the lone Klingon officer on the USS Enterprise. Poor Worf never seemed to get laid, but you got the feeling that, if the chance came along, you'd better tie the bed down, so it was a powerful signal. It sent Alison into a brief, but total astral projection—one moment she was listening with some interest to Seven describing the way she had reroofed her house with materials found at the dump, and the next she was imagining herself on top of Stacy, Stacy's mouth beneath hers. The image was so powerful she could taste the strawberries Stacy had been munching as she strolled past.

Alison came back to herself with the uncomfortable feeling she had made a fool of herself. Seven Yellow Moons was looking at her with a quizzical air that indicated a question had been asked.

"Mmm…" Alison ventured, "bigger nails?"

Seven laughed. "You're absolutely right," she said. "I'm sure that's just what's wrong with the dip." She patted Alison on the arm before strolling away. "The girlfriend's hot," she said.

Later, after they were alone, Alison remembered this line. The girlfriend's hot. How well she knew it, how many times she had whispered a little prayer of thanks and disbelief to the dancing goddesses upstairs. It had been two months, four months, six months, and even when they hit *that* dreaded milestone, that point at which so many couples were seized by lesbian bed death, Stacy hadn't become any less desirable or willing than she had been the first day she had hit Alison in the head with a soccer ball. She could still send Alison into a tailspin with the tiniest gestures—the way she wiped her full lower lip with the heel of her hand, the way that, when they were out with friends, she would look across the table and blow Alison a kiss that promised more. It was true that many nights they spent together they simply spooned, or did the quick, tired turn-taking that Stacy called 'McSex', but there were still other nights when they were up 'til two, and days when they didn't get up at all except to answer the door when the pizza arrived.

Alison had thought, from the way Stacy stalked her at the party, circling back several times to growl in her ear as she tried to make conversation with the rest of the guests, that this might be one of those times when they ended up falling upon one another as soon as the door closed behind them. They'd had many such times; they both enjoyed playing with one another almost in public, maintaining just enough decorum to say a pleasant goodnight, and then fucking hard on the stairs or in the parking lot or up against the wall of a dark back yard. This is what Alison had been anticipating. But Stacy was not a woman who liked to be too predictable.

"Twenty minutes," she whispered into Alison's ear as she made her fourth pass, and Alison knew just from the tone of her voice that she meant, twenty minutes, or else. Twenty, not fifteen or twenty-five. She watched Stacy gracefully make her way to the door leading downstairs to Alison's apartment, disentangling herself from the other guests with a word or a laugh. (Of course Alison's apartment had its own separate entrance but the house had started its life as a single family dwelling, and since it had two close families again, the doors to the inside set of stairs between the two apartments were always unlocked.)

Even though all the women at the party had arrived, as per the invitation, festively garbed, at that moment Stacy seemed to Alison like the most brilliant flower of the garden. She was wearing a long silk skirt—hand painted splotches of purple and blues—bought from the Clouddance woman at Womminfest in New Mexico the year before. Alison remembered how Stacy had tried on clothes at the festival for almost an hour, flirting with her in the mirror, before settling on this outfit. The skirt had a beautiful matching cocoon, and like many of Stacy's outfits, it could be dressed up or down. For the conception ceremony she had worn it with a lavender turtleneck and Birkenstocks, and had looked the very likeness of a suitable fairy god mother. But as she whisked down the stairs, the silk trailing after her like a wisp of perfume, Alison was thinking of the times Stacy had worn this outfit for her alone. The times she had worn it with one of the silk camisoles Alison had given her for Christmas, or with black high heels, or jewelry, or nothing at all. Twenty minutes seemed an eternity.

She joined a conversation in progress with Michelle, back on her feet, and Vicki and Nadine.

"So I don't know *what* I'm supposed to do about the sister thing," said Michelle, spreading her hands. "I mean, the money can keep, but there's all this personal stuff Tam wanted to go to her." Michelle had told Alison and Janka the day before that she was the executor of the will Liz had drawn up for Tam at the Will-a-thon as a perk from the GLBSCC. Of course, all of Michelle's old friends had known Tam from her early days on *BMR*.

"She put you in charge of it, didn't she?" asked Nadine. "Just keep the stuff, or give it to the Goodwill. If the sister's not around, who will ever know? It's not like she's got a bunch of antiques or signed first editions there, is it?"

Michelle looked disapproving. "She put me in charge of it," she said sternly, "because she *trusted* me to take care of things. I don't think having the Salvation Army come in and clean out the apartment is taking care of things. Plus, there were several other people mentioned in the will. Mementos."

"Can you even get into the apartment?" asked Vicki. "I mean, isn't it the scene of the crime, or something?"

"Alison says, in an accident, it shouldn't take more than a couple of days for that to clear, unless there was something funny in the coroner's report."

"There wasn't," Alison inserted. She had gotten this information from Robert, who was a passionate gossip, and had an underground information network at the station that put the CIA to shame. "I'll bet the landlady gets the keys back tomorrow." The Robert-vine had also told her that the death was being called an accident, rather than a suicide. Accident, right, thought Alison, but she kept her mouth shut. She had been raised with just enough Catholicism to make suicide seem repugnant, and she had seen first hand what it did to survivors. Tam did not seem to have any life insurance policies, so what did it matter what the boys downtown decided?

"I'm not worried about getting in," said Michelle, waving that aside. "I have my own keys. I'm worried about what I should do with her stuff when I do get in. She had no idea where her sister was. Did she expect *me* to play detective?"

"Well, you've got almost a month to think of something, if she was paid up on her rent." Nadine dismissed the whole thing. Nadine might wear a power suit now, but there was still a bit of that confrontive old edge on her.

Vicki was more sympathetic. "I'll come over and help you one day, Michelle," she offered. "If worst comes to worst, you can box the things for the sister until you decide what to do. How *do* they find people like that, anyway?" She turned to Alison. "Couldn't you look for her, Alison? Don't you have a huge computer net at your fingertips?"

"You are confusing us with Scotland Yard," Alison said dryly. "I can ask to have her run through motor vehicles, and if they feel like doing me a favor and not getting ugly about it," she paused, thinking of the people who ran that desk, and then rephrased. "I can have *Robert* or *my dad* ask to run her through motor vehicles. Which might turn her up if she hasn't moved or changed her name or is still driving. I don't supposed you have her social security number?" she asked

Michelle without a trace of hope.

"There's a good guess," said Michelle tartly.

Vicki's girlfriend, Wanda, joined their little circle. She put her arms around Vicki and rested her chin on her shoulder. Wanda had also been around Denver forever, but she had always moved on the outside of Alison's circle, so Alison had never really gotten to know her.

"We're talking about Tamsin's sister," Vicki explained to her. "Michelle is the executor of Tam's will, but nobody knows where the sister is."

Wanda wrinkled her forehead. "But," she said slowly, "wasn't Tamsin's sister a dyke? Didn't she work for Virago?" She named the long defunct women's production company, which, over a decade before, had brought to town Meg Christian and Teresa Trull and the Berkeley Women's Music Collective.

A brick through the window could not have caused a more surprised silence. The four women looked around at each other.

"Sary," said Wanda, dredging up a name, which she pronounced to rhyme with Mary. "Yeah, I'm sure that was it. Sary—wasn't she Tamsin's sister?"

"Well, Tam and Melanie and Sharon and I worked on *BMR* together," said Michelle slowly. She stopped and looked startled. "And two of them are dead, and one is straight now. There's a scary thought. But I don't remember Tam having a dyke sister."

"But how old are you?" asked Wanda. "Thirty five or so? See, I'm a couple of years older, and so was Tam, wasn't she? If I remember, the sister thing happened before you were on the scene."

"While you were still in junior high," said Vicki.

"Very funny. Even if the sister wasn't still around, she would have *mentioned* her, wouldn't she?"

"No," said Wanda slowly. "There was some kind of scandal. Some kind of dyke thing. God, this is so hazy. It was such a long time ago, and it was when I was still drinking. A lot of those memory cells are just plain destroyed. But don't you know other women who were in Virago? Maybe one of them would know."

Michelle looked doubtful. "That was an awfully long time ago.

I'm not sure if any of the Virago women are still in town, besides you. And I'm not sure I'd remember them if they were. Could you make a list?"

"Maybe," said Wanda, making it sound like "No."

"Research it," suggested Vicki. "That's what the Archives are for, right? I'll bet *BMR* covered Virago."

"Put an ad in *Lesbian Connection*," said Nadine. "Everybody reads *Lesbian Connection*. If she doesn't read it herself, one of her ex lovers will. And see if you can stir up the 'Pets as Slaves' issue while you're at it."

Alison looked at her watch. Twenty minutes exactly. "Excuse me," she said.

The stairwell was dark. Alison and Michelle were having a little standoff over who was going down to the basement and replacing the fuse that served this part of the house. Since it involved three rather obscure places—Alison's stairs, Michelle's tiny balcony and the basement itself, the out waiting would, in all likelihood, go on for months. It usually did.

The only light in Alison's apartment came from candles. Fat candles on the table, the window sill, and a bunch of long tapers on the mantle of the fireplace. Those, and of course the glow that came from the CD player. Stacy liked music for a scene, and she always brought her own. She was tolerant about listening to Alison's collection of Bob Wills and Patsy Cline, but rejected it as background music. The tape that was playing was not familiar, nothing Alison had heard in Stacy's workroom where she listened mostly to The Dead and the Indigo Girls. Stacy did not mix her moods. This music was instrumental and intense and exciting—Alison's heart was already pounding by the time she entered the living room.

In a fit of butch domesticity several months before, Alison had put eye bolts in her bed frame and several of her door ways. This door was the widest, the one that required the most stretch. Consequently, it was Stacy's favorite. The two sets of restraints were not hooked to the bolts, but stacked together in the middle of the doorway. This was another clue as to how this scene was to be. Sometimes Stacy liked to play rough, liked to wrestle and fight hard and finally pull Alison down into restraints through sheer force. There were other times, like tonight, when what she wanted was willing submission, total giving.

She sat in the chair across the room, dressed much in the way Alison had imagined her earlier. Silk with a twist, silk down to her stockings and panties—if she was wearing any. Her legs were crossed—she had lost the Birkenstocks and put on Alison's favorite black heels, the ones that had the little trim of gold around the edge. Someone had once asked Stacy how she managed to get around in the high heels she collected, and she had said, in genuine surprise, "Well, I don't *walk* in them! They're like pajamas, they're only meant to be worn in bed!" A waterbed would have been impossible around Stacy, she was too fond of getting right on top of Alison and riding her while wearing those heels, of wrapping her legs around her and digging one into her ass or back.

She gestured with her head, and so attuned were they that Alison knew, without a word, she was meant to remove her shirt, but not her pants. She complied , and then, at a second gesture, bent to pick up the restraints. She buckled them carefully around her wrists and ankles, not so tight that the sheepskin would chaff, not so loose that she could slip a hand or foot free. She worked with deliberate gestures, so everything could be seen and approved of, even across the room in candle-light. When she was done, she stepped back and spread-eagled her body, her arms held above her head, the clips on the wrist restraints clanking against the eye bolts in the door frame. Sometimes, in a mood like this, this was all Stacy desired. This was enough, that Alison offered herself willingly, and the test would be that she remain in the position, in the bondage in which she had placed herself, tied only by her own passion. Those were often times when Alison would end up begging Stacy to clip up the cuffs, so she had something to hang onto, to pull against.

Tonight, though, was not to be such a test of self control. Unhurried, making each move as if she was a dancer, Stacy crossed the room and knelt down to secure Alison's ankles to the door. Everything about her flowed—the silk, her dark curly hair—so she looked like some sort of water being in the candlelight. She stood, and leaned close to Alison's body as she lifted her arms. The silk trickled against Alison, and she had to close her eyes to keep from reaching out to take a handful. This was not what was desired now, and she knew, if she were able to restrain herself, whatever happened later would be that much more explosive. She allowed herself only a few silent kissing motions, grasping the air with her mouth. On one kiss she brushed the sleeve of Stacy's silk cocoon, and she held her mouth still against it as Stacy reached above her to fasten the restraint.

"Open your eyes." Stacy stood before her. She had taken off the flowing cocoon, and skirt. She was wearing the purple lace body suit they had chosen together at the very proper lingerie shop in Cherry Creek mall, laughing at the horror of the salesgirls as they went into the dressing room together. She was holding her hand out in front of her, and as Alison watched, she picked up one of the long tapers from the mantle piece. Alison watched the twin of the flame in the mirror. The cold flame dipped down to touch Stacy's mirrored hand, and in an instant, a tiny fire burst up in her palm. She watched it for what seemed to Alison an eternity, then slowly and deliberately, she reached out and pressed her palm against Alison's shoulder. The flame went out. Stacy pulled her hand back and opened it again, like a magician, showing that there was no fire, no blister, no burn mark, and Alison knew the eternity she had watched in the mirror must have been no more than a second or two. It was like this whenever they played with fire, and Stacy knew that it was like this, and that was why she had restrained her. No matter how often it was demonstrated to Alison, how often she tried it herself, she could never accept the fact the flame could easily be extinguished before there was any pain, before there was anything but the heat.

You brushed on the rubbing alcohol first, as Stacy was doing now, tracing an intricate snake that came up between her breasts and then parted to form a half circle over each. And you set the flame with a lighter, or, if you were Stacy, and liked the props and drama, with a candle or a torch. And the fire traveled up your body, and divided just before it reached your chin, and in that split second just before Stacy rubbed her hand leisurely over your torso, you could see the line of fire in the mirror. And when she had put it out you were straining against the restraints as you didn't for anything else, and your mouth was dry and you were already ready to beg, and that was why they returned to fire again and again—because she liked you in that state of fear and submission, liked seeing you trying to keep control when you wanted to scream, for the sole reason that she desired it.

And then, if you were Stacy, and you knew the woman who was bottoming for you, just when Alison's mouth was beginning to resume it's normal texture, just when she was starting to think, Why this isn't so bad, I can handle this, why, then, you added a little twist, just to make sure she was spinning off into space. Then you did something like tying a blindfold tightly across Alison's eyes. Not the silk scarves that Stacy mostly favored, but something made of sheepskin and leather, like the restraints. Something with no ends to trail down into the flames on Alison's body, just as Stacy had removed her own flowing clothes. So that now Alison was alone in the dark, unable to watch the beautiful woman in the mirror light up with the flame and her own fear, unable to see where the fire was going to strike next. So that she really did have to put herself into the hands of her top, deciding whether she wanted to hold her safeword on the tip of her tongue, ready to blurt out at any moment, or whether this was the time that she was really going to give it all over. Wondering if she was going to be able to slip past the control and place herself in Stacy's hands, as if nothing else existed....

She slipped back in fantasy, slipped back in her mind to another time, long, long before they had met. They had stood together before like this, she and Stacy, for all that she laughed and poked fun at her friends who went for channeling and told stories of Amelia Earhart and Nubian slaves. They had stood together before in dim light that smelled of smoke, with candles sputtering in the back ground. They must have stood together before, or how could this be explained? How else could Alison account for the way she had gone to Stacy the first time they had played with fire—that combination of terror and submission Alison could taste sharp in her mouth now, like a drug?

52

With her eyes closed, Alison saw another scene, cooler, underground, candles made of tallow that put out its own smell and talked
in its own language of sparks and spats.

Stacy, as always when Alison saw her in this fantasy/memory, was
older. Stacy had the kind of face that acquired beauty with age. Stacy
at nineteen had probably been gawky, face too sharp, hatchet nose too
big. Stacy at thirty-five was interesting and sexy. Stacy at forty-five,
her dark curls shot with grey, was breathtaking. She was beaded and
bangled—love of jewelry apparently followed Stacy from life to
life—but dressed only from the waist down, kirtled in a skirt made of
wonderfully embroidered cloth. A skirt on which a decade of winter
evenings had been spent, a skirt that was taken back before the fire
each year so a new row of glass beads could be added, a new labrys
worked along the border.

Because they were deep inside the cave, Alison could not tell if it
was night or day. She suspected there was a little of both in the answer,
for she suspected they had been playing this game of passion and
magic for a long time, perhaps through several nights and days. This
was why the woman who looked like Stacy liked to use the cave,
because it was impossible for Alison to tell if she had stood this way,
with her arms outstretched, for days, or merely hours. The woman in
the cave was not named Stacy, nor was she named Anastasia, which
was both Stacy's birth and play name. But Alison knew it was something *like* Anastasia. She knew, just as she knew that Anastasia
believed what they did together was magic, a magic so powerful it
could affect not only the year, but the very lives of the women for
whom they acted out the ritual. Perhaps this Anastasia was one of the
very old ones. Perhaps she was a Celt. Perhaps she was or had been
both and a touch of a dozen others. Perhaps she had been the whole
dozen—shaman, priestess, hag, witch—stoned and burned, and had
come back to this time with the memory of it all in her hands.

Always, this Anastasia had only one breast. This was the other
thing that never changed in the fantasy/dream that came automatically
to Alison's head when they played with fire. The scar that wrapped
around this Anastasia's ribs and flattened across her chest was a heavy

scar, not just webbed up from lack of skill, but deliberately darkened with ash or ink. In the waking dream Alison was not wearing a blindfold, and she stole looks at this Anastasia from underneath lids heavy with weariness and passion and terror. Sometimes it seemed to her, looking backward with her current memories, that this Anastasia was an Amazon, sometimes a woman who had simply embraced and embroidered what other might call mutilation. Self-inflicted, surgically necessary, accident, an act that saved her life—this Anastasia was beautiful, and she moved in fire.

She held out her hands again, sides together, palms up in the gesture of offering, and this time flames burned in both hands. Alison hung in their light for a long moment, and then they were gone, Anastasia's hands pressed together as if in prayer.

In the fantasy/dream Alison writhed against her restraints. They had done this before, many times, and yet each time was the first. Alison had come to a point where she had no idea whether Anastasia caressed her with a flame or her hands. Even in the fantasy, where she wore no blindfold, when she half opened her eyes what she saw was not always clear. Always Anastasia moved in fire, auraed by the candles stuck in the crevasses of the rock, lit by the flames that chased up Alison's body. The flame had become the touch of the lover, and Alison bent towards it with an undefinable longing. She knew, within the same memories, from the women keeping vigil at the mouth of the cave, that she was not chosen for sacrifice, but honor, knew also that she had hoped and dreamed and prayed for this moment. Now Anastasia, hands or flame, was, both in fantasy and reality, running her hands down over her hips, up over her ass. Part of Alison, the little part that automatically monitored those things that needed monitoring, remembered she once had been wearing black pants, and hoped Stacy hadn't cut them off. Stacy was apt to get a little knife happy when she was in scene, and there had been an argument about a favorite shirt. Then the thought was gone, unimportant in the shiver that was running up past Alison's body as she tried to push herself against Stacy's hand. In the dream/fantasy the Alison she had been yearned as well, and she knew that for this Alison, it truly was the first time. She had kept herself chaste, virginal, until this moment of offering. Now the fire, both to her blindfolded and half-opened eyes, seemed to surround her, yet she could think of nothing else but Anastasia's hand between her legs. She jerked almost with convulsion at the first touch, and began to babble as Anastasia brought her fingers up between her lips—just those same words that women have always said to their lovers—please and yes and other sounds of begging. The Alison she was now liked to be fucked and fucked hard while the Alison she had been knew instinctively this was the way she had to be taken. There was a snapping sound that penetrated both scenes, then without warning, Anastasia had three fingers inside her.

There were times when Stacy put Alison in another kind of bondage, laying her on her back and saying, "Don't move. I want to be the one fucking you," but this wasn't like that. This was about not just giving it up, but wanting to take it, begging for it, bringing her cunt down hard on Stacy's hand as if she could swallow it by sheer desire. In the fantasy/dream, Alison could see Anastasia kneeling before her, her hand up between her legs stiff and rigid. At some point Anastasia had loosed the leg restraints, and Alison threw one leg up over her shoulder, trusting the wrist restrains to keep her from falling. Both hands were wrapped around the double ended hooks, partly to keep the strain off her wrists, and partly because she had to hold something. The two scenes, which up until this point had remained quite separate in her mind, had completely merged. She felt herself two distinct persons as she rode her body up and down on Anastasia's arm. She wanted to be fucked hard and deep, and though she knew this was part of the ritual, (this was the only way to bring about the harvest, good tides and bounty for which the other women were praying,) there was another part of her who wanted it only because this was the way she could give herself totally—when Stacy reached up inside her as if she were going to take her heart in her hand.

Stacy pushed hard, and there was a brief blur of pain. It always hurt when Stacy first put her fist inside her, and she gave a cry that was part protest, part ecstasy. Stacy hesitated just a split second, and Alison found that, as well as begging, she was weeping, protesting even that tiny cessation. Stacy wrapped her free arm around Alison's ass, and now they were moving together, Stacy pumping her cunt so hard that it was jarring her, that it would have been called pain if it were not called pleasure.

The room went up in fire. Was this the final part of all those scenes they had played together throughout the years? Once again the Alison she had been was separate, and she opened her eyes wide to see the flames lapping up around both herself and Anastasia, consuming them both. She gave herself totally to the fire in a convulsion that was like an explosion, and then let herself go limp, hanging from the restraints.

Then, in the real world she occupied now, Alison smelled smoke. "Red," she blurted immediately, because that was not the way—fantasy or no fantasy—a fire scene worked. Sometimes if you weren't careful, or did it in the wrong place, or on the wrong woman, it singed a little hair. But it never smelled like this, like the house was going up in a blaze. Maybe that had happened before, maybe only in a fantasy, but here in this life she wasn't willing to do the faggot thing just to make sure the weevils didn't get into the corn this year.

"Red," she said, "Stacy, is there something on fire?"

"Oh, shit!" said Stacy and then nothing more. The other Anastasia and the scene in the cave had disappeared completely. Alison could hear Stacy rustling frantically. The one thing that kept going through her mind as she stood there helplessly, trying not to panic, was that joke that had been making it's way around the leather community. 'What's a top's safeword?'—'Oops!'

"What is it?" she asked frantically, pulling at the wrist restraints, wishing she had not decided to be quite so butch with the hardware thing. "Stacy, undo me!"

"No, no, it's okay, just let me get it under control, it's just a curtain…" Stacy trailed off, and Alison could hear her panting and straining, with an occasional, "Oh, shit!" Alison was frantic now, and the only thing that was keeping her from screaming, crying and begging to be let loose, was thinking of Stacy putting out the fire, if Stacy had to deal with her first they might all go up in flames.

"Okay, okay, there, I've got it…" panted Stacy, and it was at this point that the smoke alarms went off. "Oh, shit," panted Stacy again, but this time Alison was demanding.

"Let me loose," she said, only her butch bravado keeping back the tears of terror, of the relief she felt when Stacy's arm brushed against her.

"Alison," said Stacy, as she undid the knot on the blindfold.

And then "Alison! Alison!" came from the stairs, followed by a frantic pounding on the door. Alison had locked it behind her, but it was a flimsy lock, designed only to discourage unwanted neighbors, not prowlers, and certainly not meant to withstand the force being put on it. Michelle burst into the room, holding her fire extinguisher before her like a battering ram. She pulled the pin, still calling Alison's name, and let a stream of foam onto the floor before she looked around.

Alison followed her eyes. One of the long curtain rods had been pulled down. One of curtains was crumpled in a pile—the other was a tattered mound of singed cloth. A line of smoke told the story on the wall. Stacy, wearing only her high heels and high cut body suit, was similarly marked. There was smoke on her face and arm, and the ends of the long curls that fell around her face had been singed. Then Alison was not able to follow Michelle's glance any longer, because what Michelle was looking at, was her.

"Oh," said Michelle finally. She retreated five steps, and closed the door behind her. Alison looked at Stacy, and Stacy looked at Alison, and they both began to laugh.

6

The landlord was fairly philosophical about the damage. "We needed to paint, anyway," he said. "We might as well get the whole place while we're at it." He was a leatherboy himself, and had thought that the eyebolts did nothing but add to the property value.

The painting was a boon for Michelle—she did all of the handiwork around the house, and this was bound to be worth a month's rent at least. "So what about this?" she said to Alison, fanning her paint samples out on the table between a cucumber plant and a book on inkle weaving, and pointing to a particularly ugly shade of yellow. This had been her reaction to bursting into the fire scene—threatening to repaint with nightmare colors never seen outside institutions.

"I think not." Alison swept the samples away with one hand. Normally, she would have just told Michelle to choose whatever she wanted, and would have been delighted with the results. However, in the mood Michelle was in now, she was afraid of what she might end up with. Alison was fussing. "It's not so bad you need to repaint, why don't we just let it go..." She was allergic to the smell of wet paint, and Michelle knew it.

Michelle pointed to a particularly dreadful shade of green. "How about this for the dining room? With red trim?"

"Stop, stop!" Again Alison pushed the samples away. "I'm sorry, okay? I'm sorry you had to be there? Okay? It wasn't fun for me, having you break in, either. So stop trying to torture me."

"Yeah, well sorry would do a whole lot of good if you had burnt the house down, with all of us in it!"

"That was an accident! That didn't even come from the scene—it came from a candle. Accidents happen—you practically torched the whole national forest last year when you decided to try bean hole cooking!"

Michelle made a tight-lipped angry face, and began sorting rapidly through the color strips, looking for the ugliest paint on the market.

"How long is this going to take?" asked Alison.

"Weeks," said Michelle. "Maybe months. Stay with your girl-friend," she added nastily.

"My girlfriend beats women for a living," Alison replied, figuring that she might as well go for broke. "Clients tend to like a little privacy for that kind of thing. It kills the mood if someone is watching *Nashville City Limits* in the other room."

"Oh, well," said Michelle. "Now, do you just get hives, or is there asthma as well?"

"Stay with your dad," mercifully, Janka broke into the conversation. She was sitting on the floor and playing with the two kittens. KP and Tammy Faye were out of reach on the table, watching. They both had sad expressions on their faces, the kind of look you might wear if you knew your best friend was dating a Satanist, and was just too blind to see.

"No way. It stresses me out too much. First, my dad is so glad to see me that I feel guilty if I go anywhere. I have to spend every evening playing Scrabble and making cookies. I can do that—but then I have to sneak out when it's time to move back, so I don't have to see him cry. I can't handle it. I'm afraid if I go back, I'll end up living at home the rest of my life."

Michelle hummed a very evil and pleased little tune. She placed a purple strip with a brown one.

"He's not taking the divorce well, is he?" asked Janka.

"No," said Alison shortly. They had all—her brothers, her father, and herself—been totally blindsided when Alison's mother had served the papers in January. Alison's father, after almost thirty years of marriage, was still walking around in shock. Her mother was sending chatty postcards from Florida.

"Well, let me ask something," Alison said to Michelle. "What's going to happen with Tam's apartment? The rent is paid for the whole month, right?"

"Oh, yeah," said Michelle, flipping through the strips to see if there were any more garish oranges. "I talked to the landlady this morning. I'm sure it's going to have to sit there empty for a while, if I can't find Sary. How do you feel about the Broncos?" she asked Alison, flipping to the blues.

"Must I beg?" Alison asked.

Michelle considered. "I think so," she said. "I believe that might be pleasing." This was a line directly from Stacy, and she must have realized it a nano-second later, for she hastily said, "No!"

"How about a trade?" intervened Janka.

"Actually," said Michelle, "I hear they have some nice beds down at the women's shelter, if you get there early enough. About three in the afternoon."

"Aren't you supposed to be packing up Tamsin's stuff? You're supposed to decide where it goes, right?"

Michelle hummed.

"Okay, let me stay there while you're painting, and I'll spend all day Saturday helping you box shit."

"All day Saturday by yourself."

"All day Saturday *with* you, and an evening by myself."

Michelle picked at the dried paint on her white overalls thoughtfully. She was almost hooked. Alison hastened to sweeten the deal. "All day Saturday with you, an evening by myself, I take the kittens with me, *and* I do some research into Sary."

"Got it," said Michelle, turning back to the table, "What are your feelings about purple?"

****

"Well," said Michelle, giving the cluttered room a kind of hopeless look, one Alison knew she was mirroring. "Here we go!" She said

60

it in a brightly cheerful way, as if hoping the phrase alone would spring them into action. Instead they stood, each second making the task loom even larger. If it wasn't for the fact that her living room was already drop-clothed and taped, Alison would have turned right around and gone home.

"So what are the categories here?" Alison asked doubtfully. "I mean, is everything going to the Goodwill?" She picked up one of the smaller boxes, which they had scrounged from behind Zorba's, and then put it back down, daunted by the task before them.

"No," said Michelle, in a voice meant to still sound cheery, but sliding quickly towards depression. "I talked to Liz on the phone today, and she said, that as executor, it's my job to pack and inventory *everything* that's supposed to go to the sister. Which is just about everything. Tam left almost all of it to her sister, Sary, and Sary's daughter—no name. It's also my job to *find* the sister. Like, I'm supposed to hire a private detective if we can't turn up something here." Alison imagined Liz giving this information in a very pleased way, delighted to be a thorn in the side of Michelle. "So look for stuff like address books." She sighed. "Though I don't know what good *that* will do—I'm sure Tam didn't know where her sister was herself." She started to turn away, and then stopped. "Incidentally, after you left Wanda decided that Sary and Tam had different last names—they were only half sisters. So don't throw out papers just because they don't say McArthur."

"Pack *everything*?" Alison was horrified. "Not throw *anything* out? Not old bills? Not old clothes? Nothing?"

"Well, some specific things went to other people, and I've got that list here. We can keep them out, or box them separately, or something. But we're supposed to box everything else."

"I should have rented a hotel room," Alison muttered.

"Not too late," said Michelle. "I hear they go for about eighty dollars a night downtown. But you could probably find something really nice in Commerce City for less."

"Hmmph!" said Alison.

"But I thought we *could* kind of sort things out. You know, label things 'Garage Sale', so in case we do find the sister, and she's in China and wants us to just send the good stuff, we don't have to go through everything again." The plural pronoun rolled off her tongue just a little too readily for Alison's taste.

Michelle took a deep breath and marched into the bedroom. Alison decided that packing up dead people's belongings required a little music. Tamsin had an inexpensive—Alison didn't even know if stereo were the right word, it was so old and basic, but it had a record player and a tape deck and a radio all in one unit. She cranked the radio off the classic rock over to KYGO, where she caught Lori Morgan right in the middle of telling everyone that Monday never was any good anyway.

"Amen to that," Alison thought, as she went into Tam's little office porch. She was fascinated with the woman's writing space. As before, the clutter challenged her. Was there any method to the madness, as there was in Michelle's apartment, or had Tamsin just been a pig? Alison picked up a tiny jade turtle from the top of the keyboard, and then set it down again. The turtle was one of the items on the list, and it was supposed to go to a woman named Dana. Alison wrote the name on the side of her first box, wondering if Tamsin had left Dana's address somewhere, or if locating her was going to be another case for the private detective. Read 'Me', she thought wryly. The turtle went, in a hodgepodge way, with the other talismans Tamsin had scattered over her workspace. There was a beautiful basket made of pine needles, full of tiny, perfectly smooth river rocks, sitting beside the printer. Scattered among the papers were other tiny figures, jewelry, stones and fossils. For a moment Alison was tempted to sweep it all into a box. Let the fucking sister deal with it. Then, with a sigh, she began to sort out the papers. There were little notes all over, some stuck to the bulletin board, some glued to the wall, some actually written right *on* the wall (the landlord was probably going to have a fit, but who cared?) and others just thrown down haphazardly among the papers. A sampling read: Jefferson County has a smoke free jail. 'I'm young and I'm out'—sign at Gay Pride. Joan H. has a friend who specializes in children with shitting problems. One of Quince's clients has

a sign on the wall—'Remember to answer the phone when it rings.'
I'm keeping her typewriter—she took a little bit of me.

Michelle wandered in, carrying a box that was labeled: Crap—
throw away! "I read this," she said pointing to the note about the
smoke free jail. "This was in her last book, remember? The one called
Throw me to the Lesbians?"

Now that she had pointed it out, Alison did remember the part of
the novel where the heroine had first been taken to the local jail. It had
been, like all of Katie Copper's books, very dry and witty, so you were
laughing even while sympathizing with poor Blaze, who had been
picked up because she had put a brick through the window of the
Rocky Mountain News during a short psychotic break, and by the wee
hours of the morning was fearing for her life, watching the hookers
and drunk drivers with whom she shared the holding cell turn into
homicidal maniacs as they were forced cold turkey into nicotine with-
drawal.

"She was brilliant," said Alison, passing on to another note, something about how recycling really would not have reached its full
potential until they manufactured tampons you could later feed to your
dog.

"Oh, that's in her new book," said Michelle. "The one she was
getting ready to submit? Boy, that'd be a big seller, if I had more than
the thirty pages..." She trailed off. They looked at one another, and
then at the computer. There was a long moment of silence. Then
Michelle, who of course, knew Word Perfect, reached over and threw
the switch.

"It's not here," she said to Alison an hour later. "It is just not
here."

Alison, who was getting a little crabby about being the one going
through the disgusting cupboards while Michelle played with the computer, answered shortly. "It's on a floppy."

"No." Michelle shook her head. "I went through all the floppies.
And besides, even if it was on a floppy, she'd have it on the hard drive
as back up. It just isn't fucking here."

"She only had thirty pages written," suggested Alison, as she dropped a handful of silverware into a box labeled simply, 'Fuck this shit'.

"No." Michelle shook her head again. "That was a hard copy of a final draft she gave me—it was slick, it was finished, it was ready for submission."

"So she submitted the hard copy, and she sent the disk along." Even Alison, who was computer illiterate, had to admit there were some holes in this.

Michelle found one right away. "And didn't keep a back up? There are back ups of all her other books." Michelle screwed up her face in puzzled thought.

Alison perked up. "Cool! Can you run me a copy of *Call the Psychic*? Somebody borrowed my copy and never brought it back."

"Not now. I'm going to go get some Chinese."

"Since when do you have money to get Chinese?" Michelle and Janka had always lived pretty damn close to the bone, but ever since they had decided to do the baby thing, eating out was unheard of.

"Oh, I found fifteen dollars in a coffee can in the bedroom."

"Aren't you supposed to inventory that?" Alison lifted an eyebrow.

"Oh, fuck that. A hundred dollars, yes. A savings bond, yes. The new manuscript, yes. But I'm keeping all the change I find, and if she has any decent underwear, I'm taking them, too. Let the sister take me to court."

"Well, if I have to be an accessory, then I want some lo mein. Say, have you found Tam's keys?"

"The cops gave them back to the landlady. I told you that. She just lives around the block. You can pick them up on your way out tomorrow."

"Okay, but don't lock me in." Michelle was well known for her errands—fifteen minutes for lo mein could easily turn into an hour at the hardware store.

"Oh," said Michelle, "afraid of a fire?" She walked out without waiting for a reply, and then stuck her head back in. "Incidentally, I found Tam's address book. No Sary." She closed the door for a second time without waiting for a reply.

She had only been gone a few minutes when there was a knock on the inside door.

"What about these?" said the woman from downstairs as if Alison was going to know what she was talking about. She was carrying a cardboard box full of paperback books which she thrust at Alison.

"What *about* these?" asked Alison, taking the box automatically.

"Her early stuff," the woman explained. "She lent it to me." She seemed to be in a hurry, which was explained when Alison looked at the books. Presumably the neighbor—what *was* her name?—had not wanted to defend or discuss the fact she had been spending her nights with what appeared to be romance novels and a spattering of outright porn. Tam's early work? Surely not. But when Alison flipped open one of the romances, *Love's Lost Child*, she thought she could see Katie Copper's dry style behind the flowery phrases. She stuck the book into her backpack for another time and shoved the whole box under the coffee table to spring on Michelle when the time was right.

****

After they had spent twenty serious minutes on the vegetable lo mein and egg rolls, Alison brought out the one interesting item she had found while Michelle had been on the computer. (Actually, she had also found a huge sex-toy bag containing a selection of The Crypt's finest, but she had decided to let Michelle discover that herself.)

"Ta-da," she said, whipping out a scrap book with a flourish.

"What's that?" asked Michelle.

"Something I found under a pile of magazines."

"Oh, damn," mourned Michelle. "She cut the papers all up. If she'd saved them, we could have used them in the Archives." Michelle had been trying for weeks to get a full set of *BMR*, and the scrapbook Alison was holding was not going to help, for Tamsin had cut only local pictures.

"It's not supposed to help the Archives. Look at the photo. Look at the names! It's an article about Virago!" The photograph to which she was pointing had been taken in the pavilion at Cheeseman park.

There was a uniformity about all the women posing on the steps, as if they had all gone to the same barber, and picked out their clothes at the same Goodwill.

"Sary Riverwymon," said Michelle. "Third from the left. Oh, that name is going to help a lot. I wonder if they really were half sisters, like Wanda said, or if she actually thought someone was really named Riverwymon." She squinted at the grainy black and white photo. "Nope, never knew her. Incidentally…" she paused, as if trying to find a word. "If you find anything….personal, give it to me."

"Well, if you're talking about her butt plugs, I already found them. But don't you think Janka is going to object to used merchandise?"

"God, you're witty. Lea Delaria'd better watch her ass if Arsenio ever books you. No, I mean any personal papers. I'll go through the computer myself, but any …'personal' manuscripts, anything like that."

"Oh, so I can just box the sex toys up for the sister? That ought to be a wonderful surprise after fifteen years. She's got some dicks in there that would put Stacy to shame."

Michelle, with a will of steel, refused to follow this one up. "Okay, you're right. Box the sex toys separately, too. But what I'm talking about…" she hesitated again. Alison actually had quite a good idea of what she was talking about, but she was not about to help her out. It was rare indeed to see Michelle squirm, and it must be savored.

"What I'm talking about…."

"Yes?"

"It's just that…"

Alison took pity upon her. "Do you mean this?" She reached into the box under the table and whipped out a thin paper back. The cover showed two buxom women in leather and spike heels. The garish title read, *Butt Fucking Babes From Hell.*

"Oh, Goddess," said Michelle, covering her face, "it's worse than I thought."

"And a personal favorite of mine," said Alison, bringing out another, "*Nympho Lesbians From Mars!*"

"Oh, I hope at least that she wasn't responsible for the titles," said

66

Michelle from behind her fingers.

"Oh, look, here's one about you, Michelle. *Strapping It On For the Collective!* Your picture is on the front." The artist had gotten a little carried away—the buxom woman on the cover seemed to be wearing an MX missile between her legs.

"Tell me you're joking," Michelle pleaded.

"Just kidding," Alison assured her. "Actually, it's called *Queer Girls and the Neighbors' Dog.*"

Michelle moaned. Alison flipped open the second book. "Oh, we got some good stuff in here!" she said. "'Do you Earth girls not have a pleaser?' whispered Jarda into Dru's ear as she rubbed her shining pelt against her. 'Pah, on those ugly rubber things! You need a real woman to please you.'"

"Stop," begged Michelle. "Please. I'm begging you."

Alison thought of asking her to say, "Please, Mistress," but figured it would be pushing her luck. "I take it you were anticipating finding these?"

"No! I thought I might find a work in progress, but I didn't think she would have kept the whole bunch! I would have thought that she'd want to get rid of them!"

"Your friend was quite a little pornographer," observed Alison with a straight face. Just wait till the next time Michelle had something to say about her subscription to *On Our Backs.*

"Well," said Michelle, who recovered quickly, "she wouldn't have had to be a pornographer if lesbians supported their artists more, would she? She wouldn't have had to be a pornographer if every dyke who read her books bought her own copy instead of borrowing from a friend, or if everyone bought their Christmas presents at the Book Garden instead of Target." She fixed a beady eye on Alison.

"Oh, right, I'll be sure to get a copy of *Macho Sluts* for my dad for his birthday. He's been waiting to read it. And if I recall correctly, the main people who borrowed my Katie Copper novels were you and Janka."

"Well," said Michelle. "Still. She wrote...this shit," she gestured vaguely with her hand, unable to bring herself even to say the word,

67

"because she had to. She had to subsidize her own work because other lesbians wouldn't." She was getting warmed up now, creating a reality she could live with.

Which, Alison thought, was probably pretty close to the actual truth. She could not, however, refrain from asking, "And why did she keep them?"

"The publisher sent them," said Michelle firmly. "She was an author, it was hard for her to destroy her work, no matter how awful it was."

"Maybe it's not hers," suggested Alison. "Maybe she just liked sleazy lesbian porn."

"It's hers," said Michelle, grinding the two words out between her teeth as if they were the product of torture. "Two things. The name. Karen Caldwell. See, same initials. She told me that was a trademark. Also, the name of the woman in the book."

"Dru?"

"Yeah. I knew Dru. She was a Woman Who Done Tam Wrong. That was the other signature. Dru got it up the ass in every book."

"Oh! Yes!" Alison said, flipping through another. "Without lube, too. What revenge! I must become a writer."

"Spare me. Just put any of this shit you find, and any....accessories into a box with my name on it."

"Well, I can understand why you want them—isn't *Nymphos From Mars* out of print now?—but isn't this part of the estate? Isn't it supposed to go to the sister?"

"Get a grip!" shouted Michelle in exasperation. "I'm not planning on reading this shit, I'm planning on burning it!"

"And, I repeat, isn't it part of the estate?"

"Alison. I will personally put in ten dollars if that will make you happy."

"Look," said Alison, flipping through another book to find yet another Dru taking it up the ass. "Kidding aside, these books are worth much more than face value. Katie Copper is one of the best selling lesbian authors in the small press market. She is collectable. There are fans out there who would pay big bucks to own Katie Copper porn.

It's like that *Playboy* issue with the photo spread of Tasha Yar. It's a collector's item. If the GLBSCC had these, they could auction them off and make enough to keep you on an extra year."

"Please, Alison. Please. Don't try to put me into a moral dilemma."

"You're already there, girlfriend. You were there the minute you decided to take this shit home instead of boxing it up for the sister." Alison had not seen Michelle in such a twist since Janka had demanded they go see Woody Allen's latest flick for her birthday.

"Alison. Why do you think Tam made me the executor of her will?"

Alison had actually thought it had been kind of a rebound thing, the way you fall in bed with some gal at the bar after being dumped, but she was far too wise to bring, even obliquely, the topic of her own will up again. "I have no idea."

"Okay. She was new in town, and I was the only person she could trust. She asked me to do this, Alison. She didn't want her sister to be rooting around and find these, or even worse, find one half done on her computer!"

"Still," said Alison. "Unless she left this stuff to you in the will, I think you're doing something illegal."

"Alison. Isn't your father the executor of your will?"

"You know he is."

"And do you want him to find whatever it is you keep under your bed?"

Alison made a little moue of distress at the thought of her father gazing with bewilderment at her collection of nipple clamps.

"Fine," said Michelle. "If you will now shut the fuck up, and then promise to help me commit this felony, then I will promise the moment I hear your girlfriend has gone too far and burnt you up like a marshmallow, I will not even stop to say I told you so, but will run downstairs and have the whole place clean before your dad can send a squad car."

"Done!" said Alison, giving a high five.

Michelle brushed aside *Queer Girls and the Neighbor's Dog* and picked up the scrap book. She peered down at the photo again. "Isn't that…?" She held her thumb beneath a woman sitting on the steps beside Sary. "Is that who I think it is?"

~ 7 ~

"Is this a photo of you?" Alison handed Liz the scrapbook she had lifted from Tam's apartment. It had been opportune that she and Stacy were due to meet Liz at the Rubyfruit late that afternoon.

"Where did you get *this*?"

Alison was not sure if Liz was horrified or amused. Probably, she thought, an equal part of both. Liz, who was tiny, blonde, freckled and almost as hyperactive as Michelle, played soccer on Stacy's outdoor team, and Alison, who had ended up finishing the season in the goal when Stacy was hospitalized, had come to like her a great deal. When not playing forward or arguing the law, she was active in the leather community. She was, in fact, currently wearing a harness over her black tank top. "Where did you get this?" she asked again.

Alison waved at the woman behind the bar. It was only early afternoon and except for several pool players, one of whom was already drunk on her ass, they were the only ones in the bar. Liz was running for the title of Ms. Colorado Leather the next week, and Alison and Stacy had agreed to meet her at the Rubyfruit to help her with her speech and fantasy segment.

"Colorado Lesbian Archives," said Alison. "I wouldn't have been able to check it out if I hadn't personally known the curator."

"Well, it's only out of personal respect that I don't destroy the damn thing. God, what an incredibly shitty time period. I have not got one thing left from that era—I torched it all. I practically torched the house."

"Confrontation?" asked Alison sympathetically, pointing to the turkey sandwich listed on the menu. Liz held up her beer to indicate another.

"Worse than just confrontation. We're getting into the bad craziness category." She sighed and ran her hands through her hair. "Okay, were you around for the anti-psychiatric movement?"

"Yeah. In theory, at any rate. I never actually torched any place, but we had women who were running away from institutions stay with us. The bookstore was doing a lot of race and class stuff—kind of like *BMR*'s specialty was anti-pornography."

"Yeah, I went on a few spray paint actions myself. But anyway— Virago's thing was the anti-psychiatric movement."

"I thought you were a production company," protested Alison. Liz fixed her with a look. "Sorry," she mumbled, "I don't know what I was thinking. You were a collective. The personal is the political."

"You got it. Holly Near one night, smash the oppressor the next. It wasn't enough to bring the music to the women if we didn't follow the words ourselves. Particularly," she made a little tent with her fingers, "because we got a grant. Do you remember that? Some-fucking-how we got a six month grant—it paid five of us salaries. We were getting paid to smoke dope and listen to lesbian music, and we were real aware of how privileged we were. We were getting paid a full time salary to be lesbians and you were—what? Driving a school bus or busting tires at Sears?" She listed the two coming-of-age jobs for Denver dykes in the late seventies.

"School bus," said Alison.

"So, we were doing a couple of things. We were connected with a couple of support groups. You know, we can heal each other, it's when we bring in men and drugs that things get fucked up."

"Which is not actually a bad idea," replied Alison. "I've gotten a lot out of support groups."

"No, no, none of this was a bad idea. The groups were good. We also busted some women out of Denver General, and for the most part that was good, too. A lot of them were women who had been incested, and that wasn't acknowledged much at the time. Remember, all of us were so young at this point it wasn't uncommon for the hospital staff to contact Mommy and Daddy if someone got hauled in. So it would be one of these, 'She says her dad raped her, he says he didn't, she's a dyke and doesn't shave her legs, she must be crazy, let's lock her up.' Or, maybe she was there because her family put her there—we broke out really young women, women who were still in high school, women whose families had locked them up because they were dykes and got caught, or, again, they had been incested or abused and they had tried to talk about it and daddy thought he'd better label them crazy as quick as he could. We let them stay with us and took care of them and found them apartments and jobs and subsidized them on our pitiful little salaries and shipped them out of town to other dyke communities if their families were persistent about trying to find them. We did some real good. I believe that."

"So what was so bad about it?"

Liz tilted her chair back and gave a huge sigh. "There was another woman in the collective. She lived upstairs from me. You know how dykes are—they're worse than roaches—once you get one in the building they infest it, and we had taken this one over. So. She was my sister, my comrade in arms, and she was depressed. She was clinically depressed. She needed drugs. Now, I knew this, because I took anti-depressants myself, and so did everybody in my family. But. There was no way I was going to pass on this information because prescription drugs were bad, drugs were the enemy, and nobody even knew I did fifty milligrams a day. That was my little secret. Sharing that at this time with this particular group of women would have been like, oh, saying I blew men occasionally just for the hell of it. So anyway, she got worse and worse and we did all the things we knew to do. We tried to get her to talk about it, and we tried to distract her, and we tried to surround her with woman love and we tried to treat her with herbs and we gave her space and we took turns withdrawing because we were just too fucking burnt out. Now I know a little more about it, and maybe she could have been helped holistically. Lots of exercise, the right diet, no sugar. But I didn't know that then—christ, I wasn't any older than twenty-one myself. So she got worse, and she didn't have a job, and she was scaring the shit out of me because she was my fucking neighbor and nobody had quite said it, but she was my responsibility. I was real aware that if anything big went wrong I was going to be blamed. So one night I'm cooking curry and getting high and listening to Woody Simmons, and there's this huge crash upstairs. And I know, I instinctively *know* that this is a body-hitting-the-floor crash. I know she's cut her wrists or taken an overdose. And I can't get into her apartment. She's got the door bolted from the inside; I'm little, I don't have an ax or a saw, and I can't break the fucking door down. I also don't have a phone, because even on the grant it's a phone or dope, and I don't have anybody I need to call that bad, and so I go tearing out the front door, because the *BMR* office is only a couple of blocks away and I'm hoping there will be someone there who can help me before she bleeds to death. And on my front lawn are two policemen who are trying to arrest a wino. Now, I'm totally freaked, right? I know the cops are homophobic pigs and the enemy, but I'm freaked, and I'm high and I grew up in Iowa, and Mr. Policeman *was* my friend when I was a kid. And all I can see is that maybe I can get some help saving this woman's life."

"So the upshot was?"

"The upshot was they did break the door down and they did save her life. And they also institutionalized her, and I was totally purged from the group. Absolutely shunned."

"Oh," said Alison."

"'Oh', is fucking right," said Liz. "My whole fucking family—my friends, my sisters, my support group. All of a sudden there was fucking nothing. I mean, I can look back on it now and say, okay, this was the age of the purges, okay, this happened a lot—Didn't a similar thing go on at the bookstore?—okay, we were all twenty-one and we didn't know any better, and I still feel incredibly, incredibly bitter. I was totally thrown to the wolves. Everyone is always so sympathetic if a dyke gets a hard time about coming out from her family—you know, if she's not invited home for Christmas and all that shit. Well, that is nothing compared to being on the wrong end of a lesbian purge. You know how you get dumped by your girlfriend and it feels like it's the end of the world—you have no ego anymore because the only way you can figure anyone could treat you like this would be if you were totally worthless? You smoke dope all the time, you don't change your clothes. Life is bad, but you get through it because you have friends and they force you to go out and eat and listen to you cry, and they bail your ass out of jail or the loony bin until you're a little more functional? I had no one. Virago had been my life."

"Wow," said Alison, knowing it was stupid and inadequate. During the time period Liz was talking about, she herself had been living in a one room apartment doing pretty much exactly the things Liz had been describing—getting involved with bad crazies and breaking up and freaking out and withdrawing and considering suicide with the same attention to detail one now gave plans for a two week vacation. She didn't know how she would have gotten through the massive downs without Michelle and her other bookstore friends. "Wow," she said again.

"Yeah," said Liz. "Like I say, I can kind of talk myself out of it, but when it comes right down to the line, when I see any of those women, or read about them in *Quest*, I can't deal with it at all. There is no forgiveness. I mean, some of these women have gone on to do really good things in the community, and I see them, and I'm polite and I'm saying, 'Oh, isn't it great how you've organized this or that' and it's like my teeth are clenched the whole time I'm saying it, and what I'm really thinking is, 'You fucked me over, you bitch.' I mean, some things you just never get over—you know what I mean?"

"Oh, yeah."

"And actually, for all the shitty things my family has done to me over the years, they were never able to jerk me around to this extent. Because I didn't care as much, right? You're going to get pissed off and not talk to me for a couple of months? Okay, cool, I can handle that, no problem. They just didn't have the power to hurt me the way these other dykes did. So anyway, was there a point to all this, or were we just trying to stir up old memories? Are you working up to tell me that you're transsexual, or something?"

"No, but the bookstore collective purged a transsexual woman once."

"Yeah, us too. I spent some time thinking about that while I was locked up."

"Oh, no," said Alison.

"Oh, yes," said Liz. "You can't be a poor dyke bottoming like that without friends and not spend some time in Denver General. You ever think about that? I mean, what was so important about the work we were doing with Virago was that most of these women we were springing had no buffer what-so-ever. On one side there might be their family and on the other side there was fucking nothing—no money, no survival skills, no clue. And in my case, no job. Of course, the first thing the rest of the collective did was kick me off the board—I was the production manager—and I was too fucking depressed to look for another job. So I got evicted. So what do you do when you're a depressed baby dyke and you don't have a job or a place to live? "

"You go and stay on your friend's couch until she freaks."

"Bingo. Or, if you have no place to go, and you just kind of sit out on your lawn with your stuff for two or three days until you get locked up." She sighed again. "Sary and I should have shared the same room."

"Sary!" exclaimed Alison. "She was your neighbor? She's who I'm looking for. Tam's sister."

"Sary was Tam's sister? But, the will said… oh, okay, Sarah Jean. Sary must have been a nickname." She perked up visibly. "*That's* who Michelle is looking for. Oh, she's going to be dicked around forever on this. She's never going to find her."

"So what's the scoop here?" Neither had seen Stacy come into the bar. In a way, though she had still not gotten any information on Sary, Alison was relieved to see Stacy. She thought that Liz, too, seemed to turn to her with a sigh of relief, a way to stop dabbling in pains long past.

"Are you really sure you want to win this title?" Stacy went on, oblivious to any tension between them. Stacy could be like that. She was a great listener when she was aware there was a problem, but sometimes you had to really put it in her face. "Because, if you win, you have to go to the nationals, and if you win *that* it's this great huge pain in the fucking ass—the international title holder always has to declare bankruptcy, from what I hear."

"Oh, get a grip," said Liz, picking at the potato chips on the side of Alison's plate. "Nobody from Denver ever is a national title holder. They always choose the San Francisco and Seattle girls. The judges think that we still have cattle drives down Main Street."

"Listen, somebody from Kansas took the competition last year. You missed it because you never went out of the room the whole week end."

"Party on, Stacy!" said Liz, who had seen *Wayne's World* four times in the two months since it had been released.

"Party on, Liz!" replied Stacy, who had accompanied her to two of the showings. "So what do you want us to do?"

"I need help with this fantasy," said Liz.

"Well, baby, that's the first time I've ever heard anybody complain about you in the fantasy department. Usually what I hear is women begging you to slow down and do the vanilla thing once or twice a week just because they don't have the energy to keep up."

"Which is why you have a young girlfriend," added Alison. Carla, who was a waitress at the Blue Ryder when she was not learning to cut hair, had barely turned twenty-one.

"Fuck you both!" said Liz with unexpected vehemence. She pushed her chair roughly back from the table and stalked off towards the bathroom. Alison and Stacy looked at one another.

"Oh," said Stacy, "trouble in River City." She pulled a cottage cheese container out of her purse. It was filled with carrot sticks. For the past several months she had been trying to adapt to the Jean Brody High Carbohydrate Diet.

"Well, I kind of riled her up," said Alison. "I didn't mean to. I was only trying to track down Tamsin's sister. It turned out Liz had been a purge victim."

"You know," said Stacy, throwing back a handful of carrots, and following them with almost an entire glass of ice water, "I used to think I missed out on a lot by not coming out as a teenager. But the more I hear about this time period, the more content I am to having been married and living in Wheatridge while you all were fighting over my right to wear leather. Actually, I shouldn't have teased Liz— she said something the other day about having problems with Carla— I just forgot."

"Sex problems?" Alison was astounded. Liz and Carla had been obsessively and obnoxiously sexual since they had gotten together.

"Well, it's been six months. Everybody knows lesbians don't have sex beyond that."

"Actually, I think two months is more the norm."

"Yeah, I've sure had a lot of relationships start out hot and then go right into the 'not-tonight-*LA-Law*-is-on' stage. That's why I like you, baby. Still hot after the dreaded six-month mark." She hit Alison with the smoldering glance that could still get her hot in an instant.

"Stop," said Alison weakly, batting away the hand that reached for her knee under the table. They had already pissed off Liz—it wasn't going to help if she came back and found them in a clinch. Alison knew Stacy all too well—there had been many an innocent grope that had ended up with them fucking in a parked car or the bathroom of a restaurant.

"Oh, baby," Stacy moaned in her sexiest voice, "come on, give it up like you used to."

"She's coming back!" Alison hissed, and hastily stood up and stretched. "So what are the rules for this scene?" she asked Liz.

"About three minutes, it has to have music, no fire on stage," Liz recited in a voice much less enthusiastic than her normal tone. Like Michelle, depression on the normally hyper Liz showed up much more than a down mood on anyone else.

"I have also noticed," said Stacy, "that the judges—and the audience too—tend to like something that has some humor to it. Also, if you do win and you do get to go to MSIL (she pronounced the anagram for Ms. International Leather as M-sull) keep in mind that you'll probably have to perform with people you don't know. Do you remember Suzy Shepherd's fantasy?" she asked Liz. "She was title holder three years ago," she said in an aside to Alison.

"Yeah, it was funny," admitted Liz.

"And it was also versatile," said Stacy. "She could perform that skit with anyone. Men, women, people she had never met. She didn't have to drag her cast around with her—which is good, because I hear that her traveling expenses alone bankrupted her."

"Get off the bankrupt obsession," said Liz "I'm a lawyer. I'm a GUPPY. I can afford to go to San Francisco *and* take my girlfriend with me."

"Speaking of girlfriend, where is Carla? Are we supposed to choreograph this around her?"

"Oh, I don't know," said Liz crossly. "I don't even know if she wants to do it any more. Shit, I don't even know if I want to do it anymore."

"What's the problem here?" asked Alison. "This isn't still about the purging, is it? I never would have brought it up if I'd known..."

"No, no, it's not that. It's...Christ, I feel like such a shit about this! Look, I'm not telling you anything new if I tell you that the main attraction between Carla and me has always been sexual, am I?" As if choreographed Alison and Stacy shared a get-real look. Liz sighed. "Oh, I guess it's been pretty obvious. But the sex has been great. I'd been celibate for something like two years, I'd been hurt really badly before, and Carla wasn't anybody who could do that to me again—she was safe emotionally. And the sex was so fucking hot—she didn't have a whole lot of experience, but she wanted to try everything in a big way." This also was not news to Alison, who had been watching with interest as Carla evolved from just another girl with a leather jacket into a budding s/m monomaniac with a toy bag she couldn't lift by herself. "So, everything was cool. We loved to play together, and we had enough conversation to get through dinner if we needed to— you know, we both like *Roseanne* and *Dykes to Watch Out For* and skiing and Chinese food."

"That actually is about three things more than most couples," inserted Stacy. "This sounds like a match made in heaven."

"Well. About a month ago Carla starts having incest flashbacks." Alison winced and then was instantly ashamed. But what else could you do? A number of her close friends and ex-lovers were incest survivors, and she knew this was not going to be a story with a happy ending.

"So, she can't have sex, right?" asked Stacy. "Particularly not kinky sex."

"Actually, the kinky part is not nearly so much an issue. But, no, she can't have sex. Which is okay, I'm not a total pig. If we were in a relationship I would be willing to work this out. Except that we have fucking nothing in common besides sex. Carla is twenty-one—she wasn't even *born* when *Lesbian Concentrate* first came out. She didn't know who Alix Dobkin was until I told her. When sex is the only thing you have in common and it ends, it seems to me it's time for the relationship to end. I don't mean I want to be shitty or cut her off or anything like that! I am totally willing to be her friend and be supportive—shit, I'm paying for her therapy, and I'm totally willing to continue doing that!"

"But she really needs lots of emotional attention and support and sees a split as betrayal and a sign that you were just using her like everyone else," supplied Stacy.

"Bingo. Oh, fuck, maybe I was using her."

"You weren't using her, Liz," said Alison compassionately. "Two grown women going for a good time—that's not using. You didn't manipulate her or abuse her or force her. It's just a really hard situation to deal with, and the fact that you're not in love with her doesn't make it any easier. But I've known women who have been together for years break up around incest stuff. It's so hard to deal with, and it's so hard to do the right, supportive things without sacrificing yourself totally."

"I know," said Liz wearily, putting her head in her hands. "I'm going to come out of this one the villain no matter which way I go, aren't I?" Both Alison and Stacy looked vaguely off into the distance—this was one of those questions that didn't need a yes. "And what about this stupid fantasy? Carla has been planning on being part of it for months. Is it using her if I don't approach breaking up until after the competition?"

80

"Mmmm," said Alison, who thought that, yes, it was using her.

"You're right," sighed Liz. "The least I can do is be as honest as possible about the break. Look, you guys," she reached across the table and began gathering her things. "I can't do this right now. Let's just go home and think about a fantasy that only takes the three of us."

"Just the two," Alison put in hastily. "I'm willing to help with costumes and props and all that, but I can't appear on stage. They're watching me like a hawk at work—I can't afford to show up in *Outfront* wearing chains."

"We can get Beth or Shirley to help us if we need more people," said Stacy, naming two of the other women in their leather outreach group.

"Oh, Liz, wait a minute! I wanted to ask you, did you keep in touch with Sary? Do you have any idea where she might be now?"

Liz shrugged into her leather jacket before answering. "Not a clue, Alison. Not a clue."

At Tamsin's apartment Alison went to bed early. She had pulled a couple of night shifts the week before, and it seemed that her body could not adjust to the change. Or perhaps the continual fatigue really was part of something else, as her doctor had said. Maybe it was time to call the rheumatologist.

Either way, she was sound asleep when the phone rang. Until the fourth ring, she incorporated it into her dream. By then the answering machine kicked in, and she just lay groggily under the sheets, listening to Tamsin's voice sternly directing that a name and number be left. God, the woman even topped her answering machine. There was a beep, and an extremely irritated woman said, "Damn it, I hope you're on your way!" The phone was slammed down.

Well, that was one girl who was going to be disappointed. Where was the phone, anyway? Alison hadn't seen it at all in her travels. She finally located it in one of the cupboards under the water bed. Put there to keep it safe from kittens, or a whim of Michelle's? She shrugged. Who knows? There was half a pack of Indian Spirits beside the phone, and she lit one without thinking. She had gotten a new phone at her house last year by renewing her subscription to *Newsweek.* Tam must be a news junkie too, because her phone was identical, down to the raised *Newsweek* logo. Alison sat looking at it for a moment. God, the apartment was hot! She kicked off the covers, and both kittens went sailing.

"Sorry!" she said absentmindedly, as they meowed their indignation. She reached out a hand, and in a moment they were both fast asleep in her lap. She turned the phone over. Hers was the most high tech piece of communication equipment she'd owned since she'd graduated from rotary to push button. She didn't know how to work all the options yet, but she did know how to work the redial. Tentatively, she pushed the button. Click, click, click -the number printed on the display as it dialed. Shit. An 800 number. She had hoped for a friend—the mysterious Dana, or perhaps Judy, a name that also showed up on the list. Still, she put the phone to her ear, wondering if Tam had been making an out of town reservation, or buying concert tickets or complaining about her pain killers or toothpaste.

"The last call to your number has been traced and a one dollar fee will be added to your bill. If your call was life threatening, please call your local police. Otherwise, please call 1-800-582-0655 between nine a.m. and six p.m. weekdays to initiate deterrent action. You will not receive the name and number of the party who called you."

Alison held the receiver in her hand after the message clicked off. So Tam had received a threatening call? Not necessarily, she corrected. A nuisance call. Kids calling and hanging up? A pervert who wasn't with the program yet, who didn't realize he was going to have to change his late night ways if he didn't want the police arriving at his door along with the mail? Too late to find out tonight. She put the phone back under the bed and lay back down.

The second time she was woken by an insistent, and obviously angry knocking on the door. It was after ten, and she was naked. Hastily, she draped herself with Tamsin's robe, a beautiful butch kimono she would have liberated from the estate, had she been that kind of girl. She pushed back the curtain of the window in the door to the outside staircase. A woman, carrying a suitcase. A dyke. Femme, but it took more than high heels and a dress to throw Alison's radar off track. She had red hair, not strawberry blonde, like Janka's, but red, curly, and bouncy over her shoulders. She had that pale redhead's complexion that looked as if it would burn if she even stepped into the sun, flushed right at this moment with some high emotion.

"Hi," Alison said, opening the door while wondering just how bad her hair looked, and whether running her fingers through it would make it worse or better.

"That bitch," said the woman. She dropped her suitcase on the iron landing with a clank that set every dog on the block barking. The flush was anger. "That fucking bitch. First she's not at the airport. And now you mean to tell me she's got someone here with her? I'm going to take her fucking head off."

"No…" started Alison, with a sinking feeling that the conversation had gone from neutral to totally out of control without the ball ever even having entered her court. "I mean…" but by this time the woman had pushed past her into the living room.

"You're fucking moving in?!" she shrieked. Alison followed her eyes to the boxes on the floor and tried again, only to be shouted down. "Where the fuck is she?" The woman stalked into the bedroom. The kittens, wisely, made themselves scarce. "Oh, I should have known better, I should have fucking known better!" Out she came again. In her hand was the biggest dildo, lifted from the box Alison had started for Michelle. "You don't even know who I am, do you?" Almost casually, she brought the dildo up against one of the framed prints on the wall, shattering the glass. "She just left you here to take the heat, didn't she?" Slam, she cleared the mantle. Seashells went flying and smashed against the wall and floor. A piece of a conch shell stuck into the rubber head of the dildo, making it look as if it were wearing a hat.

"She's dead," said Alison and then, as the woman started in on a table lamp, "She's dead! She wasn't at the airport because she's dead! She electrocuted herself! They took her away in a fucking body bag!" She was horrified by the ugly sound of the words, but at least they seemed to break through the woman's rage.

"What?" she said, lowering her sword just before connecting with the wind chimes. And then, "Tamsin?" And then, like the Wicked Witch of the West, she appeared to be melting. Only as the woman sank to her knees, did Alison realize she was going to faint.

The woman had split her lip when her face hit the floor, and so she sipped at the tea gingerly. There was a plate of cheese and crackers beside her, but so far she had not touched them. Her name was Dana, and she was the woman who was to get the ceramic turtle, and the embossed prints and all of Tamsin's jewelry.

"I don't have anywhere to go," she said in a bewildered voice. It was the first thing she had said, besides her name. There was going to be a lump in the center of her forehead, as well as the split lip. "Tamsin was supposed to meet me at the airport, I have to be here for a whole week. I'm locked into my ticket, I don't have anywhere else to go." A person unacquainted with grief might have sneered to herself, and decided that this was someone who did not care about the death of Tamsin McArthur. But Alison was not unacquainted. She had stood with women who had watched their houses and children burn before their eyes, had tried to turn sons and daughters away from twisted bodies of metal that had moments before contained their parents. Sometimes they had asked about their dogs, or their luggage, or the Broncos or the weather. And what it mainly meant was "I can't deal with this, don't make me deal with this now." The brain was good about obliging. The lucky ones cried later—maybe a minute, maybe an hour, maybe a day. The unlucky ones kept the dazed look Dana was wearing—they were the ones you read about in the newspaper later, wheeling their empty baby carriages back and forth to the park, and continuing to set a table for four in a house where only three now lived.

"You can stay here," Alison assured. "I think the couch in the living room makes down into a bed."

"It does," said Dana, and then nothing more. She sipped her heavily sugared tea. Alison put a cracker into her hand, and obediently she ate it, as if it were a job.

"I can't go home," she said. "Tam said I could stay with her. She said she'd been missing me." She turned to Alison, as if for confirmation.

"She was," Alison soothed. "She would have been at the airport if she could have been. She was looking forward to seeing you." She had no compulsion about lying—shit, maybe it was the truth. Most of what she had known about Tamsin had come through Blaze Badgirl, and Blaze would have met her girlfriend at the airport, though she probably would have done it in a stolen car.

"This isn't just a…. You'd tell me if this was just a scam, wouldn't you?" She leaned forward urgently. "I won't freak out again, I promise! It's not just a scam because she changed her mind? Oh, Jesus, this isn't a scene, is it?"

"It's not a scam," said Alison gently, wondering what the hell kind of woman would plan a scene this heartless. Tam? Or was Dana just in shock, grasping at straws that could mean her lover was still alive?

"Oh, god, I could kick myself, now I'll never get the chance to hold her again…." Dana trailed off and made a visible effort to pull herself together again, taking a long hard swallow of the tea as if it were whisky. The quilt Alison had wrapped around her was falling down off her shoulders, and she absently pushed back the hem. "We had this relationship—are you in the scene, did you say?" She did a quick scan of Alison's ears and wrists, as if she was going to be wearing studs or a hankie to bed. Alison nodded. "OK, so do you know that bad craziness feeling? That 'oh-god-this-started-out-as-a-little-power-exchange-and-now-I'm-completely-lost-in-this-woman's-soul'?" Alison nodded again. She had come close, frighteningly close, to this with Stacy. It was one of the things that backed her away from merging and really doing the girlfriend thing. "Okay. Bad news. The sex is so fantastic. The s/m has gone to a totally new level—a spiritual level almost—when you're playing together it's like she's holding your soul in her hands. But outside of scenes we're eating each other alive, we're killing each other by pieces. We're doing things that she's calling scenes, but they're really just plain abusive. We're considering murder/suicide scenes, and it starts out as a joke but it's getting closer and closer to the truth, because we can't live with each other and we can't live without each other and it seems like the only damn choice. So finally," and here was where the tears began to flow, "I had to leave her. I loved her. I loved her with a passion. I loved her more than I had ever loved any other woman. But I couldn't go on being treated shitty anymore. I couldn't. She had so many issues around anger. She'd had this incredibly shitty childhood—I knew that, and I kept thinking, well, if only I love her enough, if only I'm understanding enough, if only I support her enough one day she's going to wake up and say, 'Hey, I've really been dumping on you—you're right, I do need professional help.' But she had it in her mind she could say any ugly, shitty thing she wanted to me when she was angry, and she could just brush it off because I bottomed to her. And I kept hanging on because of the connection, because of those times when all that bravado was stripped away and our souls would touch and she would weep in my arms. And then," Dana put the heel of her hand up to her forehead in a gesture of utter weariness, "it got to be so those times weren't enough. I had to leave." She used a corner of the quilt to wipe the tears that were dripping off her chin, and then leaned back in a fetal-like position, her arms crossed over her stomach as if she were protecting the feelings inside. "I have not talked to her—I haven't seen her in six months. I know she blamed me. I tried to talk to her a couple of times before I had to break it off completely. She never forgave me for leaving her—she saw it as a total betrayal, and she saw my refusing to be abused any longer as walking out on a relationship when it got tough. See, she had come from a background where constant fighting and dumping and abuse was the norm—she couldn't understand my problem with it."

"But her books," Alison protested. "Her books—they're so bright, and they're so witty and so...." She gestured towards the writing table, at a loss for words.

"Oh, yeah," agreed Dana, "she was a totally different woman when she wrote. That was one of the things that attracted me to her. I can't tell you how many times she courted me back with letters. But," and here she made herself even smaller and began to rock, "in the end it wasn't enough, oh god, it wasn't enough. It was everything she had, but it wasn't enough." Alison sat silent. She had no idea of how to comfort this woman's pain. If it had been Janka, she would have gathered her in her arms and rocked her on her lap as she cried, and perhaps added a few of her own tears for relationships now never to be resolved, and young lives forever maimed by families. But, though she would have acted spontaneously ten years ago, she could no longer do this with a stranger. All she could do was fix another cup of the tea with an extra slop of honey and then pry one of Dana's hands away from her chest to curl around the mug. There was a long pause, a pause so long Alison began to wonder if Dana hadn't drifted out.

"So finally," Dana said at last, "I just had to cut it off completely. I could not be in contact and not get sucked back in. And she was so angry! It was easier, of course, because she moved back to Denver. But oh god, it was so hard not phoning, it was like my hand had this totally evil life of it's own. Every day I'd find myself calling information for her number—sometimes dialing it, hanging up before the first ring. My friends tried to keep me straight, you know, the way you do if you're a druggie. 'She's bad news, Dana. She treats you bad, Dana. This isn't s/m, Dana, it's the mother of all sick relationships.'" She paused and blew her nose. "They don't know I'm here. They think I'm visiting my mother."

"Why?" asked Alison. "Why did you come back to her?" Because there was no doubt in her mind about what this reunion was to be— not exlovers finally becoming friends, not one old friend helping another with a place to stay. This was one woman coming back to start in again on a love that was painful and bad, for the simple reason she could not stay away.

Dana shrugged. "I don't know. No, that's another lie. I don't have to lie anymore. I've lied to my friends, and I've lied to myself, but I don't have to lie anymore—if she's really dead." She looked at Alison with a little ray of hope in her eyes, as if there was still a chance this could turn out to be the mind fuck of them all.

"She's dead," said Alison firmly.

Dana sighed. "I wouldn't be surprised, you know, if it turned out to be a sick little scene. That was the kind of thing she would do towards the end. Mind fucks. Consent didn't enter into it. Just the rush. Just the challenge of laying you wide open emotionally." She looked around vaguely. "Do you have a cigarette?" she asked. Alison found the pack of Indian Spirits, and because it seemed too cold just to hand them over, she lit two.

"Tam's," Dana said, and it wasn't a question. "Why did I come?" She blew a long stream of smoke out, and they both watched it get lost in the darkness beyond the single kitchen light. "Because she asked. I changed my phone, I sent her first letters back. And then one day she called me at work, and she asked. That was all it took." They both smoked their cigarettes down to the filter, and Alison shook two more out of the pack. "I thought it would be safe, I guess. She was here, I was there. I thought I could come and be with her for a week, and go back home where my life was safe and sane. She had a name for it, you know. For the times when we'd come back together. Maybe be months apart, and then come back together because I'd run into her in a bar, and the minute I saw her I was hooked again. Smoking just one cigarette. That's what she'd call it. Smoking just one cigarette. But you know," she said, leaning forward and flicking her ash into Alison's empty soda can, "you can never smoke just one cigarette."

9

There were three boxes of wine—the cheap kind with the spigot— on the kitchen table. Michelle couldn't drink wine, because she might be pregnant, and Janka wasn't drinking in solidarity because next month it was her turn to try and get pregnant, but Dana and Stacy both had two glasses before people even started coming. Alison suspected that Stacy, who had come over with Janka, had been into the wine all afternoon. At least she and Dana had done a little femme bonding—it had been hard to predict how Dana was going to be received as the surprise guest. They were now off fixing their hair in the bathroom while Alison and Michelle fussed with the table.

Alison didn't know who Michelle had invited. Old friends, she guessed, when Wanda and Vicki and Nadine came to the door. People who had worked with Tam on the paper. Before she had hit it so big as Katie Copper, before she had gone so bad with Dana.

"So," Michelle had said, when Alison had told her the story. "So she turned out to be pretty abusive, huh?" She was baking for the wake, and she had turned over the bread dough beneath her hands and began to use the rolling pin on the floury side. She had on a denim apron that was much too big, despite the fact the neck strap had been tied up in a knot, and she had managed to cover every square inch of it with flour.

"So the girlfriend says. I mean, I guess we all tell our own version of the truth, though." Alison hadn't brought up the s/m twist—she figured it would be more than Michelle could hear at the moment. And besides—was it even important? It was like Dana's friends had said—it wasn't s/m, it was just a fucking sick relationship.

"Well," said Michelle, beginning to spread a thin layer of margarine over the dough, "that doesn't really surprise me. I mean, I wouldn't have thought of it myself, but my first reaction is not, 'No! Never!' The signs were there. She was always a really angry woman. She had that habit of: 'If I get more pissed than everybody else, then nobody can hurt me'—You know?"

Alison ducked her head to hide a smile, for this was actually a game at which Michelle herself was fairly good.

"No," said Michelle, catching the gesture. "Okay, I might do that, but I wasn't ever in the same league Tam was in. I mean, I don't go for blood. I don't have to win at all cost. Tam did. She was very good at distracting with a political issue, you know: 'You're saying that because you're middle class and I'm working class, or you're saying that because you haven't been in an institution, and I have'—you know, stuff that well trained, guilt ridden lesbian feminists would automatically back down from. And then later you might think, 'But wait a minute, that didn't have anything to do with it.'" She was now sprinkling cinnamon and sugar lavishly. "But I kind of put that down to the climate, you know? I mean, it was the seventies, we were a collective, we were lesbians, one of our major things was preying on each other. You were positively lauded for ripping open some poor woman at a meeting—you were being upfront and not holding your anger in. I figured, I'd changed, she'd changed. I liked her. That's such a hard one to call…what do you do about a woman who's great to you but treats her girlfriend shitty? I used to feel really clear about that—fuck over my sister and death to you, oh Evil One. We'll take you to Thornton and leave you for the straight girls. I guess I actually still feel the same way. What's changed is I'm not so clear about what fucking over my sister means anymore. It's like you said—about everybody having their own version of the truth? Tam didn't talk about her break up a whole lot, but she was obviously in a great deal of pain over it. She mentioned several times that she'd been left."

"Yeah," Alison had replied, thinking back to Sandy, the ex-lover whom she hadn't seen in several years. Except far away at Gay Pride when they stayed their distance. So who had been wrong there?

So here they all were in Michelle's apartment, just as they had been gathered two nights before. Wanda and Vicki and Nadine because they had known Tamsin long ago, and Alison and Janka to support Michelle. Stacy because she was Alison's girlfriend, and Dana because she had been Tam's.

Other women whom Alison did not recognize began to trickle in, some of them carrying dishes of food.

"I called every local number in her book," Michelle said, when queried. "Shit, I don't know who they are. Go find out."

Alison had not been at many wakes, or even funerals, for that manner. She was not sure exactly what the proper manner of behavior was. Stacy, however, started mingling as if she were at a end-of-the-season soccer party, so she decided just to follow her lead. From across the room she noticed Michelle was keeping a close and cross eye on Stacy, as if she suspected at any moment she was going to empty out the funeral urn and do something kinky with the ashes. Alison wandered over to where the food was and began loading a plate with brownies. Apparently she was not the only one in the crowd who thought sweets cured all ills—the only dish that didn't contain sugar and/or chocolate was a plateful of cheese which was being largely ignored.

"Oh, excuse me!" Damnit, she had been so engrossed in brownie foreplay that she had turned too quickly and toppled another woman's plate. Oops, brownies and chocolate chip cookies all over the rug, crumbs all over the woman—another smooth move, Alison. To her utter horror, when the woman raised her dark brown eyes they were brimming with tears. "Oh, god, I'm sorry, I didn't mean...." What kind of unbalanced crazy would be in tears over a plateload of aborted brownies? Time to back out of this situation... Oh. Right. She was at a wake. Just because she and Stacy were padding didn't mean every-one was. With a new interest she looked at the woman and stuck out her hand, saying, "I'm Alison Kaine. I'm clumsy. I knock things over instead of using an opening line."

The woman laughed, though tears had began to flow down her cheeks. "I'm Marta Goichecca. I cry all the time." She put the paper plate down on the buffet table and took Alison's hand. Their hands were about the same size, which was actually a little strange, for she was a big tall woman with a good six inches and thirty pounds on Alison. She was dressed in what Alison thought of as 'old hippy femme'—a brown and maroon batiked skirt beneath a billowy top. She wore several large pieces of jewelry that didn't match but had a certain charm together. Her dark, shoulder length hair was tied back with a scarf. "I also stress eat," she said, reloading her plate as soon as Alison released her hand.

"We have an issue for bonding there. Actually, isn't there going to be a support group meeting here later?" Alison felt a little pang of guilt about joking. Was she being disrespectful? But there were other women who were talking and laughing in low voices, particularly those by the wine boxes. Marta laughed again. She bit down on a brownie and wiped her upper lip with the inside of her wrist, as if the salt of the tears did not go well with the chocolate.

"How did you know Tam?" she asked Alison. "I've only known her a couple of months, but I got the idea that she really didn't have any friends in town. I mean, that was part of her problem, she didn't know anybody except the other women in the Group."

"Oh, I'm just padding. She was really my friend's friend." She indicated Michelle with her chin, not sure if she should be embarrassed.

Marta, obviously catching the overtone of guilt, waved her hand. "Oh, yeah, I was kind of afraid there'd be nobody here, so I brought a friend for moral support, too." With a cookie she gestured over towards the bay window. Perched on the sill among the tomato plants, was a small woman in full leather talking to—of course—Stacy, who was obviously in the process of forgetting where she was and becoming tipsy and animated. Michelle was going to shit. Marta and her friend, whom she referred to as Mary Clare, were very different styles of dykes. Besides their size difference Mary Clare was doing the butch thing, but there was a similarity about their features that made Alison cut her eyes back sideways to study Marta's face again.

"Oh, yeah." Marta caught the look and was obviously familiar with it. "We are related. It's kind of obscure though—our parents call us cousins, but I'm not sure if it would actually legally be incest if we decide to do anything together. What you're seeing is the Basque thing—they don't have them down here, so we look more alike than we do at home." Alison stuffed a brownie in her mouth so she would not have to respond to this bit of information, which she found largely incomprehensible. She decided not to question—maybe Stacy would get a clearer version from Mary Clare—and asked instead,"What group?"

"Oh, crazy obsessive dykes who cry all the time. We don't have an anagram yet." Her tears, which had been flowing steadily, suddenly increased. She set her plate down on the table and used the hem of her blouse to mop her face. "Christ, I'm tired of this. I wish I felt sexual—at least I could flirt with you and it might be distracting."

"Is this an actual disorder?" Alison asked tentatively.

"God, I wish it was. Then maybe I could collect unemployment. I'm just lucky I don't work in a bank or something." The tears had stopped. Marta stood with her eyes stretched wide and tight and her head very still, as if any jarring might start the flow again. "No, it's breaking up shit. Compounded by the funeral, of course. I mean, I—we all—feel so fucking bad about this. I truly thought Tam was feel-ing better, and now I feel like we weren't listening or something. Well, I guess at least the sister won't know, and that was important to her."

Oh. Well, it was obvious that here was another woman who didn't buy the accident theory. Alison wondered if Marta knew about the official cause of death.

"Well, that...." Marta halted suddenly. "God, I have this real prob-lem with confidentiality when I'm upset. Is there Coke at that bar? Sometimes caffeine will do it for me." Abruptly she swept away, leav-ing Alison with her mouth open.

"Hey, babee," Stacy threw her arm around her neck, knocking her into the table. For the second time in less than fifteen minutes the brownies went tumbling. Stacy was a sloppy, gregarious drunk—of all her personas this was one of Alison's least favorite.

"Do you have any idea what Basques are and why they don't have them down here?" Alison asked.

"Mmm, oh yeah, it's an area in the Pyrenees, part in Spain and partly in France. They've been really successful at retaining their own ethnic identity even though they've been totally surrounded by a dominant culture. A fairly large population migrated to Idaho and Montana in the early 1900s—they were fishermen back home, but they were put to work as sheepherders over here because you didn't have to speak English…." Even when she was getting looped Stacy could kick into the computer mode which gave Alison such a laugh. True, she might have just picked this all up from Mary Clare, but it was equally likely she just happened to have two paragraphs stored on Basques and had been waiting to recall them. "Oh, I just met the cutest little leathergirl—god, I'd love to fuck her ass—"

Unfortunately, Stacy clicked out of computer mode just as Michelle came up. She recoiled from this declaration as if she had been slapped. "Oh, charming," she hissed, addressing herself to Alison, rather than Stacy. "I am so glad you brought her—it adds such a touch of class. Do you want me to just clear a table for her?"

"Oh, get a life, Michelle." For Alison's sake, Stacy was usually fairly tactful around Michelle, but it was obvious whatever she'd sucked down changed that rule. "You're just pissed off because I'm still interested in sex and your girlfriend's not." As far as Alison knew, this was a complete shot in the dark, but from the way Michelle stiffened she could see it had struck home. Michelle turned and gave Alison a betrayed look. "I didn't say anything!" Alison protested. "How could I? *You* never said anything to me."

"Oh, she didn't have to say anything. You've always been a tight ass, but you've gotten worse and worse as you've been getting less pussy," Stacy continued

Oh, christ almighty. Alison didn't know whether to try and extract Stacy from the situation before blows were exchanged or just put her hands over her face and cry. Michelle was incoherent with rage, probably over Janka being referred to, however obliquely, as 'pussy'. Alison took Stacy's hand and attempted to move her, but she was solid as a rock.

"And another thing" Stacy said, getting right up in Michelle's face, "you want to know why you're so fucking threatened by me?"

"No, honey, she doesn't." Alison tried to take Stacy's elbow, but she brushed her off like a fly. Michelle was so puffed up her head actually seemed to have grown, and it was obvious hyperventilation was not far away.

"It's not because you're afraid I'll take Alison from you—anybody can see that you'll always mean more to her than I will." Here she turned and gave Alison who hadn't even realized this was an issue, a bitter look. "You're scared of me because you're such a fucking drama queen yourself. You'd love to be in the scene yourself if you weren't such a little political tightass. You'd be great and you know it. And maybe if you'd let go a little, your girlfriend might let you do it to her once in a while. She probably just got tired of licking and rubbing."

Janka, who had been alerted to trouble by someone across the room, (by now pretty much everybody had stopped pretending to be talking and was just staring at Stacy in wide-eyed amazement) arrived just in time to hear this last sentence. What Alison was to remember was not the look of horror that froze on Janka's face, but the split second before, when something like total agreement had crossed it. Oh, dear, if what Stacy had guessed was true, there was definitely going to be trouble in the Martin-Weaversong household.

Janka gave Alison a look which she recognized, from her days as a dog owner, as an unspoken 'You hold yours and I'll hold mine'. Janka actually had hold of the collar of Michelle's shirt and looked as if she would not hesitate to twist it. Alison was afraid she might have to take Stacy out with a tackle. Abruptly, however, Stacy herself decided the party was over. She flounced to the door as if she were Scarlet O'Hara. Alison hoped she would just pass out on her bed, rather than falling down the stairs.

"Hey, hey, party girl!" Alison resisted an urge to give Stacy a hearty clip on her head, which she was resting in both hands. "Order you a glass of wine?" She settled for jarring Stacy's chair.

"Please." Stacy held up her hand without looking up. Over Alison's protests the night before, she had driven herself home, and it appeared that twenty-two hours had not been enough to sleep off the wake. She was wearing sunglasses, even though the inside of the Blue Ryder was as dim as a cave. "I will throw up if wine is mentioned. It's not a pretty sight—don't force me to make you look at it." There was a big wicker basket sitting on the table beside her, and Alison peered inside it with some trepidation. Liz had asked them both to bring props to inspire the fantasy, and she rather dreaded to see what Stacy had been carrying around in her car as if it were a family picnic.

Sure enough, the very first thing, thrown right on the top, was Stacy's biggest dildo, the one she referred to as Mr. Winkie. Still in harness.

"It's a good thing you didn't get stopped for running a red light," Alison remarked. It was even money Stacy *had* run at least one light on the way over.

"Power to the people," said Stacy. "We will fight to the death for our right to bear sex toys." She lifted the harness out and cinched it under her chin, so she was wearing the dildo pointing straight up on her head like a party hat.

Alison proceeded to remove gauzy scarves, restraints, whips and candles from the basket, allowing herself to be side-tracked by nothing but what appeared to be a huge bag of brightly ribboned party favors.

"What *are* these?" she asked. Definitely not from Hallmark.

"Gloves and lube," said Stacy, grabbing a handful of the brightly wrapped packages and tossing them out over the bar as if she were the queen of the Mardi Gras. "There must be more festivity at these events," she said, blowing on a noisemaker that unrolled like a hose and tickled Alison's nose. She grabbed her head again. "Oh, God," she moaned, "that was a mistake. Do you have any Advil?"

Alison, who had a bottle of painkillers in the car but rather thought Stacy deserved a headache for getting in Michelle's face, ignored her.

"Margie says to make sure you pick up those streamers." Oh, Carla was back at work today. She slapped their drinks down on the table in front of them in a surly way which did not invite conversation. They did not need Liz to tell them something was wrong—Carla generally spent most of her work time chatting up customers. "We were picking up rhinestones for a week and a half in here after you threw those condoms out on New Year's Eve."

"Rhinestones?" asked Alison, who had spent New Year's in bed with a sore throat and *Stone Butch Blues*.

"One can do anything with a glue gun," said Stacy. She nodded her head gravely, and Mr. Winkie mimicked the movement, bobbing several times after she stopped. A lavender streamer had caught around its base and curled down into Stacy's hair.

"Margie says she liked your New Year's Eve hat better," said Carla, still sullen, but unable to break the chatting habit completely.

"And what was that?" asked Alison.

"Don't ask," said Liz, as she slipped into the seat at the head of the table. "You don't want to know. But I'll give you a hint, you've probably had it used on you." She turned to Stacy. "Let me guess—Lorena Bobbitt?"

Carla turned pointedly on her heel and stalked away. Her hair, which had been growing out for a year after a horrible experience involving a stalker and fifty-six stitches, bristled stiffly with each step like the feathers on a plumed helmet.

"I take it you did the breaking up thing?" Alison asked.

"Oh, yes."

"And you are currently a shithead."

"I am not just a shithead, I am a manipulative, using, chicken-hawking GUPPY who doesn't care about anything but getting fucked and making money." Liz circled the rim of her coffee cup with her index finger and tried for a wry little expression, but Alison could see how Carla's anger had hurt her. "But she's going to have her therapy bills sent to my office. I guess my money's not completely tainted."

"Boy, that's really cold," said Alison.

"Oh, blow her off, Liz," said Stacy, waving both her hand and Mr. Winkie with a toss of her head. "I don't know where people get off—you're a damn good woman and you treated her as fairly as you could treat anybody. She's just striking out. It's like that Woody Allen—Mia Farrow thing."

Liz and Alison exchanged a glance that wordlessly agreed not to follow up *that* tangent.

"I hear you made a scene over at Michelle Martin's last night," said Liz brightly. "You know, if that thing was a dolphin, you could dress up like a ship, and it could be the figure head."

"I don't fuck with fish," said Stacy shortly. "Or cats. Or goddess figures. What was it, written up in the paper this morning?"

"Oh, no, I'm still in the loop. Speaking of still being in the loop, guess what I have here?" she asked. She turned to Alison coyly, flashing an envelope.

"An invitation to Madonna's birthday party. And you want to bring me as your date because you're afraid Stacy will get drunk and puke on k.d. lang after confronting Sandra Bernhardt about waffling on her character's lesbianism."

"Close," sang Liz, waving the paper up and down.

"Which part is close?"

"Well, I do think Stacy is likely to misbehave no matter where you take her. And I would love to have you for a date any old time. Is it true you can take that party hat up the ass?"

"Without lube," replied Alison not missing a beat, though the same statement would have sent her blushing from the room six months before. "Is it formal dress?"

"Oh, you know Madonna," said Liz. "Dress is optional." She handed the envelope to Alison.

"Why do I have a letter telling Brooks, Brooks and Brooks law firm that you'd be a great secretary?" asked Alison, as she looked down the typed page.

"Oh, not much of a detective, are we? What you have there, if you will look at the heading, is Sary Riverwymon's last known work address." Liz sat back, so pleased with herself you could almost hear a little round of applause.

"Where'd you get this? I thought you torched everything from that era."

"I did. You will not find one single copy of *Sinister Wisdom* on my shelves, nor a Frye boot in my closet. But Brooks, Brooks and Brooks has never torched anything in their illustrious career, and since they remember me fondly from my secretary and paralegal days, they were happy to send me copies of all my reference letters."

"Why in the world would Sary write a reference for you? You hadn't really," Alison glanced back at the letter, "worked in her business in a 'secretarial capacity', had you?"

"Oh, shit, no. I hadn't worked anywhere but Burger King and an occasional fill-in at the Velvet Hammer. We all did this kind of shit for each other all the time. If I recall correctly, I used Sary because she had a real job where she could use real letterhead stationary and was somebody who actually answered the phone with the company name instead of just saying, 'Dyke City'."

"You all were so cute," said Stacy. "I wish I had a video of the seventies."

"Well," said Alison who still occasionally put that particular salutation on the phone when the mood struck, "I wish I had a video of *you* last night."

"Did she behave *really* badly?" asked Liz with great relish.

"*Really* badly," Alison assured her.

"Oh, god," moaned Stacy. "I don't owe you an apology, do I?"

"You owe Michelle an apology. You owe me a forfeit."

"Oh, I'd rather be beaten than do either." Stacy tried to pull herself into a position that would show she wasn't the kind of girl who could be pushed around, but succeeded only in putting her elbow into Alison's cup of coffee.

"Well, don't count on that happening until you go through the social motions," said Alison, sliding into the next seat and leaving her to deal with the mess alone. "You can figure out what you need to do with regards to Dana by yourself."

"Dana?" Stacy groaned and put her head right down on the table in the coffee. Mr. Winkie hit with a plop that jarred their glasses. "That was the woman with the killer tequila, right?"

"I wondered how you got so loaded so quick on cheap wine."

"Did she behave badly, too?" Stacy brightened, obviously hoping bad behavior on the part of Dana would make her look better.

"She behaved impeccably." Alison enjoyed shooting that hope to shit. "All she did was cry. We expected that."

"Who was she, anyway?" Stacy asked, her head still on the table. "I'd like to get together with *her* again. What a party gal."

"She was the dead woman's ex."

"Oh, dear," said Stacy. "I did catch that—I'd just forgotten. Not that it necessarily narrows it down. I mean, Liz has so many ex lovers you can practically point at random into a crowd at any concert and hit one. Hey, that'd be a great idea for a *Where's Waldo?* book. Waldo in the land of Liz's exs." She put her head down on the table.

"Waldo at MSIL," said Alison absently. "Cute, but you still owe me a forfeit before you are going to be back in my good graces. I want you to come and help me and Dana pack dead girl's clothes. After you apologize to Michelle."

Stacy groaned again. Carla arrived with food and began slamming it down on the table. Apparently they were the enemy just by virtue of sitting at Liz's table. She put Stacy's salad plate beside her ear with such a crash that Stacy screamed and sat bolt upright.

"Don't you ever do that again!" she said between clenched teeth.

"Don't try to top me!" Carla flashed back. "I'm not doing any of that bullshit any more—my therapist says the s/m community took advantage of me when I was vulnerable."

"Oh, get a grip," said Stacy crossly, looking at the salad with some trepidation. "Weren't you the one who was fucking Alison in the basement before the rest of us even met you? Have you told your therapist that part of the story?" She looked to Alison for support but Alison who had been trying to erase the Carla vignette from her life, was giving full attention to her croutons. "And if you hit me in the head with a salad plate again, I won't have to top you—I'll ask your boss to do it and let me watch."

Carla stalked off, calling over her shoulder, "And I'm going to go public with it!"

"Be sure and call *USA Today*," Stacy sang back as she pushed the salad, untouched, to the side.

Alison who felt sorry for Carla even though she was behaving like a pill, resolved to talk to her alone later.

"I think you just turned into chickenhawking GUPPYs, too," said Liz. "Sorry." She picked dejectedly at her sandwich.

"If I was going to pay to send my ex to therapy," said Stacy, finally mopping up the coffee. "I'd make sure the therapist knew she wasn't allowed to bad-mouth me."

"It's not called therapy then, honey," said Alison, patting her on the head with a touch that looked caressing but actually jarred her head like a beach ball. "If you don't get to talk about your ex, it's just an infomercial." Then turning to Liz asked, "Why do you think a twenty year old address is going to do me any good?"

"For Christsake, Alison, at least *pretend* to be a detective! It ruins all my uniform fantasies when you act stupid. If they do have records on her, they're going to have her social security number, right? Isn't that going to be helpful?"

"And her real name," inserted Stacy. "I'll bet she wasn't getting checks under Riverwomyn."

"Do you think this place might still be around?"

"I *know* they're still around. I looked them up in the phone book before I came over."

"Hmm." Alison looked at the letter, and then back at Liz. She wanted to ask why Liz was giving her information that would ultimately help Michelle. Probably it was just a case of Liz going for the gratification of showing how smart she was over the gratification of knowing Michelle was floundering.

"Now, are we just going to dick around and fight with the hired help, or are we going to put together a fantasy?" Liz asked abruptly as if she had been reading Alison's mind and wanted to changed the subject.

"Actually," said Stacy, rising and holding one finger daintily in the air, "I would like to vomit first. Excuse me a minute."

Liz gazed thoughtfully after her. "You know," she said, "if she could move that fast on the field, we'd take her out of the cage and put her on the forward line. Doesn't she just behave horribly when she's drunk? We've been thrown out of every gay bar and restaurant in town, and I'm not sure if any hotel in Seattle will even take her credit card if we go to Powersurge again."

"Impressive," said Alison, resolving to jar Stacy's head again when she returned. "Do you think Sary was in touch with the rest of her family when she wrote this?"

"Oh, let me think." Liz made a little frame with her fingers and leaned her face into it. "God, it was so long ago. And, if I'm not mistaken, it was the family who had Sary incarcerated the first time."

"The first time?" Alison interrupted.

"Oh, yeah, didn't I tell you? Sary was one of our break-outs—she was like the dog who followed you home and stayed. I think that was what the lesbian thing was all about—I think she kind of imprinted on us. We were certainly the first women she saw leading independent lives. That must have been a pretty heady feeling for someone her age."

"Which was?"

"Oh, God, in her late teens at the most. But after she was locked up the second time...."

"Which was the time you called the cops?"

"Yeah. Security had gotten a lot tighter by then. I don't think they were able to get her out. Or maybe they did. I don't remember. But I believe that somehow or another, she reconnected with her parents after she was purged."

"I thought it was you who was purged!"

Liz gave her a look. "Get real, Alison. Dozens of women were purged."

"Why Sary?"

"Because she was a straight girl, Alison. You know, she was one of those political lesbians—she sang the song, but she never danced the dance. And then she became involved with one of the lefty men from RIP—let me tell you, the shit hit the fan then! This time I was on the outside, looking in. It was ugly. I think that was why Sary and I stayed in contact for a while after she was back with mommy and daddy and even after she was doing the straight scene. We'd both been through it. She never blamed me for calling the cops, like the other women did. I know I used her for references a couple of times before we drifted completely apart."

"Is that why she and Tamsin hadn't seen each other in so long?" Alison asked. "Did Tamsin join the purge?"

"Oooh," Liz pursed up her lips to think. "I don't think so," she answered slowly. "You have to remember, I was Sary's friend, not Tam's. I never hung out much with the *BMR* crowd—Michelle was way too much of a pain in the ass even then. But I don't think so. I think that came after we lost contact—if I remember right, Tam stood by her when she went straight."

"Back! Good as new!" Indeed, Stacy had lost the grey color. She had also done a little primping and, mercifully, removed Mr. Winkie who, Alison privately resolved, was going through the dishwasher twice before even shaking her hand. "God, vomiting is really renewing. I must do it more often. Now, about this scene."

Johnson Office Supplies, read Alison again on the letterhead, as the two plunged into a discussion of lighting and music and props. Definitely worth looking up.

≈ 10 ≈

"**W**hy am I here?" bellyached Michelle. "Why can't you do this yourself?"

"The question," said Alison as she drove while she checked the envelope upon which she had written the address, "is why am *I* here? This is your job, remember? You are the honored executrix of the will. I've already done my part by just getting the address."

"What did you call me?"

"The executrix. That's what a female executor is called."

Michelle narrowed her eyes suspiciously, as if she suspected Alison was using a dirty word, then said, "*You're* here because you are under the impression you are able to channel Kate Delafield. You're probably going to try to get the woman to answer personal questions while she's crying." In a move that was obviously just a distraction technique, she picked up the paperback novel lying on the seat between them. "What *is* this crap? I didn't know you were going for trashy romances these days." She gave Alison a leery look, the kind of look you might give a friendly old dog who *just maybe* was starting to foam around the mouth.

"That's not just a trashy romance," said Alison absently, as she scanned the houses for numbers. "That's a Tamsin McArthur trashy romance. It's dreadful, incidentally. Unwed mothers and children being left on door steps."

Michelle flipped the book over. "How do you know Tam wrote

this? Oh, I see—same initials again. Kim Conrad."

"Also," said Alison, "I've read a lot of her stuff now. I've read her mysteries, and I've read her porn. I'm getting to the point I can pick out her style. They don't let her do a whole lot with it in this book, but it's Tam."

Michelle flipped the book open. "It's old," she said. "This must have been one of the first things she wrote. It was put out over fifteen years ago."

"She must have figured out that porn paid more and was easier to write," said Alison. "It was the only romance in the box. Ah, here it is!"

Getting the address had been amazingly easy. The head cashier at Johnson Office Supplies, a man in his forties, had only been there five years, but he knew that the woman who ran the bookkeeping department had been there forever, and after a few questions called her up front on the PA.

"Oh, yes," the woman had told them, pleased to be chatted up. Their records didn't go back that far, but she remembered the two years Sary had been a secretary. "Sarah Jean got married right before she left. To a nice man. His name was…" she rubbed her hand back over her grey hair, trying to remember. "Well, his first name was Abel. I remember that, because Sarah Jean and I talked about how uncommon that name was now, and how no one with any sense would name their child Cain.. Although I have known women named Delila and Jezebel, and I always thought that must be a hard way to start life." She cocked her head questioningly, inviting comments.

"What was Abel's last name?" Alison had asked patiently.

"Oh, it was something very common. I know! It was *Washington*. That was another little joke we had—he was called Abe, of course, and we laughed about him being Abe Washington instead of Abe Lincoln." She sighed. "I always thought it was good that Sarah Jean got married to a nice man when she did, because her parents both died soon after. She would have been left all alone." She flashed another quick smile, tempered with respect for the dead, and urged a free notepad and pencil on Alison when she stood to leave.

The bookkeeper was their first bit of luck, and the second was that

Abel turned out to be neither a traveling nor divorcing nor paranoid kind of guy. 'Washington, Sarah and Abel', was right there in the white pages. They could have called, but Alison argued that a call seemed too cold, and besides, they had the first box culled from Tam's apartment with them.

Sary had not stayed in Capital Hill. The address Alison had scribbled on the bookkeeper's note pad was over in the Platt Park area. The house was small and brick, nothing special, but Alison knew just its location would put it in a price range not only far beyond her reach, but also that of most of her friends. Liz, maybe, could afford a house in Platt Park.

The front yard looked as if it had contained a beautiful flower display the year before. But no one had pulled out the annuals in the fall, and no one had pinched back this year's blossoms as they died. The grass had gone brown, the way it does in Denver if you don't water every third day. There was a swing on one end of the porch, but you would have had to push through a fleet of riding toys to reach it. Alison had to shove a Big Wheel and a scooter to one side to get to the door.

Only the screen was closed, and from far back in the house she could hear the theme song from *High Chaparral*, a show upon which she had been weaned. She hadn't known Big John was on in the afternoon again—having a job fucked up your TV schedule completely.

She pushed the bell. Chimes sounded four notes that hit the floor like a tree falling alone in the forest. She was just about to push the button again when a small child appeared. The child, a boy with big dark eyes and coffee brown skin stared through the screen at Alison without speaking.

Alison and Michelle exchanged a look. "Is your mommy home?" Alison asked, hoping the answer was yes. She could not respect someone who left a child of this age unattended, and lack of respect was always a bad way to start an interview.

The child did not answer, but simply turned and walked away. A moment later they heard the sound on the TV go up a notch. Damn it all! Alison hitched the box up on her hip and rang the bell again.

"Can I help you?"

There are times when you hear a voice, and you know without even looking that the speaker is ill. The voice of Sary Washington was this kind of voice—soft and hesitant, as if the woman had already begun to slip into the next world, and had no energy to project back into the one she was leaving. Her appearance only served to strengthen this impression. She moved quietly down the hall with the help of a wooden cane. She was wearing a long gauze skirt and a combination of flowing tops and sashes that had probably been expensive once, but now only served to amplify her thinness. Alison had gone to see *A Muppet Christmas Carol* twice the year before, and she was reminded of the ghost of Christmas Past, who had floated in the air, a translucent, soft-spoken head surrounded by billowing gauze and hair.

"Can I help you?" the woman asked, and those four words seemed to take such an effort that, had she been alone, Alison would have excused herself and walked away. What was the point?

But, before she could stammer an excuse, Michelle said, "Sary McArthur? We came to talk to you about your sister, Tam." The young boy had rematerialized and fastened himself to her skirt like a barnacle. He was joined by a second child, perhaps a little older. His skin and eyes were the same color as the first boy's, but his features had a slight Eurasian cast. He was a little too old to hide behind his mother's skirts, but he dogged her like a shadow. The two children peered at Alison as if they knew she could have nothing but bad news, but Sary's voice lit up with something that might have been delight.

"Tam? Are you from the agency? Have you talked to her? Do you know where she is?"

They looked at one another, each trying to say, "You tell her." In the end it was Michelle, simply because she was not the kind of woman who could out wait anyone.

"No," she said. "She's dead. We came to tell you that she died in an accident."

"I brought," said Alison, and stopped, not knowing how to tell a woman this ill she was carrying crystals and wall hangings and cat figures belonging to her dead sister. Would grief be worse if you were on the edge of the void yourself, or would you be able to accept the death of a loved one better because of your own intimacy? She didn't know, and she didn't want to know.

"Tam's things?" Sary finished for her. "But I haven't talked to Tam in ten years. How could she be dead if we never made up?" She fluttered her free hand nervously and turned her head from side to side in a jerky motion, as if unable to decide what to do, whether to sit or stand or simply fall to the floor.

"Would you like us to come in?" asked Alison, ignoring the look being sent by Michelle. Michelle was not a big one for comforting—she wanted to drop the bomb and the box and run—let the lawyer deal with the rest of it.

"Yes. Please." Sary strained with the effort of pushing open the screen door. The children moved with her, the same way Alison's father had braked on the passenger side of the car when she was learning to drive.

"This is my son Carl," Sary said to Alison, in a dazed way, drawing the littlest boy forward. "This is my son Donny." She did not ask Alison and Michelle's names. Was that merely because of shock, or was it because the boys did not even know of the aunt who had died without ever seeing them? "Why don't you guys go watch some more TV?" Sary suggested. Obediently, they left the room without a word. "It's too much for them," Sary said sadly. "Tam was the oldest in my family—our mother always used her as a surrogate—like we weren't her kids at all. I always vowed I'd never make my kids act like adults. But..." She shrugged, indicating in that childish vow there had been no allowance for tragedy.

She looked down the hall to make sure both children had vanished, and then beckoned Alison and Michelle into another room. It was one of those dining rooms into which children are not allowed except for Thanksgiving dinner. There was a soft Persian rug on the floor, and a hardwood table with hand-turned legs. At one time perhaps Sary and her husband had entertained dinner guests here. But with mom in bed the rules had relaxed, and there was a small fleet of tiny, tiny matchbox cars parked around the legs of the table and on and under sheets of the *Denver Post,* which had been turned into hills and caves.

"How can Tam be dead?" Sary asked again, as she lowered herself into a chair while Alison and Michelle seated themselves without invitation. "Are you sure it's Tam who's dead?" She looked at them hopefully. "She moved, didn't she? Years ago. You didn't see her yourselves did you? Maybe it was someone else. The picture I gave you wasn't very good."

"It's Tam," said Michelle, in a voice unexpectedly gentle. "She was in Denver—she moved back just a couple of months ago. I knew her personally."

"Are you sure...?" Sary pleaded again.

Alison flipped over a photograph she had taken off Tam's refrigerator. "Is this your sister?" she asked.

"Oh," said Sary, and then nothing more. She reached out her hand as if to pick up the photo, and then drew it back.

"She left most of her estate to you and your daughter," said Michelle, indicating the box Alison had set on the floor. "There are more."

"I don't want them." Sary cut her off swiftly. "All I want is to talk to Tam. I was done being angry years ago! But, by that time she had moved, and I didn't know how to find her. I thought she would come looking for me, eventually! I didn't know she would die, first."

"She didn't either," said Michelle. "It was an accident. A fluke. She wasn't sick...." She trailed away, but the end of her sentence hung in the air between them just as if it had been shouted aloud. She wasn't sick, like you. She didn't think she was going to die, like you are.

"I have cancer," Sary said, and it was somehow defiant, as if she were daring them to murmur condolences. After a moment, when neither responded, she let out a huge breath of air that made her collapse into an even smaller heap. Without seeming to notice, she pulled on the box. Her hands were light and thin, almost translucent, and Alison found herself straining as the children had done, willing Sary's victory against the cardboard. The lid came loose, and Alison collapsed back into her chair with a sigh of relief.

"Oh!" Sary gave a little cry, having picked up the little tiger that had flown in Tam's studio. "The flying Albert. Tam had a wonderful black cat—Albert—when I gave her this," she explained, "and she always said the tiger was his fantasy—that he imagined this was what he really looked like."

"There were two kittens in her apartment."

"No, neither of them was Albert. He died years ago. Actually, Tam had him put to sleep before it got too bad. I went with her to the vet's—they didn't want us to stay, but Tam was really firm—she said she'd told him she was going to stay with him, and by god, she was. It wasn't bad, you know. He obviously didn't suffer—she just held him in her arms, and the last thing he heard was her telling him that she loved him." She was silent for a moment, turning the flying tiger over and over in her hands. "Afterwards, there was no one who had a bad word to say about that cat. No one was angry or said, 'If only he...' That's not a bad way to die, you know?"

She paused. Who was she really talking about—the cat, her sister, or herself?

After a moment, Sary reached into the box again, coming out with a cat mug that Alison had taken down from the shelf over the sink. "Cats," she said. "Tam still loved cats, I guess. The last time we spoke, she was doing cat rescue—I'll bet five or six times a year she'd live trap some old stray, and have him doctored and neutered and fatten him up and find a home for him. All of her cats were strays. She thought strays made better pets—that they never forgot they'd been out on the street—they were always grateful for a home." She held up a little tin in the shape of a Siamese cat, and then put it down as if it were too much to look at. She put a hand up to her eye as if to wipe a tear, though Alison had seen no tears fall. "You can't understand," she said, and then stopped. "You think it will get better," she said finally. "You think eventually you're going to come to a place where there's going to be this moment of enlightenment, where you'll realize something like, well, yes, it's obvious life's like a wheel, and I'll just be passing through a door, or you'll accept that there's nothing after you die, it will just be over and whatever you did here on earth will be all that remains. But you know what? It doesn't happen like that. There's no revelation. There's no moment of truth. You just get more and more tired. That's all. Until you think that it doesn't matter what's going to happen, if only you could just not be so tired. My sister is dead," she made a motion above the box, "and I can't even mourn. I can remember the way I loved her and the things we did together, and it's as if it's just one more thing—no more or less annoying than making sure the kids all get to school, than making sure dinner's defrosted tonight. Can you understand that?" she asked, and then answered herself, "No, of course not. How could you? I can't even cry. I feel like my whole life has been blocked out, has been narrowed down to this one narrow little band of experience and feeling, and the only thing that exists in it is tiredness." She trailed her hand over the open box and came up, randomly, as if it had stuck to her hand like fly paper, the scrap book with the clippings from *Big Mama Rag*. She looked tiredly at the photo on the first page.

"Oh, Virago," she said, with something like a spark of interest. Alison was reminded of her grandfather, who had taken almost a year to arrive at the point where her father asked he be unplugged. In those last months, when all he had the energy to do on good days was sit up in the spare bedroom and play cribbage, he had often exhibited this feeling Sary described—that nothing mattered, or all things mattered only equally indifferently. Yet, even at the height of this indifference, there had still been times when he had been sparked by an image from the past. Memories, with emotions already lived out and set in stone, he could retell and relate. It seemed the same might be true for Sary, because the voice in which she reacted to the picture held a curious note, a combination of horror and something else Alison could not pinpoint.

"Our friend Liz," Alison pointed to the picture, "said that you were in Virago together."

"Yeah, Liz," said Sary. "She was a good friend. I was always sorry we lost touch. Virago. They were the ones who got me out of the hospital, you know."

Alison raised an eyebrow, and shot Michelle who was obviously getting antsy, a 'shut up' look.

"D.G., the loony bin," Sary clarified. "I had tried to commit suicide, so my parents had me locked up. Virago was big in the anti-psychiatric movement. They were responsible for springing a lot of young women at the time. They let out some crazies, I'm sure, but they saved a lot of girls. Every time I was ever locked up, there were always a couple of kids in there whose only claim to fame was coming out to their parents and or maybe telling the truth about what Daddy or Uncle Bill was up to with them at night." She had gone into a much more energized mode, as if this were a story she had told often, and all she had to do was flip the switch.

"How'd they get them out?" asked Alison.

Sary shrugged. "A bunch of ways. The wards weren't exactly secure—at first Virago people would just come in as friends or sisters, check the patients out for a walk around the hospital and never come back. The escape I was involved with was a little more complicated. I was only involved incidentally—the target was another woman on the ward. They had set her up with matches and tinder—if you could make a fire in one of the wastebaskets and hold it up to a smoke alarm without getting caught, you could set the alarms off and all the locked doors would open automatically. Anybody with any grip on reality at all knew to run when the alarm sounded. But the hospital staff would pick up most of the patients in the lobby or the park across the street— nobody had any money or any place to go—hell, most of us were dressed in hospital pajamas. The difference was that the Virago girls were waiting down the hall for this woman they were springing—with a coat, with a car outside. And I ran up behind them saying, 'Take me, take me, I'm a dyke too.'" She stopped for a moment, thinking. "You know," she said, "a lot of people might not have taken me along because they would have been afraid that I would have queered the escape—would have yelled or drawn attention. The minute those women—they probably weren't more than nineteen or twenty themselves—heard that, one of them pulled her own coat off. Huge snowstorm, pulled her own coat off to cover up my pajamas. As soon as I said I was a lesbian. They would no more have left me in that hall than they would have left one of their own—hell, I *became* one of their own at that point. They hustled us both out to this old junker—I think probably the three of them shared it—none of them were making over minimum wage, if that. We were both doing the thorazine shuffle—they'd brought shoes for her, but not for me, I'm barefoot in the snow, shuffling along, they're trying to get us past the hospital staff, firemen are coming in." She settled back her chair, eyes bright, and again Alison was reminded of her grandfather. Sary's fatigue seemed to have vanished. The difference was—well, Alison supposed the difference was that the past was done, it required no participation. It was like pulling out some old TV show you had on tape and had seen a hundred times before. You only had to recall—you didn't have to care, or decide.

"But you weren't a lesbian, were you?" Alison asked curiously. Sary stiffened, and Alison rushed in to reassure, to let her know this wasn't a confrontation, hoping Michelle wouldn't decide oh yes it was, too. It was true Alison did not understand women who had once called themselves lesbians, had lived with and dated other women and now were involved with men. This seemed to make as much sense to her as a fish one day deciding it was going to be a bird. The reverse—lesbians who had once dated or been married to men—was easy to understand. Without exception, women who had once been wives said they were pressured, they hadn't known there was another choice, they were denying their feeling. She also did not, however, understand the amount of time Denver dykes devoted to watching the Broncos, or why anyone would drink caffeine-free Pepsi or own a big dog, and that did not necessarily mean all these things should be condemned. She was interested in information, not motive.

"I mean," she said, "how did you know to say that? How did you know that was the magic word?"

Sary looked at her, still holding the flying tiger in one hand. "I wasn't stupid," she said. "People tend to think you are when you're taking thorazine—you know, 'cause you can't react right—you're ten minutes slow on everything. People will sit on the psychiatric ward—staff, visitors—and spill their guts about the most intimate things in front of you—like you can't hear a thing. I watched these women set this up—they were careful about the staff, but they weren't careful about me. And my sister was a lesbian. I knew about the sisterhood."

"So where'd you go?" Alison asked, not because it had anything to do with Tam's death, but because she was curious.

"They took us home to their own places. Little rathole places—whatever they could afford busting tires at Sears. One of them let me stay in her spare room—it was just an enclosed porch without insulation. Freezing cold, the middle of winter, but I thought I had died and gone to heaven. I'd been locked up for a while—before that I'd been with my folks, before that on the street. Drugs," she said, throwing a look down at her arm as though it might show tracks from fifteen years before. "There was a futon thrown on the floor and a light on an orange crate next to it—I could get up when I wanted to, go to bed when I wanted to, stay in bed and read all day if I wanted to. I could shower when I wanted to and help myself to food from the refrigerator. I was only sixteen years old, but they treated me like I was a grown person—my thoughts mattered just as much as anybody else's, my idea's were as good as anybody else's. They were very much into that at the time—they didn't want anyone discredited because of age or race or class background. Of course, now that I look back, I can see some of them were only a few years older than me, but it seemed like a huge gap then, and it seemed wonderfully tolerant of them to take me seriously."

"So you became a lesbian?"

"Yes." Sary laughed. "But I didn't inhale. I was a political lesbian. If you want to get technical, I still am. I *did* believe women had been screwed by men, and the only way to stop the pattern was to stop working in tandem with them. I *did* believe there was no way I could become an equal with someone for whom I was expected to cook and clean and care for—I saw those women like the slaves who stayed behind to take care of Scarlet and her sisters after the war. And I knew I wasn't up to playing games—to being with a sensitive New Age guy who talked a good game but 'accidentally' forgot to clean the bathroom or pick up the kids. Besides, I had been screwed over by guys—none of them ever broke me out of the hospital or took me in. There was a whole community there waiting to embrace me, waiting to validate my experiences. I would have been a fool to jump any other way." She sighed and then slumped. Her hand relaxed and the tiger fell down to the floor. Alison could see the tape had run out, and Sary had found herself back in the present—where people and situations required interaction, and it was just too damn hard.

"Well," said Michelle, either bored by old history or, more likely, just uncomfortable with the dying woman. "I guess I should give you the name of her lawyer."

"Oh!" Sary roused herself. "Do I owe you any money?" They both looked at her blankly. "For finding her," she explained. "It's not your fault…I should have tried to contact her long ago. It took this," she made a bitter gesture that encompassed her whole body, "to push me. Before then, I always thought there would be enough time."

"Mmm," said Alison tentatively, "I don't think we know what you're talking about. We weren't looking for Tam, we've been looking for *you.* "

Now it was Sary's turn to look blank. "You're not from the agency?" she asked. "The detective agency? The people I hired to try and find Tam? The people from the Peoplefinders Agency?"

They shook their heads. "I'm the executor of Tam's will," said Michelle. "We were trying to find you because of that. We have all this stuff that belonged to Tam—there's some money, too, royalties."

"Royalties?"

"She wrote books," said Alison, for the first time really realizing there actually had been a fifteen year gap between these women, and they knew nothing at all about each other. "She was very popular— she took the Lambda Award for mysteries several times." She dug through the box, and took out a copy of *The Neon Cat Trap.* "Tam wrote this," she said, holding it out. "I have another of her books in the car, a romance. I can get it…."

Sary cut her off with a short, bitter laugh that sounded close to tears. "*Love's Lost Child*, I suppose? I don't want any of it. I don't want any of her things." With her eyes closed, she thrust the flying tiger out in front of her. "It would be too hard. She was here. She was right here, where I could have called her or gone to see her! If I hadn't been so...if I hadn't told her I never wanted to see her again!"

"Why weren't you speaking?" asked Alison, but before Sary could answer, they heard the screen door open and shut, and a man's voice called her name.

"Sarah Jean?" he called, and then a pale, redheaded man.stepped into the room. He looked at Sary, and the box, and Alison and Michelle, and then back at Sary's face. She had begun, quietly, to cry the moment she had heard his voice, as if it were not something she could do until he was in the house.

"Please," he said, in a voice that was tired and angry at the same time. "Please, can't you people ever leave her alone? Even now? Please!" Alison looked at Michelle. What people were they? she asked silently, and Michelle shrugged. Oh. Dykes? Was that it? Had other dykes come by before to hassle Sary?

"No," choked out Sary. She wiped her nose on her sleeve as naturally as a little child. "That's not why they're here, Abe. They came to tell me that my sister had died. Tam is dead."

"Oh, honey!" He took three steps across the room and gathered her to him.

Now we escape, Michelle shot in a look, and she popped to her feet to put the idea into motion. She had reached the door, Alison close behind her, before Sary extracted herself.

"Just throw it away," she said. "Throw it away, give it away. I don't care! I don't want—it would be like the pieces of one of those awful puzzles that can be put together a hundred ways. I'd never know which way was right!"

"But what about your daughter?" asked Michelle.

"Oh god." Sary leaned her head back into her husband's shoulder. "She didn't know, did she?" She buried her head in his shoulder, and began to weep anew.

"Come *on*," said Michelle out of the side of her mouth like a little kid. Michelle did not do other people's emotions, though she had a broad range herself. Alison allowed herself to be pulled.

The two little boys were standing in the front hall. They looked somberly at Alison and Michelle, and then back down towards the dining room. The weeping was audible. Alison's heart went out to them.

"Your mom heard some bad news," she said, squatting down to look the littlest one in the eye. "It made her really sad. You know?" They looked at her for a moment without any acknowledgement at all, and then the older boy gave a tiny nod. Then both heads bobbed up and down.

"Your dad's in there helping her. Maybe it would be better to leave them alone for just a little while."

"I'm hungry," said the littler boy, and because this was a need she could actually meet, this was not like, 'My mother is dying,' Alison said, "Let's go in the kitchen and see if we can find a snack." Michelle had beaten a hasty retreat to the car and was already listening to an Indigo Girls tape and reading *Lesbian Connection*.

The kitchen looked as if the children had been foraging for some time. Everything that could be reached had been pulled out and then left—cracker boxes, cereal boxes, cartons of milk. Alison bit back a reprimand—it was probably hard enough at this house without a stranger chewing you out. In the freezer she found a loaf of seven-grain bread, and with a little help from Carl, the older boy, she located the toaster. It was the kind that took four slices at one time, and she filled all four slots. There was no butter, but there was some crystallized honey in a high cupboard. There were clean plates in the dishwasher, and while the boys were eating the first slice of toast, she quickly unloaded the clean dishes and placed them in the cupboards, consulting the boys when she wasn't sure where something went. She loaded it again with dishes and glasses, and ran a sink of hot water for the pots. Most of them would need to soak a good, long time. The boys were thirsty, and she found a can of juice in the freezer. When she picked up the pitcher—dirty, of course—she saw someone had abandoned a cordless phone on the counter. Probably one of the kids because it was still turned on—there was a weak dial tone—and the low battery light was blinking. She picked it up and turned it off, looking to see where it went.

"On the wall," Carl volunteered. He indicated with a hand, and then looked away quickly, as if he knew more about how the phone had gotten to the counter than he was willing to share.

Alison poured two glasses of juice, handed out the second pieces of toast, and checked to make sure the toaster was unplugged. Michelle would be fuming by now.

"You okay now?" she asked the boys, and they nodded, knowing that she was referring only to their immediate need, and that things would not really be okay in their lives for a long, long while. "I have to go now." They nodded again, solemn little good-byes. One of them raised a hand. She wondered where their older sister was. Was she old enough to be away at college? Were they trying to spare her until the very end?

She picked up the phone, meaning to place it in the recharger on her way out the door. Like everything else in the house, it was very state of the art. There was a little plastic window in the receiver—you were supposed to write the home number on a tiny piece of paper and insert it. Alison's phone had the same window, but she had just slapped her number on with a piece of masking tape, and then only when Stacy complained. Sary's home number—333-4456—had been typed on a computer, and someone had centered it in the window with patience. Alison glanced at it, and then looked again.

"More juice," said the littler boy, and absently she responded, still clutching the phone in one hand. After his glass was full, she put the pitcher down and put her hand into the pocket of her shorts. She pulled out the piece of police stationary—Our Job is to Serve!—upon which she had written the number given to her when she had called US West that morning before her shift and asked about the trace Tam had put on that last call. She held it up to the phone.

The two numbers were identical.

≈ 11 ≈

Though the sun was almost down, it was still hot when Robert dropped Alison off at Tam's house after work. Robert had been in fine form that day, rolling along on a cigarette and sugar high that made every encounter with the public a little drama. Not until late afternoon had he mellowed out enough for an update on the Tam and Sary situation, which he had been following with great interest all week. Robert was a good sounding board.

"You'd better call those homicide dicks and tell them you found this woman," he had said as soon as she had filled him in. He was not using the word 'dick' as slang for police officer. He was a loyal partner, and anyone who tried to railroad Alison was an asshole in his book.

"Why? I mean, what do they care?"

Robert had given her an arched eyebrow that many a drag queen would have died to duplicate. "Because they're looking for her, too. They always look for the next-of-kin in this kind of thing. Send notices out to other stations. Run them through the motor vehicles. And if all they had was the first name…"

"Oh, yeah," Alison had said, trying to look as if she had known this. Robert always had a better pulse on procedure in other departments than she did. But she hadn't called the Homicide Bureau. Fuck them—they had jerked her around, and she saw no reason not to wait on the information a few days. She had a feeling finding the sister of a dyke who had killed herself by being stupid and clumsy was not high on their list anyway.

But, even though she had not called the Homicide Bureau, she had called Michelle around noon to inquire about her apartment. That call had elicited a spat of crabbiness that had contained no real information, except for the fact that painting while the weather was hitting the high nineties was pretty hellish. Alison just hoped Michelle wouldn't take it out on her woodwork.

She ground the Camel Robert had given her beneath her heel before she opened the front door, and pulled her shirt out of her uniform pants as she walked up the inside stairs. Whoever had designed the uniforms had never worn one during a Denver summer. They needed to imitate the British and get a version with shorts, or even short skirts. She'd be willing to wear a short skirt in this weather. Hell, *Robert* would be willing to wear a short skirt in this weather. She could hear the water pipes banging in the walls—Dana must be running water upstairs. The whole system was noisy—she had come down to get the mail once while Dana was filling the tub, and it had sounded as if the ocean was going to break through the walls.

She had just reached the landing when the door marked Two opened suddenly, and a man about the age of Alison's father popped his head out.

"This isn't right!" he said sternly, shaking a finger in Alison's face. "This just isn't right! I come home and find that everything in my refrigerator is spoiled or melted, and all because you're too lazy to change the fuse! I know the landlady told you to flip the switch if any of your lights go out—she tells everyone—she knows I'm gone for days sometimes! And then to lock the fuse box! I had to cut it off! It isn't right!" He popped back into his apartment before Alison could either defend or explain. Well, that explained the candles and the extension cord—apparently Tam's house was wired as haphazardly as Alison's.

Alison could hear music coming from the apartment, and for a moment she wished, selfishly, Dana had somewhere else to go. She didn't want music, and she didn't want conversation. She wanted to sit naked in the dark and watch mindless sitcoms. She wanted to think about the visit to Sary's house, and the random patterns of fate that had allowed Tam to die even as her sister was searching for her. If there was a God, she did not appreciate His humor. She wanted, too, to think about what the phone number meant. Had Sary called Tam? If so, that meant she had lied about not knowing she was in town, and if that was true, failing to call Jones and Jorgeson became a little bit more than a jerk back.

"Hey, baby!" She had not expected Stacy, as well as Dana, to be in the living room, and to be truthful, she was no more happy to see the former than the latter, though Stacy looked charming in a blue and green sundress, with her hair pulled back in a ponytail. Small strands had escaped and curled up all around her face, just as they did when she was playing soccer. She was wearing big, funky earrings—one brushed Alison's cheek as she bounced over to give her a hug. Alison hugged her carefully, trying not to let her crankiness show. She had lived alone too long—as charming as Stacy looked, all she wanted was a cold drink and something to eat, and Stacy was worthless in that department. If it didn't come in carry-out, you were out of luck. Half the time, if she bought a six pack of soda at 7-11, she didn't even bother to put it in the fridge.

"I've been helping Dana," said Stacy.

At the same moment Dana, who had disappeared into the kitchen, reappeared and said, "Here." She handed Alison a huge Marguerita in what appeared to be a soup bowl with the tail of a whale. In her other hand, on a matching plate, she was carrying a pile of nachos. The cheese was still steaming.

"You are a goddess," Alison told her after the first sip and mouthful, and gave her such a grateful look Stacy felt it necessary to slap her on the butt with a rolled up magazine.

"Be careful what you wish for," Stacy warned as Dana once more went into the kitchen.

"You went to Powersurge," Alison complained.

"Fine. You can go to Seattle and spend a weekend having women in Birkenstocks feed you homemade meals. Just don't look at other women like that while I'm around."

Just two sips of the drink had mellowed Alison enough so she was able to hug Stacy again, this time as though she wanted to.

"I've been helping Dana pack," said Stacy again, half a bowl of guacamole later. From the glasses and plates and ashtrays it looked more like she and Dana had been drinking and getting high all afternoon. But there were some new boxes, the biggest reading, 'Don't open in front of your Mother'.

"Well, that's the forfeit, then," said Alison. Her Marguerita bowl had been magically refilled. "I don't suppose you apologized to Michelle?"

"Kind of."

"Which means?"

"Well, I said, 'Alison says I owe you an apology.'"

Figuring this was not only as good as it was going to get, but also about what Michelle could have been forced to say had the tables been switched, Alison didn't push. She sat contentedly on the couch, watching Dana pack up books. For all that she was obviously trying to put on her best face, Dana looked wretched. There were huge circles under her eyes, and she had probably been crying within the hour. Alison remembered two years before when her grandfather had died, and she and her father and brother had spent the week packing his house. It had been horrible, but soothing all the same. She hoped that Dana was getting some kind of closure from the task.

"Michelle said the sister didn't want anything?" asked Stacy, who was going through the videos. "Really? Cause I want this copy of *Arobasex Girls*."

"Well, there's a surprise," said Alison. "And your tastes are usually so much more refined."

"Well, I'm taking *Desert Hearts* to balance it out. If that's okay."

Alison threw up her hands. "That's what she said. But I think we'd better talk to Liz. Maybe Sary needs to sign a release first." She wandered into the bedroom and changed into a pair of gym shorts and a lavender t-shirt Michelle had brought her from the March on Washington. If Sary really didn't want anything, she was going to go put dibs on the old posters and Casse Culver records. She figured she had first choice after Dana. She heard a knock on the door, and when she went back into the other room, a third woman, also in a long skirt, had entered.

"Oh, hi," she said to Alison in a voice that said she expected to be recognized. Alison spread her hands helplessly. "Oh, maybe you don't know me without the brownies. Marta? From the wake?"

"Oh! Hi! I have a drink here somewhere—would you like me to spill it on you?" Something had changed while she had been out of the room—suddenly everyone seemed tense.

"That's okay," said Marta. She waved away Dana's offer of a drink. "I actually came by to pick up something I had loaned Tam. I feel a little bad about it—I mean, if I could I'd just let it go, but I don't have the money to get another blender."

"Oh, dear," said Dana, "We've been using it to make drinks. Let me—"

"Maybe Alison could get it for me," said Marta, without looking at her. Okay. Alison wasn't sure what the problem was, but she led Marta into the kitchen.

"Just let me rinse…" to Alison's dismay, when she turned, Marta had begun to cry.

"Oh, no," said Alison. "I mean, is there anything…."

"No, no," Marta waved her down. "Remember, I do this all the time? My therapist says it's healthy. Just ignore it—that's what I do."

"Well, uh, is it polite to inquire what's wrong?"

"Oh, just this." She waved her hand around at the half dismantled room. "I hadn't known Tam for that long—I think I told you. But I got such a fucking kick out of her! She was so alive! I mean—she was right there. She had been through so much shit with her family, and with this abusive relationship, but she was still so funny. Everything was funny to her…I mean, look at her books, and look at all this stuff." She motioned towards the wall of notes that had amused Alison so. She still had not removed them, for she still had no idea what to do with them. Marta stood up and wandered over to the wall. "Listen to this," she said. 'Hazel's list of things to talk about included

Unforgivable Things Roy Has Done' What a laugh. I'll bet that would have turned up in her next book."

"Actually," said Alison, "that *was* in her latest book. You know, the one that came out this spring?"

"Oh. *The Neon Cat Trap*? I'm on the waiting list at the library."

"I have a copy, if you'd like to borrow it."

"I don't know if I can deal with it right now. I just fucking hate it that she did this right now. I hate it! I mean, I really thought things were going better."

"Did you know," asked Alison tentatively, "that it was officially ruled an accident? I mean, there wasn't a note or...."

"Well," interrupted Marta, "she did a good job."

"Why...?"

"Look," said Marta, "were you ever in this apartment before she died?" Alison shook her head. "Now, this is a woman who has something up on every square inch of wall. Doesn't it make you wonder why there's nothing up in there over the bed? Big prime space, right?"

"Well, yeah...."

"Well, there used to be a bunch of nudes there. Some friend had done a whole series of Tam a couple of years ago—they were really nice. So have you found those anywhere? No," she answered herself. "And why would she take them down in the first place? Because she didn't want her sister to come in and find them?"

"That's kind of thin evidence," objected Alison

"It doesn't matter, I guess. I mean, I suppose part of the reason she did it was to spare everyone pain. Suicide is really hard to accept, you know? All you can think about is what you could have done, what you should have done. I've heard Tam talk about suicide, about how people should try to consider the mind of the suicide, if she really made a choice that made her happier...," she trailed off, and Alison suspected that again she was afraid of breaching confidentiality.

"You know," Alison said, "she used that in her new book, too. Blaze has a discussion with her therapy group about a woman's right to commit suicide and whether or not it is ever the right and sane decision."

"Let me guess" said Marta, holding up her hand. "Umm, she starts with people who are terminally ill, and gets you to agree that suicide is really sane in some of those cases. She talks about the quality of life and the Hemlock society. She talks about people in concentration camps—would it be insane to kill yourself in those circumstances? So why is it worse to kill yourself when you're in long-term emotional pain that is just as bad and isn't going to get better?"

"Yeah," admitted Alison, "she covered all that."

"What about the emotional manipulation of others in our lives? Did she talk about that? About how, as lesbians we spend our whole adult lives trying to not be overly influenced by other's reactions, to get away from our traditional training as women, but still we have this huge blind spot around suicide? Hundreds of people are stuck in really hateful and miserable existences which cannot be changed, but don't consider suicide an option because it will upset those left behind?"

"I actually don't remember that," Alison admitted.

"Well," said Marta. She picked up the blender, and looked around for the lid. "I guess it doesn't matter. She was just as tied up by convention as the rest of us in the end, wasn't she? I'm sure as hell not going to say anything to anyone." Alison wondered how she had obtained the status of being no one, but she didn't ask. "I mean, she obviously wanted to spare feelings."

"Do you want anything else?" Alison asked, moved by the fresh flow of tears that began as Marta stood looking at the room. Marta was one of the few people who seemed to truly mourn for Tam.

"Oh, no," Marta said. "I couldn't deal with it. I absolutely couldn't. This is so weird. I mean—sure, I knew Tam was telling her side of the story. We all do—that's the whole point of the group. But even with a grain of salt, she made that woman in there," she inclined her head towards the other room, "sound like a monster. I don't even know what to say to her—everything that comes to mind is something like, 'Oh, so you're the one who ripped Tam's heart out, huh?' I never thought I'd see *her* crying."

"Yeah," Alison said. She located the lid of the blender and held it under the faucet. "Does it make you wonder if your ex is crying over you?"

"My ex," said Marta in a voice that was cold enough to freeze stone, "picked up a twenty-three-year-old the same day we broke up. The same day. I think there is very little crying going on in that household."

Oh, overstepped herself there. As it seemed too big a faux pas for backpedaling, Alison went straight into the living room without saying anything else. Dana had obviously made some attempt at pulling herself together—she had wiped her face and blown her nose and was looking out the window.

"I am so sorry," she apologized to Alison. "You really got into the middle of this by accident, didn't you?" Alison made a soothing, never mind sound. It was the only thing she could think to do, as telling the truth would mean agreeing totally, and that seemed ungracious. "This has just been such a kick in the gut. To get all screwed up to see her again—that took weeks—and then to find…this." She lifted her hand and then dropped it again in a gesture of total helplessness. "And what a fucking stupid accident."

"Oh, come on." Only the one sentence, but Alison could tell just by the sound of those three syllables that Marta's trigger had finally been tripped. She had shown something almost like sympathy for Dana in the kitchen, but her voice was now cold and hard.

"What?" Alison winced for the total innocence in Dana's reply. She moved towards Marta as if she could somehow cut her off physically, but the other woman was too fast for her.

"It wasn't an accident," she said. "I mean, you can think that if it makes you feel better, but that's not what happened."

"What are you talking about?" All the color had drained out of Dana's face, and the hand in which she held her cup was slowly going limp, almost as if her finger bones were melting. Alison was torn between the two of them, wanting to comfort the one and shut down the other.

"Marta," she said, with all the warning she could muster. But it was no good. Marta was wound up in a knot of grief and anger herself, and Alison could see she would have to be restrained physically to be halted at all.

"Tam killed herself," she told Dana bitterly. "Can't you see that? It wasn't an accident. She killed herself." Unspoken, but still hanging in the air, were the words "Because of you. She killed herself because of you." Alison looked at Dana. Her face was completely frozen with horror, and she recoiled before each of Marta's words as if under a blow.

"Marta," Alison said desperately, "confidentiality." For a moment she thought she had hit the button which would stop the assault. Marta stopped in midsentence, looking chagrined. Alison put a hand out to Dana, hoping to draw her into the other room while she tried to send Marta packing. But the tall woman regained her composure before she was able to get Dana to her feet.

"No," she said. "It doesn't matter what the official line is—you agree, don't you? You arrived at that yourself—without any help from me. I'm not breaking anything at all."

"Maybe not," hissed Alison, getting right up in her face, "but you sure as shit are trying to hurt her because you feel bad about not being able to stop Tam! You're assuming every fucking ugly thing she said in the heat of anger about Dana betraying her is true!"

"I didn't betray her!" protested Dana. "I left her because she was abusive to me! For Christ's sake—I hung on months after my friends were begging me to go!"

"Wait a minute," broke in Stacy. She was still in front of the VCR and, frankly, she looked about half looped. "You're saying you think Tam killed herself?" She looked at Alison.

Alison spread her hands. She would have liked to protect Dana, but this was something she had indeed suspected from the beginning. She had been suppressing that little voice in her head all along—suicide was always so ugly—but she just couldn't bring herself to lie anymore. "Stacy, come on. She dropped a vibrator into the tub with her. I don't care what Michelle says—nobody uses a vibrator in the tub."

"Tam would!" said Dana, with a fresh new volley of tears. She turned to Alison. "Let me guess what else you found by the bathtub.

A bucket of ice, right?"

"Yeah, maybe," said Alison, thinking of the water in the blue plastic bucket.

"Tam had arthritis in her hands—when it got really bad she'd sit in a hot tub and ice them—alternate the heat and the cold. *And* she'd use a vibrator on her hands as well." She turned defiantly to Marta. "If Tam killed herself, it wasn't because of me. Or, at least, not the way you're saying. If she was going to kill herself because of me, she would have wanted to do one last big mind fuck. And if she'd done that, she would have waited a couple of days. She would have wanted me to be the one to find the body."

Before anyone could say another word there was a quick, courtesy knock on the door, and Michelle stuck her head in.

"Hi! We were just on our way back from two-stepping lessons, and we saw the light."

"How's the packing going?" asked Janka, coming in behind her.

"Oh, are there any more nachos?" asked Michelle. "I'm starving!"

Dana and Marta both burst into fresh tears. Alison, faced with the prospect of comforting, beat a hasty retreat into the kitchen. Michelle was on her heels.

"What are you doing, having group therapy?" She poked her head into the refrigerator and pulled out a huge pitcher of Marguerita mix. "Oh, gimme a glass, I want one of these."

Alison handed her another whale bowl. "I thought you weren't supposed to be drinking."

Michelle filled the bowl to the brim and looked into the pitcher critically, as if calculating the chances on seconds and thirds. "It didn't take. I started my period today. We must have been way off with the ovulation time." She set the pitcher down and did a little dance of victory before taking a huge hit from the bowl.

"I thought you *wanted* to get pregnant!"

"Fuck no! I want a kid. I want *Janka* to get pregnant."

"So why are you blowing a two hundred dollar shot of sperm on yourself every other month?"

Michelle looked pained. "I know you and Stacy are into the

butch/femme thing. It's none of my business, so I don't say a thing about it." This was such a blatant lie Alison could only give her a look. "But *we* believe butch/femme stuff is just another way to feed into the patriarchy, *we* believe traditional mens' and women's jobs should be shared equally and..."

"And you think you're too butch to be pregnant, but you don't want to say it," Alison finished for her. "Actually, I wondered how you were going to reshingle the roof in your third trimester."

"Give me another hit of those," said Michelle, holding up the empty bowl. "It was Janka's turn to lead this week at class—that always stresses me out."

"Remember that book of Tam's I was showing you?" asked Alison, dividing the last of the pitcher between them. "*Love's Lost Child*? Did you ever read it when you were younger?"

"No—unless it was a Blaze? I think I've read all of those."

"No." Alison started putting another bowl of nachos together. "It's way earlier than that. It's a straight romance."

"That leaves me out," said Michelle. She looked at Alison curiously. "Why?"

Alison answered with another question. "Do you think that Tam borrowed a lot from real life?"

"Oh, absolutely," answered Michelle immediately. "That's one of the reasons I liked reading her. I've been to Seattle, I've *been* to The Wild Rose and some of the other places she talked about. It was fun to recognize them."

"No, I mean more like...well, in the porn she cameoed women she didn't like. I wonder if she did anything like that in her other books."

Michelle shrugged. "Yeah, I'll bet she did. Didn't Blaze work on a lesbian paper for a while? That's got to be *BMR*. But, again, why?"

Alison pulled the copy of *Love's Lost Child* out of her day pack, which was sitting on the table. "I told you I was reading this, and as near as I can tell, it's just a rip off of Sary's story. Oh, yeah, a few things have been changed to make it flow and provide the romance, but there's the sister and the illegitimate baby and the druggie mother—the whole cast."

Michelle looked at the garish cover, which showed a woman who was probably, considering when the book was published, meant to be a flower child, pregnant, and sitting forlornly on a curb.

"It's not a very kind portrayal," said Alison. "I wonder if this is what started the bad blood between Tam and Sary. It came out around the right time."

Michelle chased her Marguerita down with a handful of chips and said, "Do you think they're done crying in there?"

"Maybe, but keep in mind it's only a lull."

Everyone was, in fact, done crying. They were sitting in a close group around Janka, who had a notebook in her lap.

"So what do you think?" she asked Alison abruptly when they walked back into the room. "Did she kill herself, or was it an accident?"

"She killed herself," said Michelle cheerfully as she plonked down on the futon, sloshing her drink onto Dana's pillow. "Why the hell else would she have a vibrator in the tub?"

"You were the one who had the theory about the stuffed up head," protested Alison.

"I was just trying to help her save face," said Michelle, taking another huge swallow. Janka was going to have to drive home tonight. "She had the vibrator because it was the only thing anybody could accept, even with a stretch of the imagination. What else did she have in the house that was electric? Her printer? Her blender? Her radio was built into the stereo—anything else, and the police would have called it suicide right off the bat."

"She *didn't* kill herself," said Dana. "Okay, let's say she wouldn't have used the chance to fuck with my head—which, believe me, she would. But what about those kittens?" They all looked around, but the two kittens had gone into deep cover. "She loved cats, she wouldn't get two brand new kittens and then kill herself without providing for them."

"There wasn't any cat food out," remembered Alison. "and there wasn't any water."

"Right," said Dana. "And there's no door on the bathroom. I don't know how long...I mean..." she backed away from a topic obviously too graphic.

"The current," said Janka, writing in her notebook. "If one of the kittens had drunk from the tub when the current was active, he would have been zapped. She would have thought of that."

"She killed herself," said Marta. "She was in pain, she thought the move would help, and it didn't. She killed herself and tried to cover."

"You're all wrong," said Stacy suddenly. "Someone else killed her."

There was a sudden and total pause. k.d. lang spoke yearningly from the stereo of being down to her last cigarette. "What are you talking about?" said Michelle. "Who would want to kill Tam?"

"I don't know who, but I sure as hell can see how." Stacy took the notebook from Janka. "Okay, everything that you've got listed here under suicide fits murder as well. She used the vibrator instead of the blender so it would look like an accident. Okay, *the killer* used the vibrator for the same reason. Did you ever actually see Tam use a vibrator in the tub?" she asked Dana.

"Once or twice," said Dana tearfully. "Mostly not. It made me too nervous."

"Okay, the nudes are gone. Marta says Tam didn't want her sister to see them. But Tam didn't know her sister was in Denver, she didn't know she was anywhere near. And, just in case, she gave Michelle who is the executrix of the will, orders to clean-sweep the place if she died."

"I still think you made that word up," whispered Michelle to Alison.

Stacy frowned them into silence.

"Who's topping this scene?" she inquired frostily, slipping for a split second into her Anastasia mode. "Are you done? Thank you. So she had no reason to clean up after herself in advance, because Michelle would do it after. But Michelle and Alison *couldn't find* everything she told Michelle to look for—am I right?" She looked at the two of them over her glasses, giving permission to speak.

"Couldn't find the porn," agreed Michelle cheerfully, without excuses or explanations. They should keep her half drunk all the time.

"Or her new *Newsweek* magazine," said Alison. "Well, it should be here," she defended when Stacy gave her the over-the-glasses look again. "Mine came the day she was killed—why isn't hers here?"

"Wait a minute, I saw the porn," protested Janka.

"Those books weren't here," explained Alison. "The neighbor had them. What we couldn't find was anything on the computer."

"You can hide things on a computer," pointed out Marta.

"Tam couldn't," said Dana with a touch of scorn. "The computer was like a big typewriter to her. She barely knew how to use Word Perfect. She was always losing stuff and asking me to get it back for her. I know she kept the porn in the hard drive—if she got really low on money she'd take out an old story and doctor it a little and sell it to another fuck and suck company. The file was *labeled* 'Porn' She wasn't one for subtlety".

"Not any more," put in Michelle. "I looked. And we couldn't find the rest of her new manuscript, either."

"And I can't find her notebook," Dana said. Everyone looked blank. "She kept one in her fanny pack," she explained. "She made notes all the time—story ideas, character ideas. I wanted to see if she'd been writing down anything that would give a clue as to what she was thinking." She furrowed her brow. "You know what," she said slowly, "Maybe Stacy's right. Maybe somebody did kill her."

****

Dana had been at the computer when Alison, far too early, had left for work, and she was still at it when Alison returned. A full ashtray attested to a hard day's work.

"Okay," she said, not bothering with a greeting. Alison thought longingly of the night before. She would have liked to have been greeted with a drink and dinner again. "Michelle's right. It's just not here—not on the hard drive and not on floppy, either. And Tam *always* backed up—she learned that the hard way after losing almost a whole book."

"It's still not murder," said Alison grumpily. When was the heat wave going to break? As always, domestic violence rose with the temperature, and a day spent hauling fathers and boyfriends to jail had not improved her temper. She saw, with a sigh, that the living room and kitchen were just as they had been left the night before. The debate had turned into something of a party. Dana had left the room to make drinks several more times, and when Alison had finally retreated to the bedroom, everyone else had been going strong with theories and suppositions. She saw now that, sometime after she had fallen asleep, the notebook had been abandoned and someone or two had started writing directly on the walls. In among Tam's notes was written several times, "Who killed her? Why?" Alison salvaged one of Dana's butts that had only been smoked half way down and walked into the kitchen to light it off the stove.

The phone rang. "Is Janka there?" Michelle asked crossly, without bothering to identify herself. "Why in the world did you let me drink so much? You know I'm always sick the next day when I drink."

"You're nicer when drink," said Alison. "Besides, it's good practice for morning sickness." Michelle hung up without saying goodbye.

The door burst open, and in came Stacy, Janka, and Liz. Stacy and Janka were both wearing cotton skirts and tank tops and carrying grocery sacks. Liz was wearing a corporate lawyer suit that made her haircut look even worse and a cuff in her nose.

"No files," said Dana to Stacy. "Nada. And I still can't find her little notebook, either. I found a bunch of old ones, but the last one stopped a month ago."

"I knew it," replied Stacy in a satisfied voice. "Is it possible," she asked Alison, "that you are in a service mode? Because we brought stuff for dinner."

"If I can get it up to melt some cheese on a tortilla for myself I'm going to be lucky," said Alison shortly, wishing she were back in her own place. Since when had Tam's apartment turned into Ten-forward? Everyone seemed to be thinking of it as the scene of the crime, without realizing she was trying to *live* here.

"I could be in service mode," volunteered Janka, heading for the couch, "if one of you could top some picking up in here."

"Dibs on topping," said Liz quickly. Obviously everyone was in high spirits. Janka slapped a cold can of Diet Pepsi into Alison's hand as she pranced into the kitchen.

"What did you find out?" demanded Dana. "Incidentally," she said in an aside to Alison, "I did find the *Newsweek*, so *that's* not a clue."

"Where have you guys been?" Alison asked grumpily. Why was it always her clues that didn't pan out?

"We have been to see Sary Washington," said Liz.

"Why?"

"Because you always get to pretend you're the detective," answered Stacy, swishing past her with an armload of dishes. "Today," she called from the kitchen, "we were the Delafield sisters. And Liz was the bait."

"The Delafettes," called Janka. There was a crash. Stacy really was not very good in the kitchen.

"God, how did that poor sick woman react to you?" asked Alison, remembering Sary's frailness.

"Alison," scolded Liz, "you don't do us justice. And you don't read detective novels, either. We didn't charge in with a rubber hose. I went as an old friend. Janka and Stacy cleaned the kitchen and made dinner and watched the kids." There was another crash from the kitchen. "Janka cleaned the kitchen," amended Liz. "Stacy took the kids down to the playground. The woman was grateful."

"And was this outfit you're wearing supposed to inspire confidence?"

Liz looked hurt. "Alison. This is my court drag." Alison tapped her own nose, and Liz put her hand up to her face. "Oh, shit, did I have that on in court? Oh, well, I won anyway. But, Alison, the reason we went to see Sary was..." she paused dramatically, "...who do the police investigate first in a murder case?"

"Oh, good," said Stacy, "It's *Jeopardy!*" She was carrying a plate of sliced apples and oranges. There was a new band aid on her thumb. "And the answer is?"

"Their spouses," said Alison.

"In the form of a question, please."

"Who are their spouses, which means that Dana is the prime suspect, not Sary."

"I've got an iron clad alibi," said Dana, leaving the computer and lighting up. "I spent twenty-four hours at a sex club. And I have a very distinct birthmark on my ass—dozens of women can testify for me."

"Cool," said Liz, perking up. "I've always wanted to go to one of those. What…."

"Down girl," said Stacy, who was gathering up another armload of dishes in a manner that guaranteed another disaster. Alison, who quite liked the whale plates, and hoped to take them home if Sary really didn't want them, rescued them.

"But who else?" called Liz after her, as she went into the kitchen. "Who else do the police suspect?"

"Actually," Alison called back, "the police suspect no one, because it was an accident. Or maybe suicide." She knew this from her short and curt call to the Homicide Bureau that morning. Her information about locating Sary and the traced number had been received by a man who had not bothered to hide the fact he thought she was wasting his time.

She took one look at the kitchen and left quickly, afraid she might click into submissive mode at the sight of so many dishes. Janka was happily cutting up vegetables on the one clean counter. There was broken crockery all over the floor. "But, if they did, they'd look for someone who stood to gain financially. Which is Sary, right? We knew that all along. But Sary doesn't even want Tam's stuff."

"Sary said she didn't want Tam's things, right," said Liz. "But is she going to turn down Tam's royalties?"

"Tam's royalties?" asked Alison. She picked up Dana's ashtray and began looking for another butt. "Are Tam's royalties even worth fucking with? I mean, if the woman had to write porn to make it on the side, that indicates that she wasn't pulling the big bucks in."

"You're pitiful," said Dana. "Here, I don't like to see a woman humiliate herself outside a scene." She handed Alison her pack and lighter. "Maybe Tam wasn't Dorothy Allison," she said, blowing the smoke from her own cigarette out her nose, "but she was pulling an okay amount. Sure, she was with a small press, but she had seven books out, and everyone of them hit Lambda Book Reviews' top ten for months. And they all were bringing in foreign royalties as well. She got a check for a couple of thou four times a year. It wasn't enough to live in luxury, but she didn't have to work full time, either. Most of the porn was written years ago—she'd do something new if she had an emergency at a bad time. Like, once she had to have major dental work in January, right after she'd spent her first of the year check."

"And amount isn't always a consideration, either," pointed out Liz, who had abandoned topping the cleaning scene and was picking up napkins and chips herself. "People have been killed for as little as five and ten dollars. I know. I've seen some of them in court."

"Then you know," said Alison, "that they're usually junkies who pulled the trigger because they were freaked, and they usually thought the victim had more. You don't go through an elaborate set-up with a family member for five dollars."

"How about ten thousand a year?" asked Dana. "That's more like what she was bringing in. And that's not counting the new manuscript—her death is going to make that one gold."

"And the old books," reminded Janka. She was carrying a pitcher and glasses. A wonderful smell trailed her from the kitchen. "You told Michelle they'd be collector's items."

"In the lesbian community," protested Alison. "For something like a charity auction. You couldn't just walk into a rare bookstore and get money for them. And another thing. Sary is ill. Sary is fucking *dying*. What is she going to do with all this money? She's not up to going to Disneyland."

"What about the daughter?" asked Janka, passing out glasses. Alison looked quickly into the pitcher, and was relieved to see it was only orange juice. Good, another night of partying would kill her. "Maybe what she wants is to get the daughter set up before she dies. Mothers do strange things for their children."

"Hmm," said Alison. She wanted to protest, but it was true, mothers did do strange things for their children. And why had Sary—or someone at that house—called Tam's number the night she died?

"Texas cheerleader mother," inserted Stacy as an example of aggressive mothers.

"Wait a minute," said Alison. Janka was now passing out plates of stir fry, and she accepted one gratefully. "This is getting too complicated."

"I wrote it down," said Stacy, flipping open Janka's notebook. "Okay, twenty years ago. Tam has taken off from her family to join the lesbians. This is the time period during which she is working on *BMR* with Vicki but before Michelle."

"Sary," continued Liz, looking over her shoulder, "is the younger sister. She is also having problems at home, and is probably clinically depressed. She runs away from home and does drugs for the first time, is brought back, attempts suicide, and because she is under age, she ends up locked up at Denver General. There is a breakout, and she ends up with the dykes."

"Where she passes," Stacy took up the story again, "for several years. She is in contact with Tam, her older sister, the whole time. In fact, at least once they share an apartment."

"Then," said Janka, who now was carrying a wok, "Sary falls into another depression. She is living upstairs from Liz, and as a result of calling the police, Liz is purged from the newspaper, and in fact spends some time in DG herself."

"Sary," said Stacy, "is welcomed back into the lesbian community when she gets out. However, around this time she becomes involved with a man from R.I.P., gets pregnant with a child who was obviously not conceived with a turkey baster, and feels the wrong end of a purge herself. The only people who stand by her are—"

"Liz," said Janka, "because she'd been through it herself."

"And Tam," said Liz. "Her sister."

"Sary and Tam are planning to keep the baby. At this point, Sary and Tam have some kind of huge fight and Sary moves out."

"What was the fight about?" asked Alison.

"Don't know," said Liz. "She wouldn't say. Just that it was silly, and she couldn't believe she'd wasted all those years over it."

"So," Stacy rode right over the top of the sidebar. "Sary, who is like now eighteen or nineteen with a kid and not even a high school diploma, ends up breaking totally with the lesbian community, and eventually going back home. "

"Tam moves to Tacoma," said Stacy, "which cuts off an easy reunion with her sister. Sary gets married and changes her name. Tam spends a decade in Tacoma, writing the Blaze Badgirl books, and pretty much operating under the name Katie Copper."

"And jerking me around," put in Dana.

"Well, yeah. After she breaks off with you, she moves back to Denver. Her sister is on her mind, so at the Will-a-thon she arranges to have her estate benefit Sary and her niece, who she either hasn't seen since she was a baby, or maybe never at all. Tam dies unexpectedly, leaving her property and her royalties to Sary and the kid, who incidentally is about eighteen now and is named Kathy. So all you have left to find out is—"

Liz finished the sentence for her. "—did Sary know about Tam being in town before you and Michelle went over that day?"

"Well…," said Alison uncomfortably, as if she was breaking confidence. But that was silly, how could anything be confidential if there was no investigation? "Actually, I think maybe Sary did know." Quickly, she explained the telephone report from US West.

"Yes!" Stacy and Liz did a high five which splashed soy sauce on Stacy's shirt. No one even commented—Stacy stained her clothes as if it were a hobby. "Okay," said Liz, "She knew, she came over, they fought—maybe the old stuff blew up again? Did Tam tell Sary about the will? Of course, if Sary is her closest living relative, she might have assumed Tam's assets would go to her as a matter of course."

"Would they?" asked Dana.

Liz shrugged. "I don't know. I'm a criminal lawyer, not a probate lawyer. I brushed up enough to fill out the forms at the Will-a-thon, and even then the other guys had to help me if it was anything out of the ordinary. Different states all have their own laws."

"And how did Sary, who weighs maybe ninety pounds and who probably can't even drive herself any more, get Tam into the tub?"

asked Alison. "With a wheelbarrow?"

"She didn't have to get her into the tub," said Dana. "Tam put herself in. Her arthritis had really started bothering her this last year—she'd gotten so she'd do the hot bath thing no matter who was in the house. She drew the bath herself, and told Sary to come in and talk to her while she was soaking. After all, they were sisters."

"Who hadn't seen each other in almost twenty years," pointed out Alison. "Isn't that kind of an instant intimacy, particularly if they've stirred up an old quarrel?"

"That was Tam," said Dana, around a mouthful of cabbage and sprouts. "I've seen her do something like that a hundred times. You'd be right in the middle of a fight, and suddenly she'd stop and do something like make herself a sandwich or hop in the tub. Queen of the Mind Fucks."

"So there it is." Stacy beamed, as if they had just given Alison a fine present. "We've done all the work for you."

Alison was uncomfortably aware that four sets of eyes were on her. "And what, exactly, do you expect me to do?"

"Call the detective agency," said Stacy. "We got the name—they'll verify that Sary knew before."

"Call the cab company," said Liz. "Won't they give you records?"

"Talk to the daughter," suggested Janka. "Find out what the money situation is at home. It must be tight, or they'd have someone staying with Sary during the day. And isn't it about time for the kid to be going to college? That's bound to put a real twist in their budget."

"Is she already at college?" asked Alison. "I mean, there wasn't a sign of her when we went by."

"I don't think so," replied Liz. "Sary referred to her a couple of times in present tense. I'll bet she'd be a wealth of information if you just leaked a little about her mother's past."

"Liz! God! You mean you want me to go back to that house and pick the kids' brains by telling them their mom used to be a dyke? That seems to go a little beyond human decency!"

"Liz has no ethics," said Stacy in a surprised voice, as if she couldn't believe that Alison hadn't known this fact. "She went to see

Basic Instinct at the dollar movies last week."

"With you!" protested Liz.

"Yes, but I felt guilty."

"Oh, how was that?" asked Janka who, it went without saying, had supported the boycott with Michelle.

"Weird," said Liz. "I sure as hell didn't come away thinking it was a poor portrayal of lesbians, I just thought everybody in it was crazy. And I've never seen so many ice picks in my life. I don't even know where to *buy* an ice pick."

"Well, I do have some ethics," said Alison. "The woman is dying, and the police have accepted it as an accident. That poor woman is going to die without having anything resolved with her sister, isn't that enough?"

Everyone looked pouty. "Well, rain on *our* parade," said Liz in a sulky voice. "Just wait and see when I do undercover work for *you* again."

The outside door flew open, and in came Michelle, who had obviously decided that her barging in privileges extended, not just to Alison's apartment, but anywhere Alison happened to be staying.

"Oh," she said to Janka. "Hi. I wondered where you were." It was obvious to everyone that what she really wanted to do was channel Archie Bunker, asking where the hell Janka had been and where *her* dinner was. Liz brightened and opened her mouth to stir the pot, but Alison nudged her with her foot.

"Janka has been playing Nancy Drew," she said. "These are her dear friends Beth and George."

"Dibs on being George!" said Stacy and Liz together.

"Have you ever noticed how there aren't any femme detectives?" asked Stacy.

"That's because dykes think femmes are stupid," said Dana. "I *had* noticed *that*."

Before this could take off, Michelle broke in crossly, "God, are you still going on about that? She lived in an old house, she didn't have a ground fault detector outlet. That's all there is to it." Michelle, who had supported the suicide theory so strongly the night before, had no trouble at all switching back to the accident side.

"What?" asked Alison.

"You know," said Michelle. "A ground fault detector outlet. They cut the circuit when this kind of thing happens. I put them in our bathrooms a couple of years ago."

"Why wouldn't she have one?" asked Dana.

"It's an old house," explained Michelle "An old house like this—the wiring is probably grandfathered—well, grandmothered. New dwellings, they have to be up to the current code. But an old house like this doesn't necessarily have to be updated."

"Wouldn't they do that automatically when they remodeled?" asked Alison, remembering the stacks of plywood in the downstairs hall.

Michelle shrugged. "Maybe. I would if it was my house. Safer that way. You know, you don't even have to be immersed in water to create a current. I got one going one time by standing with my hand under the faucet and reaching over and touching the electric stove. All it takes is a little faulty wiring. But who cares why not? She obviously didn't have one, or she wouldn't have been able to zap herself in the tub."

"How does it work?" asked Alison. "I mean, not how does it work, but what does it cover? Is it something you do at the fuse box to cover the whole building? Or does each apartment need one?"

"Neither," answered Michelle, shaking her head. "It goes right into the outlet themselves. You generally only put them on outlets in the bathroom or the kitchen. In the laundry room, I guess. Or a dark room. You know, you don't bother with the living room or the bedroom because you're not so likely to set up a current there."

"Is this a clue?" asked Liz brightly. Alison, sitting on the futon, her shirt stuck to her back with sweat, said nothing. What she was remembering was the extension cord that had snaked out of the bathroom, and plugged into the socket in the pantry, and the fuse box neighbor number two had said was locked.

❧ 12 ❧

Some idiot in a Volkswagen, trying to beat the light, shot across the intersection at Downing after Alison had already put her car in gear, and she had to slam on her brakes to avoid a collision. The continents might shift, and the Berlin Wall come down, but Newton's first law was a constant, so the glass casserole dish she had unthinkingly placed on the front seat beside her went shooting forward. Only at the last moment, and twisting her wrist, was Alison able to keep it from spilling onto the floor. Glass, sour cream and cheese sauce, rice and chicken—that would have been a disaster. Alison made a universal gesture of disapproval at the Volkswagen—a gesture in more ways than one, for the car was by now too far down the road for such communication—and cautiously pulled through the intersection. The car behind her honked—so she had almost been totaled, get over it!

She had not wanted to bring food. What she had wanted, what she had wanted more than anything else in the world was not to get involved. She had wanted to pack up the rest of Tam's things in cardboard boxes that could be dropped off on the shaded porch at night— no, better yet, sent through UPS—it didn't matter if it took a week. What she wanted was to drop a nice, impersonal card to Abel Washington when she eventually saw by the obituary page that Sary Washington had died. She had not wanted to bring food, to see the face of either Sary or her children again.

143

But the damage, unfortunately, had already been done by the one visit. No matter what Sary had said, Alison as she had sat alone at night, watching reruns of *Star Trek* and sorting through Tam's life, had found herself placing fewer things in the box marked GLBSCC and more things in the box for Sary and her family. Now that she had seen the children she could not just discard the box of Christmas ornaments—cats of tin and glass and porcelain and straw—she had found in the closet. She could not just consign to rummage the old, well worn fairy tale books in the bookshelf beside the bed, nor could she give away the handmade quilt—a Broken Dishes pattern—that covered the bed, to be sold to a stranger for five dollars.

And, once there were names and faces, a casserole was inevitable. She had two strikes against her to begin with—a Polish mother who comforted, celebrated and even censured with food, and of course, the lesbian potluck curse. Alison thought that the various groups of religious crazies who spent their time trying to destroy gay life—get them into twelve step groups and they'll go away, get them denounced by the church and they'll go away, take away their civil rights, close their bars and they'll go away—were approaching the issue all wrong. Stop their potlucks instead and dyke social life would be brought to a grinding halt. Stop lesbian potlucks and no one could meet new lovers, no one could break up in ugly scenes witnessed by so many old friends that getting back together was out of the question, no one could find someone who would mulch her yard in return for having her car tuned. Soccer and softball teams would dissolve. It would be the end of lesbian civilization as Alison knew it.

Luckily, the Colorado Family Values (and where did that name come from, anyway? Did they think gays had no families, they just hatched on the beach?) people had no idea this cornerstone even existed, so they had shot their wad on Amendment Two, and that was going to get shot down by the Supreme Court if there really was any justice in the land. That was fine, it kept them busy. But, at any rate, that was the reason half of Alison's famous Mexican chicken dish had almost landed on her grey floor mat, while the other half, carefully covered to thwart kittens, cooled on the counter at home. You brought food when there was a tragedy. That was what you did. And the fact that Sary was now, in the minds of the Delafettes if not the police, a murder suspect, did not mean that Alison could skip the casserole. It only meant she felt bad about bringing both it and the box, as if her real motive canceled the original kindness.

The fleet of riding toys was still sitting on the porch, but it did not seem as cheery to Alison as it had the week before. She noticed that each bicycle and wagon was propped in exactly the same place, and imagined the two children retreating further and further from death into the rays of the TV. Nothing, Sary had said, mattered when you were dying. You wanted to shield your children, to ease their way, you thought there would come a time when the universe revealed to you all it's secrets and you accepted your place on the great mandala. But what really happened was that you became more and more tired, until being tired filled up your head and your life and your day, and your children stopped going outside to ride their bikes and instead spent their days with Gilligan and the Skipper while they waited for Mama to die. Alison almost turned around.

But she had the box, and she had the casserole, and so she worked one finger loose to push the gentle chimes. As before, only the wrought iron safety door was closed.

"Yes?"

"Uh, I..." Alison stood there stupidly with both hands full. All of her speeches had begun with, "Your sister" or "your aunt"—she had known it might be Sary's hitherto unseen daughter who opened the door. What she had not counted on was knowing the girl. Several times she had failed to recognize leatherwomen later in their street clothes, but the girl from OUTEEN was too striking for that. Alison flashed back on the way the girl had flirted and postured with the other youth. What was her name? Something made up. It was Jasper or Olivine...no, Obsidian. Even though she was wearing a huge t-shirt and equally baggy shorts—black, but nothing any teenager couldn't get at Target—instead of the chaps and jacket, the sexual overtone, as well as the shaved patches and nose rings, were still right there. She seemed to have no discomfort with Alison's fumbling, but stood, holding the door open with one hand while she looked her up and down slowly like someone getting ready to make a big purchase—not as big as a sofa or microwave, but, still, a comforter or a set of dishes.

"Umm," said Alison finally, when the covered dish got to be too heavy to hold and she was burning from the experience of being window shopped as well, "I thought maybe Sary...."

"My mom," the girl supplied, looking for the first time at anything but Alison's body. "Yeah, it would be nice if we had something to eat." There was a slightly angry tone to her voice, as if she found Sary's illness rather inconsiderate and certainly selfish. "I know you, don't I?"

"OUTEEN," Alison said. "Career day."

"The cop," said Obsidian. "The uniform." Alison braced herself for the dreaded remark to follow. The girl said nothing. Instead, she wet her index finger in her mouth, dragging it along the inside of her full lower lip rather than using her tongue. Delicately, she touched the finger to Alison's straining wrist. "Ssst," she hissed, water hitting the frying pan.

"Could you please take this?" Alison said brusquely, thrusting the casserole towards her. Perhaps she would have been more impressed had she not seen the girl's performance at the GLBSCC the week before. She didn't go for jailbait, they only made her nervous.

"Don't! *Don't!*" The cry from the other room was fretful and whiny, the kind of cry a five-year-old can conjure up only after hours of delicate torture by an older sibling. Alison, an older sister, knew this. She knew about poking your feet under your brother's butt as you lay on opposite ends of the couch, about chanting his name endlessly and then saying, "Oh, nothing." She was amazed, sometimes, that her younger brother still spoke to her.

The whine escalated into a full fledged wail. Obsidian looked crossly over her shoulder, but made no move to intervene.

"Could you please...." It was only at this second meeting of Sary's husband that Alison realized she had come away from the first meeting with no image at all of the man. He had been as weary and washed out as an overlay, as one of those maps her fifth grade librarian, Miss Miller, had been so fond of putting on screen via an overhead projector. Only now, as he came down the hall towards them, carrying a basket overflowing with small t-shirts and little pairs of jeans, did it occur to Alison that this man could not be the father of the two boys Sary had introduced as her sons. He was not black, or Latino or Indio—anything that could have accounted for their soft brown skin and black eyes. He was, in fact, one of those red-headed men with the white freckled skin who sunburns at the beach before he gets out of the car. At another time, in another life time, when his wife was not dying in the next room, he was probably a handsome man. But he was too much now like those plastic drawings of Miss Miller's—once you took them away from the light and held them up, they were nothing but a few lines.

"Could you please," he said to the girl, "see what the problem is in there? Maybe make them something to eat? There's peanut butter, if there isn't anything else." He spoke in a perfectly neutral, polite voice, asking, not telling, but at the same time somehow managing to convey a whole host of unsaid complaints—why do I even have to ask you, why aren't you doing this on your own, can't you help out at all?

"Oh!" he said, noticing Alison for the first time. "I don't remember...."

"Alison Kaine," she said. "Tam's friend? I brought Sary some more of Tam's things."

"Oh," he said. "She's sleeping." He looked back over his shoulder towards the sound of discord, and then back at Obsidian. Again there was that whole volume of the unsaid: at least she *was* sleeping, it'd be a miracle if anyone could sleep through that noise, why do I have to tell you to be considerate to your mother, what the hell is *your problem*? He looked at the box Alison was holding with a marked lack of enthusiasm.

"I brought you some dinner," said Alison, thrusting forward her other hand, and he brightened.

"Great! Maybe...." he said to Obsidian, and this was when Alison noticed he had not yet called her by any title, but rather addressed her in that nameless way one uses when uncertain of protocol, the way Alison's sister-in-law had addressed her mother for the first six months of her marriage, when Mrs. Kaine was too formal and 'Jean' not quite comfortable.

Both boys burst out into the hall, both crying, both vying for the right to tell his story of wrongdoing first. "Daddy!" they cried, and he squatted down to draw them both close, not bothering to try to sort the accusations out.

"Maybe," he said to Obsidian over the top of their heads, "you could take that in and put it in the oven," there was a small space, "Kathy?"

"Okay," she said, and then, mimicking the pause perfectly, "Daddy." The man and the girl looked at one another, and the man looked away first.

"Maybe we could take the boys for a walk," Alison suggested. She didn't know where that suggestion came from, except that, just as you brought food to the house where there had been death, you offered to help however you could. She could have offered to do the laundry, or mow the law having done both things for bereaved gay friends upon their partners' death. AIDS had made her all too familiar with death at an early age—but she was called by that sad pile of bikes on the porch.

The man brightened, and she could see the thoughts running through his head—then I can get some dinner on the table and the clothes out of the wash, and maybe if they're gone long enough I can sit with their mother and won't have to feel bad about doing it because they'll be out getting some exercise and not vegged out on *Roseanne*... The boys themselves looked skeptical. They looked over at the bikes with a kind of longing surprise, as if riding around the block was a memory—pleasant, yes, but barely within recall. They held onto their father with both hands.

"I baked some bread," said Alison, remembering the paper sack she had thrust into the top of the box. "We could have a snack on the way." She opened the top of the bag, and the boys inched closer to the fresh baked smell, still clutching their father's pants in their fists.

In the end, it took not only the enticement of the bread, but also two dollars in change, doled out from their father's pockets and placed in their *very own* hands for sodas on the way, to complete the enticement. Obsidian was not included in the negotiation, and Alison could feel Abel Washington carefully not looking at her, carefully not suggesting that perhaps she could help with the laundry or make lunches for tomorrow. At the last minute, she caught the screen door and trailed out behind the boys. She stood at the bottom of the steps as Alison helped in the choosing and disentangling of vehicles, looking down the street with her eyes shaded—for what, Alison could not tell. She seemed not to belong either to the street, nor to the two little boys who had not turned to her even once.

"Uniform girl," said Obsidian in her sultry voice, once they were finally on their way, trailing half a block behind the boys.

"Old married lady," said Alison firmly, though she felt none of the three things—she just wanted to get it clear that these were the terms on which they were going to relate, that she didn't want to be breathed on and clung to by someone who could almost be her own daughter. Obsidian gave a breathy sigh that sounded almost like relief. Well, it was probably exhausting to keep up that sexual energy and put it out to everyone.

Without any planning at all, they had arrived at a playground, and the boys threw down their bikes and swarmed back for hunks of cheese bread. Obsidian tore a piece herself, touching her fingers to Alison's, but the gesture was more reflexive than heartfelt.

"You go to OUTEEN much?" asked Alison, picking this question from all the others that seemed so much more interesting, but so much less polite. Like, what's the scoop between Abel and you, and why do you act like your brothers are strangers and are you a sex worker, like I thought and if so what are you doing living at home and calling someone at OUTEEN 'boss'?

"Mostly," replied Obsidian, stuffing the bread into her mouth with no more finesse than the older boy, Donny. She caught Alison watching, and suddenly changed her whole style, taking little, cat-like bites, as if she were doing a Playboy video. It was very odd to see the bits of little girl that kept peeking out from behind the sophisticated, sexual image she wanted so hard to project. She shrugged, a shrug that, with the right combination of lingerie, might have been capable of toppling empires. "I like being around the other gay kids."

"There aren't a lot of girls in the group," said Alison, more to make conversation than anything else.

"Ha!" laughed Obsidian, low and sultry again. "Those girls are afraid of *me*." She said it as though she couldn't quite believe it, and yet was rather proud of it at the same time. "I just talk to the guys— they don't want anything. One of them got me a job."

Donny came running back again, aiming for the can of soda sitting on the ground between them. He careened into Obsidian's leg and she shook him off angrily.

"Fucking kids," she said angrily. "I hate kids."

"Well, little brothers," said Alison soothingly, surprised by the vehemence of her tone.

"They're *not* my brothers," the girl said, in a tone so harsh Alison was glad the little boy had moved out of earshot.

"They're your half-brothers, aren't they? Sary's their mom, too, isn't she?"

"No." Short, vehement, no room for argument. "Sarah is *my* mom. Those guys are adopted."

"Well, but...."

"No." Obsidian held up her hand. "Don't try to tell me. Don't try to tell me that love makes a family or any of that crap. I was adopted myself for a while. I know. She just adopted *them* because she felt guilty about *me*."

There was a horrible howl from the jungle gym, and the next ten minutes were spent dealing with baby Carl's lower lip—stanching the blood with a shirt tail, talking calmly to soothe the screaming while inside trying frantically to decide if it really was okay, (just a mouth wound, and everybody knew they bled like crazy,) or if it was going to take a trip to the hospital. That would be a wonderful help to their parents, thought Alison, and she was relieved when the bleeding suddenly stopped and Carl abruptly pulled away to go jump on the swings.

"You're all covered with blood," said Obsidian, who had stayed far in the background.

"Yeah, well, kids," Alison started to, and then stopped herself suddenly when she realized this was not what Obsidian was saying, that Obsidian was referring to Sary back in bed. Oh, shit, thought Alison, maybe she doesn't have cancer, maybe she has AIDS, if she has AIDS, maybe the kids do, too, and they keep telling us to use gloves at work and I forgot all about it because he was just a little kid and he was hurt....

"Don't worry about it." Obsidian said, as if she had been able to read every thought, and was pleased at the panic she had created. "She has cancer. I know—they made me go in to the doctor and get a bone marrow test. They thought maybe there'd be a match. Ha! Can you believe the nerve? The minute I got here, taking me into the hospital. Not even a how are you, or gee, I'm sorry."

"I don't understand," said Alison. Obsidian turned to her, seductive face back in play. Before Alison realized her intent, Obsidian lifted Alison's hand and licked a dainty bit of blood off her forefinger. "Don't worry," she said. "She doesn't have AIDS, and they're not her kids."

✍ 13 ✍

Perhaps Liz, who didn't have any ethics, or even Stacy who was just hard to throw, would have been able to pull their finger out of the girl's mouth and continue questioning. Perhaps they would have come back with a page full of answers that reached all the way back into Obsidian's infancy. Alison, however, had barely been able to muster enough composure to make small talk along the walk home. Which had happened almost immediately. As much as she would have liked to have given Abe Washington an hour, or maybe two, she could not bring herself to continue standing there with the girl who flashed her sexuality off and on like a firefly. The girl knew it, too, and she prefaced each innocent answer with a kind of secret smile—yes, she was out of school, no, she hadn't graduated, but was working on her GED—as if it were something suggestive.

"Go back again," Stacy had said, when Alison told her the whole story over the phone at work, failing only to describe the way the father's face had fallen when they returned after only forty five minutes. It was not advice Alison felt she could take, not so soon, not with her ears still burning from the way the girl had bested her.

Since she had failed so miserably with Obsidian, Alison consoled herself the next morning by looking up the detective agency Sary had mentioned. It wasn't in the phone book, but Information (who she had to call with her own quarter from a pay phone, because the staff room phone blocked all pay calls) had a Peoplefinders. She dialed that number while Robert forced the desk sergeant to look at photos of Timica.

"Peoplefinders." The call was answered by a girl who sounded much too young to be doing anything except flip burgers.

"I heard," Alison said, "that you were looking for a woman named Tam McArthur? A friend told me. I know where she is." The incomplete truth required her to explain nothing.

"Hey, way cool!" said the voice on the other end. Alison winced. If and when *she* ever hired a detective, she did not want one whose main source of transportation was probably roller blades. "We've been having a terrible time tracking her!" Well, at least it told her Sary had not known about Tam through this angle.

"The thing is, she's dead. It was in last week's obituaries."

"Damn!" said the girl on the end of the line. "Just our luck—I'll bet we don't get paid again! I'm about ready to throw it up and get a day job!"

"Well, maybe you'll still get paid," said Alison, watching Robert with one eye. He had just cornered a new victim—she had a good ten minutes. "I mean, if it was about a will or life insurance, they'll still get the money."

"No good," the girl said chattily. "She needed to be alive to help our client. You know, cancer? They were trying to find her to see if she'd be compatible for a bone marrow transplant."

"Um," said Alison, and then, taking a chance, "well, maybe you'll have better luck with the daughter." Robert had left his cigarettes—he bought a new pack from the machine every morning—sitting on the table beside her. She eyed them longingly, but smoking was forbidden in all Denver city buildings.

"Nah," said the girl in a disgusted tone. "We found the adoptive family right away. But the kid had split. Runaways—they're impossible to find. They don't have jobs, they don't have drivers' licenses, they're not paying taxes." There was a sound in the background. "Hey, my dad is calling me. Do you know what day the obit ran?"

Alison gave her the information, and then went outside to wait for Robert. She didn't bother to tell him where she was going. He had a homing signal where his cigarettes were concerned. She stood far enough away from the other smokers to discourage chatting, though a couple of them raised a hand. They had a strict set of protocol—no one would bother her as long as she kept the right distance.

So Sary had lied about her daughter. No, not lied, but not volunteered the whole story to either her or Liz. She had carried the child to term, but what had happened then? She and Tam had planned on raising the child—but that possibility must have fallen through when they quarreled. Sary had eventually moved back home…was that because of money? And, if she hadn't been able to keep an apartment for herself, she wouldn't have been able to pay for a child, either, would she? Or, had it been a demand from the parents? Did they even know they had a granddaughter? Would they have let Sary come home with an illegitimate child? And if what the girl from the detective agency had said was true, how did Obsidian go from being a runaway to being back with her birthmother? Obsidian. A street name—she had thought that when she had first seen the girl at OUTEEN, and she had not changed her mind. Whatever else had happened, she was willing to bet the girl had spent some time supporting herself with her body.

She had tried to find that out, calling the GLBSCC.

"I can't tell you that," Marnie had said in a shocked voice, when the staffer called her to the phone. "That's confidential. The youth groups are like therapy groups, everything that's said here stays here."

"Oh, come on," Alison had argued. "When I went out for a smoke break, all the kids did was dish the dirt. And a couple of them went to use the phones to fill their friends in on what had happened so far."

"Well," acknowledged Marnie. "That is a problem. But I don't have to provide a poor example! Besides, she's in her home now. What does it matter what she was doing before?"

Alison had hung up without saying good-bye, but not before Marnie had tried to get her to agree to chaperon their Senior Prom. Maybe Marnie was right. What did it matter what path had led Obsidian back to her mother's door? Yet, it seemed funny she would appear just when she was about to inherit money. Would the whole ten thousand go to her? That was a lot of money for a street kid. And what about the bone marrow transplant? It almost gave Sary an alibi—she was the last person who would want Tam dead—but why had she not mentioned it?

Alison lit another cigarette and thought of the conversation she'd had with Stacy the night before. "Do you suppose Sary's baby finally showed up to haunt her?" she had asked, and then winced at her own choice of words. Surely, if you had given up your first child when you were as young as seventeen, you would welcome her return into your life eighteen years later. Or was that just a story-tale response? Alison suspected it was. Eighteen years was a lot of water under the bridge, and it couldn't be easy to welcome a virtual stranger into your family under the very best of circumstances. And how had it felt to Obsidian to find her mother just in time to be abandoned again? No wonder things were strained at Tam's sister's house.

Stacy had not tried to correct her unfortunate choice of words, but rather just nodded in thoughtful agreement, as if Alison had done all her processing aloud.

"How hard is it to find your birth parents these days?" asked Alison.

"Not hard at all," Stacy said, "if you both want to be found. There are agencies where you can register from either end of the spectrum, the parent or the child, and if both of you are looking and you both have a little information, you might find each other easily. Or not. There's still a lot of closed adoptions, a lot of birth parents who don't want their kids to find them, a lot of adoptive parents who don't want their kids to find their birth parents. It's a whole huge can of worms to open."

"Jealousy," said Alison. "Maybe your kid will like her birth parent better than you. After all, she wasn't the one who had to tell you 'no' your whole life."

"Or disappointment. Maybe your birth mother won't be someone who pined for you and celebrated your birthday in secret. Maybe she won't even remember the baby she gave away. Or maybe your birth child is going to be some kind of hood, maybe she's in the court system because you gave her to somebody who was neglectful, or abusive. How are either of those going to make you feel?"

"Or maybe just bad craziness. Maybe you're going to uncover a crazy—on either end—and she's going to want to cleave right onto you and your family. Want to make her problems your problems."

"Want a place to stay."

"Want to use the car and an allowance." They both sat quietly for a moment, thinking of Obsidian. A moth had flown through the open window, and was fluttering about near the ceiling. There was no more chance of either kitten catching it than there was of Will Perkins inviting Alison to dinner, but they were tracking it from the floor, like a u-boat doppelgänging a submarine from the surface. Back and forth they went in tandem, around and around in circles that sometimes went behind and sometimes beneath Alison's chair.

"Want a lot of attention when you were sick and couldn't give it," said Stacy finally, scarfing up the very last cookie on the plate just a moment before Alison could reach for it.

"Want to resolve issues while you were just trying to die." The little black boy kitten suddenly leapt five feet straight up into the air, which of course took him nowhere near the moth, but was still quite impressive none-the-less. The women and the other kitten stared at him with an equal amount of surprise, and as they looked, the moth flew straight down into Alison's cup of hot tea. Stacy, looking just as horrified as if she had accidentally added the moth herself, grabbed for the cup, but Alison had pulled it away. Pensively, she had stared down at the insect as it struggled feebly. Was this, she had wondered, what it had been like for Obsidian to come home?

Alison brought herself back to the here and now just as Robert came charging out of the building. He grabbed her third cigarette from her hands and stuck it in his mouth, grabbing the pack with the other hand.

"You either stop or you buy next time," he told her. "And I'm choosing lunch." She did not argue, even though it meant they'd wind up someplace where everything was fried. She secretly suspected Robert would eat Crisco with a spoon, as long as it was sprinkled with sugar.

"And you got a message," he said, after three drags. He fished a crumpled paper from his pocket. "The phone people called back." He knew about the bits and pieces, the strange things that didn't fit into the official accidental death of Tamsin McArthur, because they spent a lot of time together, and you had to talk about something, and she didn't like football or care about the Rockies. "They said there was a second number."

She looked at the number. Tam being hassled from two separate numbers? She sighed. Tonight, she thought, after work. She would try to talk to Sary again.

****

It was good to be at Tam's apartment. Even though Alison longed for her own home and kitty and bed, Tam's was quiet and dark, and with the two fans going, even cool. To Alison's relief, no one was there making drinks or dinner.

There was a note from Dana stuck on the refrigerator. Alison had thought at first, because Sary was so much on her mind, that the note read, "Call Sary." Just Dana nagging at her. It took reading it twice to see that it really said, "Sary called." No sooner had Alison figured this out, when the phone began to ring. She looked around. Dana was nowhere to be seen. There was a second note on the stove that read, "Helping Liz and Stacy."

"Hello?" The voice was soft and weak, and even though Alison had only talked to the woman once, she knew her again immediately. "Is this Alison? I need to have you come over." Alison had been planning that very thing, but something about the insistency made her balk.

"I just got home, I need to shower and get something to eat…"

"No. You need to come right now. While Abe is gone. I need to tell you something."

****

The house was dark, and Alison stumbled on the porch. Sary must have been waiting inside, for she pulled the door open before Alison could ring. Again, in the evening light, Alison was reminded of a wraith, or a ghost. She beckoned to Alison—speaking seemed beyond her. There was a straight-backed kitchen chair just inside the door

157

where she had been sitting. Instead of the dining room, she led Alison to the back of the house, to the one room where a light was burning. The master bedroom.

Sary crawled beneath the covers, though the night was warm. Alison sat tentatively in a chair that had been placed by the bed. Beside the chair was an end table, and on it was a book, an ashtray, and several empty bottles of spring water, as if Abel Washington had taken up vigil here often.

"What?" began Alison, and then stopped herself. Because Sary's face was torn with pain. She waited.

"I wanted to be a lesbian," said Sary finally. "I tried so hard to be a lesbian. No one had ever cared about me like those women did. No one had thought what I said mattered. I looked at the straight feminists, and I thought, 'How do they put up with that shit every day? How do they try to keep things equal in their relationships *every day*? The kids. The chores. The outside work. How do they have the energy to do it?' I *wanted* to be a lesbian."

She had been speaking to the wall up to this moment, now she turned her head to Alison. "But I wasn't a lesbian," she said. "Tam said once, 'I'm not a lesbian because I can't have sex with men. I can have sex with men, they just can't tear my heart out the way that women can.' It was like that. I could pretend, I could do the sex, but when my heart went out, it went out to a man." She turned her head away again. "And even though they all said *they* didn't have a choice, they acted as if *I* had a choice. And I didn't. Because if I could have chosen, I would have chosen to be a lesbian." She sighed heavily, and Alison shifted in her chair, wondering if this was what she had been called to hear. "I thought," Sary said, "that maybe things could go on kind of the same way. I could have a husband, and still have women close to me." She blinked rapidly—her eyes were glittering with tears. "Do you know what one of those women said to me? 'I've wasted my time,' she said. 'I don't waste my time on straight women.'"

"It was the climate," Alison said, aching for her, aching for Liz. "Maybe now," she said, and then stopped, because the truth was that neither she nor any of her close friends really hung out with straight women, and though they didn't say it out loud, it was because it wasted their time. Or, maybe, not wasted it so much as squandered it. You only had so much time for work and friends and lovers, and you chose to give it to other lesbians.

"I wanted to find Tam because she would help me," said Sary.

"The bone marrow," said Alison, but Sary waved that away.

"I didn't even let myself think of that. I've been sick a long time—there've been too many false hopes. I wanted Tam to help me. I want you to help me. Because I tried hard to be a lesbian."

"I don't know what you want," said Alison, though she was beginning to have a terrible suspicion, a suspicion so strong that all she could think of doing was standing up and getting out of the place, getting out of the sickroom, getting out of the house whose only soundtrack was sitcoms, getting out of the nice neighborhood made up of single family dwellings too expensive for either her or her friends to afford.

"You do," said Sary. "You know what I want. I want you to help me die."

Alison closed her eyes. This was the kind of thing that she discussed with Michelle or Janka or her father, the kind of plans you made with your family, whoever you had chosen them to be. I am willing to live like *this* but not like *that*. Pull the plug if *that* happens. Tell them to remove the feeding tubes. Don't try to revive me if it looks like a major attack. It was not something you discussed with a woman you knew a little less than two weeks. This was what happened when you went against your better judgment and brought a casserole.

"Sary," she said, half rising from her chair, "this isn't...." And then she stopped, for Tam's sister had fixed her eyes upon her face, those burning, feverish eyes that were the only thing about her that seemed still alive. Alison was drawn to her against her will, remembering the story Sary had told about the three young women who had taken her out of the hospital with them, about how one had taken off her own coat in the blinding snow, though she was not the one they had come for, because they believed that she was a lesbian.

So right, said the small voice of Michelle, so she scammed a couple of dykes before, and now she's going to scam you the same way. She's not a dyke, she's a straight girl with all the heterosexual privilege in the world. Let her nuclear family take care of her.

"This is something your husband should do," said Alison, standing now but unable, somehow, to begin her move towards the door.

"No." Sary shook her head, a move that was, for her, vehement, though it barely fluttered her hair and her earrings. "He's going to have it hard enough as it is—if it ever comes out, he could never bear it if one of the children accused him of killing me. He would crumble under that, and he has to be there for them.

Alison put her hand up to her face. "And what if it comes out, and I'm implicated?" she asked. "What about me?"

Sary said nothing. You think, she had said, that you will come to a place where you will know all the answers, or where you at least will be resigned. Instead, you come to a place where you are merely tired. And now she had come to a place where all she could do was wait. She had asked the question, and now she would wait for the answer to be yes.

"I can't..." began Alison, and Sary swiftly interrupted.

"Tam would have helped me," she said. "Tam would have made sure that everything went right," and it was as if she had said, 'But she was killed, she was murdered, and you don't know who, and your people don't even know that it happened.'

"Sary," Alison said, "I'm not ready for this. Let me...."

"No," said Sary, "it has to be now. While everyone is away. I made Abe and the kids go to his mother's, and Kathy's at work. We need several hours." She opened her clenched, claw hand and a pamphlet fell onto the coverlet. Alison did not even have to look at it to see that it was from the Hemlock Society. She had been around too many AIDS victims to be unfamiliar with that cover.

"No," she said, wanting to be back in her own place, where women were discussing quilts or houses or babies or soccer—anything but killing themselves, and what role you would play in the death, "I...."

"Alison," said Sary, "it has to be you. It has to be you, because I have something to tell you."

☞ 14 ☜

Sary had everything they needed in the table beside the bed. She had the painkillers, carefully stashed in a box with a lock. Children in the house. Alison remembered, mainly because of her mother's hysteria when she was discovered, a hot afternoon decades before in the back of her parents' closet, eating the entire pink contents of a bottle of baby aspirin as if they were dinner mints. It had been the taste that had hooked her, though. She could not imagine Carl or Donny being attracted to the shiny capsules that looked more like plastic than anything edible.

Sary had the bottle of Scotch. She had, and this was the worst of all, the roll of Saran Wrap. The widest roll you could buy, the kind that clings. Alison wondered how she had explained that to her husband, stashed there among the Michener novels. Or was he just operating on the Clinton plan—'don't ask, don't tell?' I won't ask if you please, please, *please* won't tell me. She had a big towel to put under her, because she was afraid that, at the last, she might shit the bed, and that was not the way she wanted her husband to find her. She gave Alison the clean up instructions without asking if she would mind—she had already put all the energy she could spare into asking, and the one question would have to cover everything. As she tipped her head back and began swallowing the capsules, one by one, Alison became aware of how much that agreement meant. Don't let him find me in my own shit. Don't let the kids find me at all. If something goes wrong, don't let him call the ambulance, and if you can't stop him, don't let them revive me. Protect me. Protect me.

She swallowed the capsules fiercely, by handfuls, as if she were going towards something joyful, the way Alison had swallowed peyote (capsuled because it upset her stomach) in her druggie days. For a moment Alison was afraid Sary would choke, would bring it all back up again, but she knew herself. She had been a druggie herself, Alison remembered, and just because heroin had been her Drug Of Choice did not mean she had not snatched and tried everything that came along. Alison again thought of mushroom trips up on the cliffs that gave Red Rocks Park its name, and the ritual with which they had prepared, Michelle bent over her mortar and pestle for up to an hour, while Alison used the kitchen to prepare treats that would delight them hours later. In the background, Alix Dobkin and Baba Yaga would play.

As if she had read her mind, Sary paused a moment to instruct her to turn the tape player on. Alison had almost expected something from the years Sary had mimicked the lesbians, but what came on instead was Woody Guthrie, singing about Geronimo's Cadillac.

"I can't stand New Age music," said Sary, catching her eye. "Gotta have something upbeat." For a moment they both smiled at one another as the music took them back, and it was as if they had both forgotten what was happening. Then Sary put her hand up to her mouth one last time. She laid her head back against her pillow, her eyes closed. Could it be working so soon? The pamphlet was still on the bed, unopened. Everything had happened so quickly Alison had not even looked at it. She cleared her throat.

"Yes," said Sary, as if it were a question. She did not open her eyes. Alison damned her and damned herself. Sary she damned because she had used the exchange of information as an enticement. Herself she damned because she had fallen for it with open eyes, acting not with compassion, but her obsession with Tam's death.

"Yes," said Sary again, and this time she opened her eyes. "Yes," she said, "I did it. That was what you wanted to know, wasn't it?"

"Did what?" Alison asked, thinking that it was already too late, that she had lost her lucidity, and she would carry any information with her to her grave.

"I killed her," said Sary, and she turned upon Alison eyes that were not yet clouded with drugs, but as burning and intense as the moment she had asked for her help. "I killed my sister."

There was a moment of silence, or rather a moment in which there was no talking, for in the background Woody sang about setting the Indian Nation free. Absently, Alison turned the stereo down, turning the sentences Sary had said over and over in her head, as if they could be made to mean something else.

"But, why?" she asked, and then remembered the romance she had read, the one that had used Sary's pregnancy for it's treacley plot. "*Love's Lost Child,*" she blurted, even at this moment feeling a little embarrassed by saying the name out loud.

Sary shook her head, a movement much heavier and slower than it had been a half an hour before. "No. I was angry about that, furious. My tragedy, my life—she took it and turned it into a dime store novel! Like what I had been through could be brushed away as easily as closing a book. I didn't want to talk to her, be around her. I didn't think ahead, didn't realize I'd have to give up the baby without her. And after I had done that," she shrugged, "I was afraid to go back to her and tell her. So I became angry about that. And when I finally wasn't angry anymore, she'd moved, and no one knew exactly where to find her."

"Then why," began Alison, and then stopped. She looked at Sary with something like horror. She couldn't have been that selfish, could she? She couldn't…she braced herself, waiting for Sary to say something about the journey, and company and fear. Waiting for her to say that she had needed to have her sister waiting at the end of the tunnel.

"My daughter," was what she said instead. "My own daughter. Do you have any idea what that felt like—to have lost her for so long, and then to finally get her back? I'd registered with Birthparents years ago when I thought she'd be old enough to start looking. I'd almost forgotten. Then to get her back again when I was dying! To want to know everything about her, and be too tired? I'd snatch at her during my up moments, like she was some kind of treat I only had so long to stuff down. And what did I find out? That she was a prostitute." She shook her head, and the movement was perceptively slower than it had been just a few minutes before. "The apple doesn't fall far from the tree, does it? I was out on the street when I was sixteen, too. I know how you get money. It was bearable. But to have it be your child who's telling you these stories....it made me want to weep. I knew that was part of the reason she was doing it. She wanted to make me know how badly she had suffered because I had abandoned her. Maybe if we'd had more time, it wouldn't have all had to come out in such a gush. But there was only so much time, and she wanted to make sure I knew it all. The way she had been abused in her home. They shoved their religion down her like they were force feeding a goose. The main part of it was that she was bad. Everything she did, everything she felt was bad. She never mentioned sexual abuse, but I'm sure it was there. She went into the sex trade so easily. Or maybe it was just a way to show her parents. Do you know—I don't even know their names. She just called them 'they'. Not Mom and Dad. 'She' did this, she would say. 'He' did that." She closed her eyes and then opened them again. The effort was becoming obvious. "She was a lesbian. That was why she ran, they never could accept it. I could celebrate and honor that. She was a prostitute. I could understand that. And she was into the s/m scene. I couldn't even grasp that. I had never understood that, not even with my own sister. With Tam I always wondered if it wasn't because we had been abused as children, if part of that hadn't gotten accidentally mixed in with her sexual stuff. And my own daughter—it was like another point in the case. She had obviously been abused, so what was all the beating and hurting about if not reliving, trying to come to terms with that?"

Alison opened her mouth. *I* wasn't abused as a child, *I'm* in the scene and *I'm* not living out anything from my past. Ready to defend her honor on the edge of a woman's death bed. She closed it again.

"Yeah," said Sary, "I know." she shot her a look that would have been wry, were she not losing control of her features. The edges of her mouth and forehead were melting, as if she were being redrawn by

Picasso. "She told me you were in the scene, too. She told me everything you had done together."

"I never touched—!"

Sary held up a finger the way another person might have held up a hand. "I know. She had a story about everyone. Everyone had beaten her, fucked her, stuck their fist up her ass. Anyone she thought might hurt me. She tried to tell me it had happened with my husband, with my friends. That's why I didn't believe her at first when she told me what she had done with Tam." She was fading, and this was something Alison needed to hear. She put her hand on Sary's face, hating herself for not just allowing her to slip quietly out to Woody.

"But why," she asked, bringing her face close to Sary's, "would you believe anything she said? Why would you believe it more about Tam than me or anyone else."

Sary recalled herself with an obvious effort. "You know," she said, "how your mother used to go through your things? You're born with that! It's an instinct! It's genetic!" She closed her eyes as if she were going to sleep, and then gave a little start. "My own sister," she said and closed her eyes again.

Alison could not bring herself to try to shake her awake again, despite her unanswered questions. She was already disgusted with herself for making Sary's last minutes a confession rather than allowing her to send fond little messages. And who was going to listen to this death bed confession? Was she—a policewoman whose possibility of promotion was never more than slim to nonexistent—going to get on the stand and describe her part in another woman's euthanasia? Better that Tam's death went down as an accident than that.

Sary looked as if she were sleeping peacefully. Alison knew that this was when she was supposed to cover her face with the plastic, just in case something went wrong. She picked up the roll of Saran Wrap and then put it back down. She could not do it, not now. She was not sure what it was that made her hesitate. Was it the knowledge that, if she covered Sary's face now, she would be the one killing her, no matter what she had ingested? Or was in more the image she had of herself lifting Sary's head, wrapping and sealing her like leftover turkey from Christmas? Either way, it was just not possible.

Perhaps it would be possible when Stacy arrived. Alison did not know what part of Sary's cryptic phone message had made her beep Stacy (the beeper was the new toy of Mistress Anastasia), and she suspected she was being selfish to drag her into this mess, but she was glad she had done it, none the less. She looked at her watch. Stacy had said she would be along as soon as they were done rehearsing Liz's fantasy. Make it another half hour. She could not just sit here and watch Sary.

She located the laundry room, started a load of towels. The bunk beds in the boys' room were long overdue for a change—not just the sheets, but the bedspreads badly needed washing. She stripped them, and decided to do Obsidian's as well.

The room in which Obsidian's clothes were hung seemed almost unlived in. Perhaps, before her arrival, it had been a guest or storage room. Probably the latter, for the bed was a futon couch like Tam's, and the cover underneath the sheets matched the decor of the living room. There were no posters on the walls—none of the things with which Alison had claimed her territory as a teenager. The few items sitting on the dresser and the window sill—an alarm clock, a radio— were brand new, as were most of the clothes in the closet. She must have come off the street with virtually nothing. Perhaps Sary had mustered herself for a shopping trip or two. Obsidian's leathers were nowhere to be seen. What kind of job, Alison wondered, did she have that allowed her to wear them to work?

She was leaving the room with the bundle of laundry when she suddenly remember Sary asking, "You know how your mother used to go through your things? It's genetic!" Had Sary found something in here that had sent her to Tam's house with murder on her mind? She looked around. There were few places to hide things in the almost empty room. On impulse, she lifted the mattress. Bingo—resting on the slats was a whole hoard of magazines. *On Our Backs, Venus Infers, Bad Attitude* and the lesbian issue of *Newsweek*, which looked almost like a Norman Rockwell compared to the others. Alison hesitated. If she took them with her, Obsidian might realize that something was amiss with her mother's death, but she could not bring herself to sit down and look at paper skinflicks with Sary dying two rooms away. Finally, she looked at the cover of each sex magazine carefully. They were all recent copies—she could find them either at the Book Garden or Stacy's house.

On her way to check on the wash (anything to keep her from checking on Sary) she remembered the crumpled paper Robert had given her earlier, and made a quick detour to the kitchen. She unloaded the top tier of the dish washer while she waited for the phone to be picked up.

"AT&T research," said a voice that sounded both giggly and a little confused.

"Oh," said Alison. How did this fit? Had the *phone company* been harassing Tam?

"I've never been *called* before." Another giggle. "Mostly *I* call."

Before she could process any of this, Alison heard a car door slam. Hastily she replaced the receiver and hurried to the front of the house, leaving the sheets in the hall. She almost cried with relief at the sight of Stacy's station wagon. The front door locked with a dead bolt—she removed the key from the inside and locked it behind her as she went outside to greet her. She didn't want anything weird to happen, like a solicitous neighbor slipping in unnoticed and calling 911 in a panic.

"This better be good," said Stacy, and then, catching sight of her face, "Oh, shit, what happened?"

"Sary called," began Alison. "Sary called," she said again, like a broken record. Then, suddenly, she was crying, and Stacy was holding her as she choked out the story—the phone call, the pills, the confession, and the dreadful roll of plastic wrap still waiting beside the bed.

"Oh, no," breathed Stacy, and nothing else, because there was nothing else to say.

Finally Alison mopped up her face with the tail of her shirt, blew her nose on a Kleenex offered by Stacy, and looked back at the house. This, she knew, and she knew by a glance that Stacy knew, was it. This was the moment to go back inside, and put the towels in the drier, put the sheets in the washer, and then finally seal Sary's doom as she had asked. Stacy took her hand, and she took a deep breath.

Then the car pulled up.

It seemed, at first, something out of a bad dream—because Sary had sent her husband and children to his mother's, so it could not be him climbing out of the driver's door. And Obsidian was at work, so her appearance was equally impossible. It was not until Abel Washington spoke that the dream sequence ended and the panic set in.

"Oh, hello," he said to Alison, in a voice that wondered what she was doing in front of his house at night and then, as if his explanation might spark hers, "Kathy got sick at work. She needed a ride home."

Alison opened her mouth, and then shut it, because Stacy was twisting on her hand so viciously it could only be a command, and the command could only be, "Shut the fuck up."

"We just dropped by," said Stacy, as if they were making polite conversation at a party, or in a store, or any place but in front of a house where a woman was doing her best to die. "We wanted to see if you needed anything, but when we saw the lights were off, we figured everyone was in bed." Obsidian had trailed over to stand beside her mother's husband. She did look ill in the street light, but perhaps that was only because of the dead white makeup she wore. She was dressed, as Alison had surmised, in leather, and her lips had been painted black. Where the hell did she work?

"No, nothing," said Abel, accepting the explanation and dismissing the offer all with the two words. He turned to the house as if they no longer existed.

"What are you doing?" hissed Alison to Stacy as he went up the walk. "I can't let him walk in there!"

"You can't stop him, babe." If Stacy's voice had been full of bravado, or carried a hint of order, Alison would have rushed up the walk and seized the man's hand as he bent to the lock. But there was nothing but compassion in the sentence, and as it washed over her, Alison suddenly knew Stacy was right. She had promised Sary that she would protect her, but Abel's arrival had made that promise worthless. Because Sary, one way or the other, was going to die within the next few months, and Alison had ahead of her forty or fifty years, and a career that could not afford to be besmirched with charges of assisting a suicide. Maybe if it had been Michelle, maybe if it had been Stacy. Someone she loved. But it was just a straight girl who had hung out with dykes a while, just a woman who, by her own confession, had killed one of their own.

****

The story of Sary's suicide attempt was not even big enough to be in the paper the next day, but there were only a few hospitals in town, and Alison's third call had revealed the information that Sary was fine, able to see visitors and resting at Rose Medical Center. She said thank-you and hung up the phone. She would not visit. What could she and Sary say to one another after what had been said the evening before?

Stacy owned the copy of *On Our Backs* that had been beneath Obsidian's mattress. It was the one with the telling photo in it, although it's evidence was redundant. "Is that the kid?" Stacy had asked the night before, after Abel had opened the door and Obsidian had stood outlined in the light. "Is that Tam's niece? I know her," she said, "I saw her at Powersurge." And that was when it all came together. Your friend Tam likes the young ones, Stacy had said. Her own aunt! Sary had said. Of course, Tam had not known that when she played with the girl at Powersurge....

Obsidian was just a kid who knew enough about dykes to be out, and enough about the scene to attend a lesbian leather event. It was just fate that, when Obsidian ran from her adoptive parents, she ran to Seattle, and Tam lived only forty-five minutes away, just fate that some photographer had captured the two of them together at a dungeon. Without that photo, more than likely Sary would have dismissed Obsidian's accusation of Tam with all the rest. With it, Obsidian had been able to destroy a family. Yet, thought Alison, she had kept it hidden, rather than using it as a weapon to back up her story. What had been going on in her mind? And what was it about the *Newsweek* magazine? Alison had gone through her own copy, and found nothing that would horrify a snooping mother. So why did she keep coming back to it, even now as she sat in the semi-darkness of the Rubyfruit, working on getting beer drunk? Carla had been short with her, on an obvious tear from having to wait on the leather women.

I can't do this tonight, Alison thought, and then thanked her lucky stars that all she *had* to do was sit in the audience alone, drinking beer after beer while the crowd howled at the MSIL Contestants. The place was packed—Alison was saving the seats at her table only by force. She had ordered several pitchers from Carla early in the evening, realizing that the crowd was soon going to make waitress service to the ringside seats a thing of the past.

Stacy stuck her head out from backstage, and then made a little dart down the runway to Alison's table. Her dark, curly hair had been brushed and fluffed and glittered by the gay boys at the hair place that afternoon. Stacy liked being on stage, and she liked looking good while she performed. She was wearing a pair of her long, dangley earrings, and as she bent over Alison for a kiss, they brushed down across the top of her head and her shoulder, just tiny feather touches. Maybe she *could* do this, Alison thought, trying to clear her mind of all thoughts of Sary and justice and Tam cold and stiff underwater. Tam was the one for whom she should feel sorry, so why did she feel as if she owed Sary an apology?

There were three women vying for the Colorado title and they had already given their speeches. Now it was time for the fantasy. Stacy was on the stage setting up, ignoring the whistling and calls. Packaging was not what had sold Alison on Stacy—she thought she was hot in her soccer uniform or her old jeans with her hair pulled up in a pony tail. But she loved her play outfits as well, loved the way she was able to shake off her everyday shit and don the persona of what Alison thought of as the Evil Femme. Stacy worried about money and her cat and recalling Amendment Two just like the rest of them. The Evil Femme existed only for her own pleasure. Alison loved the way the Evil Femme mixed up every straight boy/bad girl/leather dyke fantasy and fashion and stuck them all together, assuming they would please others because they pleased her. Right now, for example, while all the other femmes who expected to go on stage were wearing spike heels, the Evil Femme was wearing a pair of short black cowgirl boots. She owned the spikes, but they were too expected. Her short skirt was black with metallic silver spots, and the two ruffles that made the skirt climbed up high on her thighs and made a point four inches lower in front and back. She was wearing a heavy, majorly bad girl jacket over it—a motorcycle jacket with chains and studs that you'd expect to see on a big butch woman. The hair, the skirt, the jacket, the boots—it worked. She was helping Dana, who *was* wearing the spikes, move a huge roulette wheel—six feet across—onto the table. There was going to be some major femme energy on the stage— the third woman who was helping was Stacy's friend Beth, and she, too, was decked out femme and bad and wild.

Dana looked down at her hand, and swore. She said something to Stacy and Beth, asking a question, and then turned and came down the ramp to Alison's table.

"Let me see Tam's keys," she said, putting out her hand. "I broke a nail."

Puzzled, Alison fished the keys from her jacket pocket and placed them in Dana's palm.

"Damnit!" said Dana, loud enough for the girls in the ringside tables to follow with interest. "You've taken her clippers off!"

"I didn't do anything," Alison protested defensively, but Dana was not listening.

"These aren't Tam's keys," she said, holding the chain up to the light. "Where's her clippers? Where's her roach clip? Where's her whip?" She tossed the keys disdainfully back onto the table and strutted back up the ramp to whistles.

Alison picked up the ring of keys that Tam's landlady had given her, the ring *she* had said the police had given *her*. She had not really paid much attention to them before, but now that she was noticing, wasn't it odd that the ring held only the keys to Tam's apartment? Alison's own key ring held her car and bike keys, plus a spare to both Michelle and her dad's place. This was much more like the ring upon which you might keep your spare or visitor keys.

The music came on suddenly, something with a hard, pounding beat that made you want to fuck immediately. Beth gave the wheel a good hard spin. The three women stood there as if oblivious to the crowd, each clutching a fist full of money as she watched to see if her number would come up.

The lights went out suddenly, and there was murmuring as the crowd wondered if this was part of the act, for the music was still pounding. Alison heard a slurping sound behind her as if the girls at the next table had seized the moment to hop right up on the table and do the nasty. The lights went back on, and now Liz was *on* the roulette wheel, her arms and legs spread-eagled and strapped down. Alison's heart skipped a beat as, for a moment, she imagined herself in Liz's position, helpless and open to the women spinning the wheel. It was a fantasy from hell and it pulled her and teased her and made her close her eyes and then open them again and lean forward. Out of the corner of her eye, she saw Obsidian sitting at a table across the room. Right after her mother almost died? she thought and then, No, I'm not going to think of that. Distraction was not hard—the wheel had stopped with Liz's legs open to Dana, and she had crawled right up on the table and pulled on a glove like she was going to fist her right there. Maybe she did fist her right there—it was hard to see because Beth had set the table spinning again. This time, instead of waiting for the stop, Stacy grabbed a peg and slowed it just enough to catch hold of Dana's foot as she knelt over Liz.

For a moment you thought she was going to pull Dana off the table, but what she did was use Dana as a handle to leap up on the table herself. Again Alison flashed herself into Liz's position. God, she loved femme women, loved their power. The wheel was spinning again, fast enough to ruffle Stacy's short skirt as she stood with her legs spread and braced over Liz's body. Three minutes—the maximum time that could be used—was not enough for her to do all the things that Alison wanted to see. She wanted to see Stacy sink to her knees and bring her cunt down hard to Liz's mouth, the way that she sometimes did when Alison was bound beneath her. She wanted to see Stacy flip up her skirt to reveal Mr. Winkie, and then she wanted her to fuck Liz's mouth hard while Dana slammed her fist inside her. She wanted—but the music was slowing and the lights were going down, and the three minutes were coming to an end. Which was the point, Alison realized—every woman there was left wanting, imagining the fantasy she desired most. Stacy reached into the pockets of her bad girl jacket, and began throwing the bundles of gloves and lube as the wheel continued to spin. Women in the audience leapt for them as if for a bridal bouquet. One landed on Alison's table. She pulled the glove onto her right hand, giving it that little snap. All over the room women were doing the same—snapping instead of applause.

The lights dimmed again. Alison was close enough to the stage to see that Liz had been released, and was being helped backstage. Stacy and Dana were trying to move the wheel, but it was giving them trouble. Rolling it out had been easier than tipping it back onto its side. The natives were getting restless and calling for more. Alison hopped up onto the stage to give a hand. The second contestant who was dressed like a baton twirler, was waiting impatiently in the wings. The woman running the lights was having problems—they were switching on and off in front, and it was almost pitch black back behind the curtain.

"Com'ere," someone said right into Alison's ear, seizing a handful of her hair and throwing her back against a wall. She was fairly certain it was Stacy. But what if it wasn't? It was not just Liz's crew that was behind the curtain, but also everyone involved in the third performance. Alison enlarged the thought into a fantasy—an unknown woman taking her and then disappearing before the lights came on; leaving her forever wondering, Was it you? You?

"I want it now, give it to me now," the woman was demanding in Alison's ear. She had wrapped one leg around Alison's waist to anchor herself, and with a last, "Now!" leaned backwards, holding onto Alison's shoulders. One false move was going to topple them both, but Alison was not thinking of that as she ran her hands up the woman's thighs. She was wearing stockings, but no panties. Her cunt was wet and open enough to fall into.

When she first came out, oral sex had been Alison's perversion of choice. It was partly safer sex that had changed that. It did not seem worth it to use a dental dam—part of what she had liked was how messy women were, how they got all over your chin and nose—yet it did not seem safe not to use them. S/M dykes were the only lesbians she knew who took safer sex seriously, and they tended to be obsessive.

And, she had changed partly because Stacy really liked to be fucked. Liked to be fucked hard—chided Alison if she wasn't really putting her back into it, if she wasn't going in all the way, if she wasn't making her scream and cry. Gradually, her preference had become Alison's. And wasn't that the perfect set up—you liking to do what your girlfriend wanted best? So Alison got a huge rush when she pushed three fingers into the woman's cunt. The lights could come back on at any moment—she knew that—and it just made it more urgent. Because of the position, there was little room to move her arm the way she wanted to, but the woman was taking care of that for her, riding her hand up and down. She gave a little hop, and suddenly she had both legs around Alison's waist, and her arms around her neck, and she was sliding her cunt up and down on Alison's whole hand like she was jumping on a bed.

"Fuck me, fuck me hard!" she was saying, and it wasn't a whisper in Alison's ear anymore, it had become way louder than that and the other women backstage had tuned in to what was happening and were adding their own chorus: "Take it girl, make it yours, make her give you what you want!" Was that Stacy's voice off to the left, instead of in Alison's ear? Alison almost lost her stride, but the woman would not allow this—now she was clutching Alison's head with two handfuls of hair while she drove herself to orgasm. She gave a moan that was almost a shriek, and the sound was echoed by the unseen audience. Suddenly in a hurry, she unwrapped herself and, feet on the ground, pulled away from Alison. Fifteen seconds after Alison had peeled the glove, the backstage lights came back on.

The second contestant's music had come up, and one of her people stuck her head back behind the curtain with a curt "Shh!" because every one of the ten or so women backstage was laughing and talking, "Was that you? It sure sounded like you! It must have been Stacy—nobody else screams like that! No, it was Liz, she got all hot from the fantasy!" Unobtrusively, Alison kicked the glove back behind the props. The stage manager, a round little butch woman wearing a vest with a Sisterhood of Steel logo, came back to hiss the extras into their chairs. Everyone from Liz's fantasy hopped down into the ringside chairs Alison had saved for them. They were one short, so Stacy sat on Alison's lap, her short skirt riding up as Alison placed a hand on her leg. Was she acting this way because she had been the one, or was she just excited by the voyeurism? Covertly Alison glanced around the table. All of the women wearing skirts—Dana, Stacy, Beth—were flushed and excited. Had it been one of them, or one of the women waiting to go on stage? Would she ever know?

The music was going, but nothing was happening on stage. Abruptly the sound was cut and those in the front rows could hear the second candidate arguing furiously with the stage manager. The words 'respect' and 'apology' rang through over and over. The women at Alison's table all looked guiltily at one another, and then ducked their heads to hide smiles. Liz poured beer for everyone. Stacy tried to engage Alison in a little tongue activity, but Alison, suddenly shy, ducked her head.

"Aw, dammit," said Liz, and everyone looked at the stage. Carla had stepped onto the stage, a determined look on her face. She must have slid past the stage manager from the back, because there was now no way to reach the stage through the audience. Stacy and Liz exchanged a hopeless look and then both turned to Alison who shook her head. Whatever Carla had to say was going to be bad, but trying to remove her would only make things worse.

"I know that a lot of you have seen me around in the leather scene in the past year," Carla said into the mike that had been left on the end of the runway from the speeches. The light tech, who was getting a little bored now that everything was under control, hit her with a spot. The audience, who had not yet realized this was not part of the show, cheered and shouted that, yes, they had seen Carla, and would like to see more.

"I'm here to tell you that I consider everything I've done over the last year in the name of s/m sick, that I consider myself used and preyed on by the s/m community." There was a startled silence. One woman started to call out that that's why *she* was there, prey on *her*! but was shushed by her partner. "The women in this community took advantage of me when I was vulnerable—and I know I'm not the only one! I know there are women out there *right now* who are wondering how the hell they ended up like this! Am I right?"

"Get me a vodka tonic, Carla!" yelled someone in the back, and Alison winced, because she didn't want Carla to be harassed any more than *she* wanted to be harassed by Carla. Damnit, why hadn't she taken the time to talk to Carla—she had known she was upset. She turned her head to see if she knew the woman yelling and when she turned it back, another woman was climbing up beside Carla. At first she thought it was an audience member who was tired of the preaching and wanted the show to go on, and she tensed herself for a fight. But the second woman conversed with Carla in whispers and then stepped up to the mike herself.

"I can validate every word this woman says," Obsidian told the audience. Her hair was blonde tonight, and she had accessorized her leather pants and tank top with a little dagger strapped to her upper arm. "I am not afraid to say that the women's leather community has nothing but using on their minds." Both she and Carla were being caught in the smoky mirror paneling, imperfect images that followed their movements only vaguely. Alison was reminded of the window at the GLBSCC, the one that had reflected the two dim shapes of two people arguing. She looked from the mirror to the mike and then back again. What was it that was giving her such a strong sense of déjà vu? She looked at the long, white shape into which the panel translated Obsidian's hair. Of course, that was it. The person at the center also had long blonde hair. Alison had seen Obsidian only with purple before. "It meant nothing," one of the people had said. Why was Alison, who had thought only in generics before, thinking now of both people as women? 'That one, at least, had kind of a happy ending,' Marnie had said. What else had Marnie said? 'I think not', coldly, when Michelle tried to push Tam as a guest speaker. Did that mean she knew something the rest of them did not? Like, for example, that Tam had been the woman with whom Obsidian had been pleading? Was it Obsidian who had been calling Tam, rather than Sary? Was it more than coincidence that she and Tam, after playing at Powersurge, had ended up in the same town?

There was more commotion on stage. The manager had turned the mike off from the back, and had one hand under Carla's elbow, one under Obsidian's. Carla started to balk, but the manager whispered something that made her surly but silent. She climbed back into the crowd. Margie, her boss, was waiting. She went right into a furious whisper—you could tell that what she really wanted to do was grab hold of Carla's ear and keep twisting. Obsidian, wisely, decided to go off the other side of the stage. The audience was packed in far too closely for her to jump down—Dana, who was closest to the runway, reached a hand up to steady her.

"Pick your glasses up," she warned, and everyone hastily complied. Obsidian stepped down onto the table with a thump that rattled the pitcher. Her situation, however, did not seem much better. There was no way she could squeeze through the crowd—and into an audience who was largely hostile about being called jackals—without a major commotion, and the music for the second fantasy was restarting. They couldn't just toss her back up on the stage—if their group caused any additional commotion, Liz was going to be disqualified for sure. Liz shrugged—Hey, we might as well be good sports—and moved over to sit on Beth's lap. For a moment it looked as if Obsidian might choose to continue standing on the table. Finally, grudgingly, and with the air of doing a favor, she stepped down and sat in the empty chair.

There was so much lying going on, thought Alison. Sary had let Alison think that Obsidian had been living with her all along. Why was that lie important? Obsidian had lied about her sexual activities to punish her mother. Sary had lied about her motive to find Tam, never once mentioned the bone marrow. Tam had lied to Dana, telling her she has been wasting and celibate without her, when she really had been partying. What else was a lie? What about Sary's suicide attempt? Was that a lie, too? Alison had believed, while it was happening, that Sary only had a stranger to turn to when it came the time for death. But was that, too, a lie? Had she needed a deathbed so that there could be a deathbed confession? Mothers do strange things for their kids, Michelle had said so back at Tam's, referring to money and cheerleading. And they protected them as well. Was that what the scene, played out with Woody in the back ground, had been all about? A mother protecting her daughter? And what was it that was bothering her about that fucking *Newsweek* magazine?

"Obsidian," Alison said, sotto voce, leaning across Dana, "Have you met Dana? Dana was Tam's lover."

There must have been a lull in the music at that point, because everyone on the floor heard "You fucking bitch!" though Obsidian's voice went right back to a whisper immediately afterwards, "You fucking bitch!" she hissed again, while Dana looked bewildered and, as she had for the past few days, about to cry.

"Yeah," said Alison conversationally, "Dana was the reason Tam couldn't be with you any more. Dana wouldn't have allowed *that* for a minute. All she ever allowed her was a party fling. Just one cigarette."

Obsidian was quivering now as if the last phrase had gone to her heart just like an arrow. "I could have taken care of her," she said slowly. "You weren't even giving her what she wanted. I knew there was a reason she was holding back."

"I guess you killed the wrong person after all," said Alison casually.

"I guess so," said Obsidian slowly, without surprise. "But, I guess it's not too late, is it?" Her hand went to her arm.

"Watch out, Dana!" Alison tried to rise, to fling out a hand, but at that moment Stacy shifted, crossing her leg close up under the table so that both were pinned. Obsidian brought her hand up, slashing the sleeve of Dana's dress. Dana did not move, not even to put her fingers up to her arm where the blood oozed. It seemed to Alison almost that she leaned into Obsidian, going as eagerly towards her death as Sary had done. Obsidian raised her arm again.

"You asshole," said Liz, and it was impossible to tell whether she was more pissed off by the knife or the interruption of the contest. She picked up the half full pitcher of beer and threw the whole thing sideways into Obsidian's chest, so that she was hit with the heavy glass. Everyone within ten feet was drenched with Miller lite. Obsidian's chair toppled backwards, knocking her onto a neighboring table. The boot knife flew out of her hand.

"That is it!" said the stage manager angrily, leaning down off the runway. She pointed at Liz. "I am not going to put up with any more of this crap! You are *out!*!"

～ 15 ～

"What'd ya bring?" asked Stacy, rooting around in the box that was sitting on the front seat. "Pie! I didn't know you could make pie. Can you make pie?" she asked, as if suspecting Alison had made a quick stop at the Blue Note Bakery on the way. She herself was carrying her standard potluck contribution, two bottles of apple juice.

"I can make pie," said Alison. "But only one of those is for us. I want to drop the second one off at the Washington's on the way."

"Boy, that's going beyond," said Stacy, shaking her head. "After the way Sary tried to use you?"

"She was a victim, too," said Alison shortly and then, "What I can't believe is that, even though we knew Obsidian lied about everything else, we didn't even think of her lying about Sary."

The weather was doing the Denver thing, which meant, though there had been a thunderstorm earlier in the day, it was now as balmy as spring. The sidewalks were clear, and Carl and Donny were riding up and down the block. Abel Washington was sitting on the steps.

"We brought you a pie," Alison told him shyly.

"Thank you," he said simply. "Thank you for getting her out of this house. I knew there was something wrong with her, but I didn't know it was that bad. When I think that I left Sarah Jean and the kids with her..." He shuddered.

The screen door opened, and onto the porch came Sary

Washington. Walking, instead of wafting. Up five or ten pounds. Smiling. The new bone marrow match had been good.

"I couldn't understand," she said to Alison, as if she had somehow tapped into their conversation in the car, "why she was so reluctant to have our bone marrow matched. I thought she was just angry—I had abandoned her, and then wanted her to save me. She must have known what the test would eventually show. You know, the day Abe finally forced her to go in was the day she confessed. Told me the whole story. Told me her life was over—unless I saved her. Told me she'd had no idea who Tam was until she saw her photo in the book you left, and showed me that photo of her and Tam. Told me she'd freaked out and killed Tam when she found out she was her aunt. I think she knew I thought she had been sexually abused as a child—she plugged right into that. She was the one who planted suicide in my mind—I had the pills, but I wasn't ready to use them yet. She pointed out that a death bed confession is not regarded as hearsay, and suggested hiding those magazines to make it look more real." Including the *Newsweek* with Tam's mailing label. That was what had been bothering Alison—the others had come from a store, but the *Newsweek* had that little white label that said it came from Tam's house. Obsidian had been in Tam's house, *that* was what they should be thinking about. Obsidian must have picked it up at Tam's. Maybe she had read it as she sat on the stairs, waiting for the tub to fill.

"It's over now," said Abe, taking her hand.

The door opened again, and out came a young girl of about seventeen. She was dressed all in black and her manner was a little leery like a feral cat's.

"Come here, Kathy," said Sary, holding out her hand. "Come and meet a friend." She turned back to Alison. "She lied about everything," she said, "and yet we never thought she'd lie about—"

"Who she was," finished Alison. "It never occurred to you that she wasn't your daughter. How did you meet her?" she asked the girl. "How did she get to know you well enough to have your mother's name?"

"At the shelter in Seattle." The girl hung her head down and gently Sary tipped it back with a finger beneath the chin, so that she was looking at Alison.

"There's no need to be afraid," she said softly. "You didn't do anything wrong."

"At the shelter," the girl said again and then shrugged. "There were a bunch of gay kids there—we'd all been thrown out. I guess I bragged a little—maybe my folks had thrown me out, but I had a *real mom* somewhere, and someday *she* was going to take me in. You know?" She spread her hands imploringly. "And one day I couldn't find the number any more."

Sary broke in, "Obsidian had been dogging Tam ever since she met her at Powersurge. That was probably one of the reasons Tam decided to move...as an attempt to shake her. She didn't have to be secretive about it—she thought that the cost of the plane fare would stop a street kid. It did stop her for a couple of months. But when she found out this was where Kathy's birth mother lived, she saw us as a free ride. We paid for her plane fare. Of course! A call from my daughter! Catch the next plane! All she wanted was a place to operate from, a base to pursue Tam. She didn't even know Tam was my sister. She didn't know until after she had killed her. Then she saw the photo in the back of one of the books you'd brought over. By then you were suspicious, and she'd realized she'd made a mistake by taking Tam's keys instead of the spare set, so she showed me the photo in *On Our Backs* and told me the story she'd made up. Crying. She had been taken advantage of, she had her whole life ahead of her. I played right into the script."

"But *why* did she kill her?" asked the girl.

Alison shrugged. "Nobody knows. I'd guess that Tam told her to get lost, Dana was coming, and she couldn't deal with it. Probably up 'til that time Tam had been putting up with her, probably playing with her. But Dana was Tam's one love—she couldn't have a kid coming around when she got here. Tam must have cut her off totally—she even called US West to register a complaint when Obsidian persisted in calling her from home and work."

"Working doing phone surveys," said Stacy softly. "That's why she could wear her leather to work."

"All her validation came through sex," continued Alison as if she had not been interrupted. "She had nothing else. She pulled the switch downstairs—she knew about it because it had blown once while she was visiting. She put the lock from her nose onto the box to keep Tam from resetting it, although she probably waited to pull it until she thought Tam was undressed. Easier to use an extension than to put everything on again to go downstairs. She waited until she could hear Tam running the bath water. Then she went up again, quietly. She had lifted Tam's keys, used them to let herself in and then lock the door behind her. She had seen Tam use the vibrator while she was in the tub. All she had to do was surprise her and drop it in the water and…" Alison raised her hands, "that's all she wrote."

"Speaking of writing," said Stacy, "why did she take Tam's notebook and mess with the computer?"

"I know that," said Sary before Alison could speak. "It was because she was doing her old thing, wasn't it? Making a story out of the truth."

"That's what we guess," agreed Alison. "She wrote about Obsidian and she didn't do it with love. We called Tam's publisher—we know from her that Tam used Obsidian as a minor character in her new book—a fuck of Blaze's who was eventually thrown aside. But Tam was having a cash flow problem—the move had drained her, and her royalties weren't due for another two months so she sat down and wrote a quick piece of porn. Using her experience with Obsidian as the main story line. It must have been heartbreaking when she found it."

Sary closed her eyes. "I never thought I'd say this about her," she said slowly. "And I feel bad about it. But Tam almost brought it on, didn't she?"

"Nobody deserves to be killed," said Alison shortly. But she knew what Sary was trying to put to words. Tam McArthur had made her living by feeding off the emotions of others and finally one of them had fed off her. The only person she had seemed to care about had been Dana, and that 'love' would take Dana years to recover from. As much as she mourned the passing of Katie Copper, Alison had shed no tears for Tam McArthur.

"What about the photos?" asked Stacy. "I never did get that. If Obsidian was trying to make it look like it was a suicide, why didn't she take the sex toys, too?"

"I don't think she was trying," said Alison. "All she really destroyed were the things that pointed directly to her. I think she took those picture because she was obsessed with Tam. If I had gone ahead and looked through the magazines here, I would have found them. They were stuck inside the *OOB*. I'll bet I would have found the keys, too. She was amazingly lucky that *we* found the body, but the cops found the extra keys and passed them back to the landlady. That would have been the tip off right there."

"So, if she couldn't have Tam, nobody else could either?" asked Stacy. "She must have lost it completely when she realized who Dana was. In her mind, it was Dana who had made her kill Tam. Everything had been fine up until then. She must never have realized that for Tam, she was just one cigarette."

"You know what I can't understand?" said Sary. "She really was angry with me. She *really* felt that I had abandoned her."

"Someone abandoned her," said Alison. "I'll bet Tam was only the last in a long line."

Stacy broke in before they could follow this tangent. "Well," she said to Sary. "We gotta go. We've got a soccer potluck." The children had put down their bikes and climbed up onto the steps. Donny wormed his way onto his half-sister's lap.

"Good-by," said Sary, raising her hand. The last thing that Alison thought, as she drove down the street, was that she was glad she had put the pie into a disposable pan. Because now she had no reason for ever going back.

Kate Allen lives in Denver, Colorado, where she is supported in her writing by a loving and long time lesbian extended family. Since her last book, she has had to send two cats on ahead. Both she and her other four cats are still grieving for the losses, but they are also enjoying a new living space with a back yard. Kate is particularly enjoying not having her computer in the kitchen any more. For those of you who were looking for the phone psychic in this novel, look for Kate Allen's next book, *I Knew You Would Call*.

TELL ME WHAT YOU LIKE   Kate Allen
Alison Kaine enters the world of leather-dykes after a woman is brutally murdered at a Denver bar. In this fast-paced, yet slyly humorous novel, Allen confronts the sensitive issues of S & M, queer-bashers and women-identified sex workers. $9.95   ISBN 0-934678-48-0

IF LOOKS COULD KILL   Frances Lucas
Fast-paced mystery featuring Latina lesbian lawyer Diana Mendoza, currently scriptwriter for a TV series about a woman detective and a hollywood actress suspected of murder. ISBN 0-934678-63-4 $9.95

NUN IN THE CLOSET Joanna Michaels
Probation officer Callie Sinclair takes on a vehicular manslaughter case involving the beautiful owner of a women's bar and the death of the nun who was her passenger. An intriguing mystery exploring the issues of alcoholism and repressed sexuality. ISBN 0-934678-43-X $9.95

MURDER IS MATERIAL Karen Saum
The third in the series of Brigid Donovan mysteries. Brigid searches for the clues in the death of a self-styled Buddhist guru. $9.95 ISBN 0-934678-57-X
Earlier Donovan mysteries—Murder is Relative and Murder is Germane are now available from New Victoria at $8.95

EVERYWHERE HOUSE Jane Meyerding
Seattle in the seventies. A professor is stabbed and a lesbian is arrested. *Jane Meyerding's touchingly innocent hero makes her way through the 70s, revealing familiar lesbian types and an amused look at our own past, in addition to some unsavory villains.—*Alex Dobkin ISBN 0-934678-54-5 $9.95

THE KALI CONNECTION   Claudia McKay
Covering a seemingly simple drug overdose, reporter Lynn Evans finds herself investigating the murder of a member of the Kalimaya Society, a mysterious Eastern cult. ISBN 0-934678-42-1 $9.95

DEATH BY THE RIVERSIDE J.M. Redmann
Detective Micky Knight, hired to take a few pictures, finds herself slugging through thugs and slogging through swamps in an attempt to expose a dangerous drug ring. $9.95 ISBN 0-934678-27-8

DEATHS OF JOCASTA J.M. Redmann
What was the body of a woman doing in the basement of the Clinic? Micky Knight investigates before the police and the news media find their solution. *"Knight is witty, irreverent and very sexy."* $9.95 ISBN 0-934678-39-1

HERS WAS THE SKY ReBecca Béguin
Sabotage, betting and intimate rivalry cloud the first women's flying race in 1929 as pilot Hazel Preston despite personal cost searches for the truth. ISBN 0-9-34678-47-2 $8.95

ALSO AVAILABLE— SIX STONER MCTAVISH MYSTERIES BY SARAH DREHER

STONER MCTAVISH

The first Stoner mystery introduces us to travel agent Stoner McTavish. On a trip to the Tetons, Stoner meets and falls in love with her dream lover, Gwen, whom she must rescue from danger and almost certain death.
$9.95   ISBN 0-934678-06-5

SOMETHING SHADY

Investigating the mysterious disappearance of a nurse at a suspicious rest home on the Maine coast, Stoner becomes an inmate, trapped in the clutches of the evil psychiatrist Dr. Milicent Tunes. Can Gwen and Aunt Hermione charge to the rescue before it's too late? $8.95 ISBN 0-934678-07-3

GRAY MAGIC

After telling Gwen's grandmother that they are lovers, Stoner and Gwen set off to Arizona to escape the fallout. But a peaceful vacation turns frightening when Stoner finds herself an unwitting combatant in a struggle between the Hopi spirits of Good and Evil. $9.95   ISBN 0-934678-11-1

A CAPTIVE IN TIME

Stoner finds herself inexplicably transported to a small town in Colorado Territory, time 1871. There she encounters Dot, the saloon keeper, Blue Mary, a local witch/healer, and an enigmatic teenage runaway named Billy.
$9.95   ISBN 0-934678-22-7

OTHERWORLD

All your favorite characters—business partner Marylou, eccentric Aunt Hermione, psychiatrist, Edith Kesselbaum, and of course, devoted lover, Gwen, on vacation at Disney World. In a case of mistaken identity. Marylou is kidnapped and held hostage in an underground tunnel.
$10.95   ISBN 0-934678-44-8

BAD COMPANY

The latest in the series. A Maine B&B resort, summer home to a feminist theater troupe, experiences mysterious and ever more serious "accidents."
An intricate, entertaining plot, with delightfully witty dialogue.
ISBN 0-934678-66-9 $10.95 paperback
ISBN 0-934678-67-7 $19.95 hardcover

Order from New Victoria Publishers PO Box 27 Norwich VT. 05055
Or write for free Catalogue